METHUSELAH'S LEGACY

T.W. FENDLEY

Soul Song Press, LLC

Published by Soul Song Press, LLC, in St Augustine, Florida, 2020.

www.SoulSongPress.com

ISBN 978-0-999-8434-5-1 (Paperback)

To remote viewers worldwide, with great hope for the future.

September 2029

OGDEN, UTAH—The word "cancer" lingered on the air like a ticking bomb. At ninety-two, Lilith Davidson had lost more friends and family to that disease than any other. And now cancer had come for her. It felt personal.

Seth wrapped his arm around her shoulders, and their daughter Gemini held her hand. Bad news loomed above them. Stomach pain, nausea, loss of appetite, and shedding thirty pounds without trying had to be caused by something, and the benign answers had already been ruled out.

"This is an aggressive disease," the oncologist continued, "but with a combination of radiation and the new immunotherapy drugs, we should be able to slow it down and relieve some of the symptoms."

"What about surgery?" Seth asked.

"It has already spread to the liver." The doctor took off his glasses and rested his elbows on the desk. "And at her age… well, it's just too late for surgery." He looked at Lilith. "I'm sorry."

Lilith heard the words, but focused on Gemini's reaction instead of letting the meaning sink in. The appointment had been for her benefit, to help Gemini come to grips with what they faced. Her daughter fought back the tears. Having both her parents given a death sentence in the same year had to be tough to handle.

Seth's right kidney and adrenal gland were surgically removed five months ago. His follow-up scan scheduled for next month would've let them know if the targeted therapy had kept the cancer from spreading to his lymph nodes. But he wouldn't be keeping that appointment.

Lilith squeezed Gemini's hand and stood. "I think I need a little air."

"I understand." The doctor stood. "But don't delay starting treatment. I'll have my office call you tomorrow."

"Thank you, but I plan to get a second opinion," she said.

Gemini stared at her, mouth open.

"Of course." The doctor frowned slightly.

Lilith took Seth's hand as they walked out. When they got to the car, she said, "Looks like it's time to try the serum."

Gemini slid into the back seat. "Mom, you can't mean that." Her face taut with stress, Gemini's voice drifted an octave higher. "Dad, talk some sense into her." When he remained quiet, she persisted. "It's an experimental treatment you've never tried on humans."

Lilith turned to look at her as Seth pulled out of the parking lot. "People don't survive Stage Four pancreatic cancer," she said calmly. "You know that. I don't see that I have a choice."

"Your mother's right," Seth added. "It may be experimental, but we've been working on the treatment for more than a decade."

Gemini sighed. "I'm sure a dozen people who know nothing about biology or medicine have found the cure to cancer."

Lilith huffed. "As I've told you before, many times, it's not about cancer—it's about longevity."

"That means more than curing diseases," Seth said, "although that's a critical part of the process."

"I know you've never been interested in what our group does, Gem, but you've seen some of the results," Lilith said. "It paid for our home and for your kids' college education, yet you still doubt it works?"

"Mom, please don't do this," Gemini pleaded. "It's one thing to do woo-woo stuff to raise money, and entirely different when your life is on the line. You could go to M.D. Anderson. The Mayo Clinic. Anywhere in the world. Get a second opinion, like you told the doctor."

Lilith shook her head. "I tried the Mayo Clinic. I'm sorry you don't understand, Gemini, but this is my life, and my decision."

The silence stretched on for several minutes. They pulled into the circle drive in front of a modern two-story building made of glass and flat, tan stone. In the middle of the circle, a bronze sculpture of the Renu Tree of Life rose from a pool of water. Its trunk and branches were entwined DNA ladders.

Located down a private road off the Ogden River Scenic Byway, Renu's research center lay nestled in the foothills of the Wasatch Range east of Ogden. Though isolated enough to discourage curiosity seekers, it was not so far away from the city to appear secretive.

Seth parked, popped the trunk, and handed Gemini the keys. "We won't be needing the car for a while."

"Dad, you're not thinking of being a guinea pig, too?" Gemini said, her face drawn.

He hugged her. "I love you, girl. Maybe I wouldn't try it if I were still in my sixties like you. But we have thirty years more experience, and it makes a difference in how we view our risks."

He and Lilith each retrieved two suitcases from the trunk.

"You were already planning this," Gemini said.

Lilith nodded. "I didn't know how bad the diagnosis would be, but I didn't think it would be good. Besides, this just makes it easier to take the next step with our study...and it's going to be amazing. You'll see." Lilith hugged Gemini. "Don't worry."

"Right. What's to worry about?" Gemini snipped. She got in the car and rolled down the window.

"I love you," Lilith said.

Gemini locked eyes with each of them, then the fight went out of her. She opened the door and rushed back to Lilith, hugging her fiercely. "I love you, too, Mom." Tears streamed down Gemini's face as she turned and wrapped her arms around Seth, laying her head against his chest. "Please be okay!" Reluctantly, she returned to the car. Her voice broke as she said "I love you" once more, then drove away.

Lilith turned to Seth, "I wish I felt as confident as I sounded."

"That makes two of us," Seth said.

As he signed in at the security desk, Lilith messaged the group to confirm the human trials would proceed as planned. Hers was the final diagnosis they'd been waiting for.

Chapter 2

RENU CENTER, OGDEN RIVER SCENIC BYWAY—The next morning, Lilith waited in the conference room, smiling at a hologram they'd just taken outside the research center. She remembered when they'd dubbed themselves the Methuselah Pioneers more than a decade ago after their group of twelve decided to focus its efforts on longevity research. Within the past year, all of them had signed up for the first human trials.

As others entered, Lilith smoothed the creases from her T-shirt, which bore Renu's Tree of Life insignia. Marketing had rebranded their company after focus groups showed few people remembered anything about Methuselah—the Bible's oldest reported human— but the founders maintained their identity.

With the aches and pains she had at ninety-two, living to nine hundred sixty-nine like Methuselah sounded more like a curse than a blessing. Unless the Pioneers could access the secrets locked within their genes—the legacy of the ancients.

Her friend, Ralen Alexander, sat beside Lilith. "Are you nervous?"

She nodded. Who wouldn't be? "But optimistic," Lilith said. And that was true. They'd taken every precaution, but this was uncharted territory.

Seth handed Lilith a glass of water as he sat on her other side.

"Hey, Seth," Ralen said.

"Hi, buddy." Seth gave Ralen's shoulder a light knuckle-bump. "Guess this is the moment of truth."

"Looks like it." Ralen brushed back his white hair and grinned. "Besides, it's not like any of us has a good alternative."

"So true," Seth said.

At their age—ranging from Seth's ninety to Ralen's ninety-three —actuarial tables insurance companies relied upon showed it was no riskier to take the experimental treatment than not to do so.

The Pioneers all turned to greet Kate Flowers, the marketing director, as she entered the room.

"Glad to see you brought a videographer," Lilith said.

"We're making history here," Kate said, "so we want to get everything on record."

They'd banned the media because of their lawyer's concern about the treatment's experimental nature. "No sense in flaunting human trials until you have the science behind you to prove its merits," he had advised.

The videographer lifted a palm-sized digital camera, and the red indicator light popped on.

"Give us a little background about how you got selected," Kate said, playing the role of reporter.

"Where to start?" Lilith glanced at Seth. "You could say it began thirty years ago when we formed an online group to study remote viewing."

"That's a scientific protocol developed at the Stanford Research Institute and used by the military during the Twentieth Century's Cold War," Seth explained.

"Yes," Lilith said. "It involves gathering information using intuition rather than the intellect or the usual five senses."

"At first, we started using our sessions to predict the outcome of sporting events or to forecast stock market changes," he said. "We were part of a bigger, global group, but over time, a core group of twelve stayed together."

"We kept trying new ways to use the protocol," Lilith said. "Our results were far from being one-hundred percent accurate, but we came to understand how powerful even a slight edge over chance was."

"Explain what you mean by that," Kate said.

"Say you have a binary choice—yes or no, up or down," Lilith said. "Just based on random selection, each choice will occur fifty percent of the time. With remote viewing, more than sixty percent of our predictions were correct."

"That's not much of a difference," Kate said.

"To put it in perspective," Ralen said, "casinos can make money winning only fifty-three percent of the time."

"When we added the Kelly Wagering method—where the percentage of your stake that's bet each time is based on a mathematical formula—we saw even greater financial gains," Seth said.

"How successful were you?" Kate asked.

"Within five years, we were able to pay cash for stunning homes in Park City, if that gives you some idea," Ralen said.

"But we wanted to use the money to make a difference in the world," Lilith said. "And we weren't getting any younger."

The others laughed. "That's a bit of an understatement, don't you think?" Ralen said.

"As more of us faced life-threatening illnesses, we started looking at projects that could cure diseases or improve our quality of life," Seth said.

"About fifteen years ago, we decided to focus on longevity," Ralen added. "Lilith came up with the name—Methuselah Pioneers. It just stuck."

"What do you mean—longevity? Seems like curing disease would have that result," Kate said.

"It's kind of a chicken-and-egg issue," Seth conceded. "But telomeres are key—if you keep them from shortening or get them to elongate, you avoid the ravages of old age, including disease."

"Plus, it's a quality of life issue," Lilith said. "Just being disease-free doesn't help if you're too feeble to enjoy life."

"We wanted to find a way to help people stay at their peak for as long as possible—to be modern-day Methuselahs," Kameitha added.

"How did you get the scientific knowledge to make decisions about medical issues?" Kate asked.

"None of us had medical training, but that worked in our favor," Lilith said.

Kate scrunched her eyebrows together, really getting into the part of a skeptical reporter. "Did I hear you right?"

Lilith laughed. "No, it's true. Remote viewing techniques often work best when viewers have no knowledge or are "blind" to the target."

"So, you guided research without knowing anything about it?" Kate said.

"Exactly," Seth said. "We set up sessions so we could view for simple outcomes. For instance, should we hire geneticist A or B?"

"Using double-blind protocols—where both the researcher and viewer didn't know the precise target—we guided the research, too," Ralen said.

"I'm having trouble envisioning how that worked," Kate said.

The videographer shifted positions for a different angle when Lilith opened her tablet and drew three boxes on the screen, labeled A, B and C.

"Say person A knows what the target is, but only gives person B a number that is linked to the target," she said. "Person B assigns person C to remote view the target associated with the number."

"Since neither B nor C knows what the target is, it's a double-blind study," Seth said.

"As we came to decision points, we used remote viewing to give the researchers direction," Lilith said.

"Again, it wasn't foolproof—we followed some wrong leads," Ralen said.

"But it didn't take long for our group to make breakthroughs in areas that still baffled other researchers," Seth said.

"And one breakthrough led to another—a kind of synchronicity," Lilith said.

"Even so, it's taken us more than a dozen years to get to this point," Ralen said.

"Aren't human trials a big step?" Kate asked.

Ralen shrugged. "As Lilith said, none of us are getting younger."

"And it's not like we have a lot of other choices," Seth said. "During the past year, all of us have been told our time is running out."

"Yesterday I learned I have pancreatic cancer," Lilith said. "Even with the latest treatments, my doctor said I probably have only a few months to live."

"It's the same for the rest of us." Ralen motioned to the others, who were taking seats around the conference table. "We have nothing to lose and a lot to gain."

"Time to see who's going to make history today as the very first person to take the treatment," Kate said.

Chapter 3

The twelve Pioneers each checked the slips of paper they'd drawn from a box when they entered the room.

Hector waved his paper and held up one finger. The doctor walked over to him, followed closely by the videographer and Kate.

Kate gestured to Hector. "Our attorney, Hector Juarez, has the winning number! Congratulations on being the first to receive this historic treatment."

He nodded and faced the camera. "This treatment holds out hope for more than simply living longer—it's about improving the quality of life. It opens the possibility of living full lives for many more decades. Imagine if Thomas Edison, Henry Ford, or Albert Einstein had been productive for twice as long, and you'll see the impact this could have on humankind."

Kate's head bobbed. "That's so true, Hector."

In the background, the other Pioneers gave him a "thumbs-up" salute.

Despite his glowing words, Lilith thought Hector's smile looked forced as the silver air gun hissed and the serum entered his bloodstream. The doctor lingered for several minutes before moving to the next person, his distant expression making Lilith wonder if he, too, had second thoughts about going forward with the treatment.

Or maybe it was just her imagination. Lilith's pulse raced as the doctor stepped in front of her. She braced her arm to hold it steady and willed her body to relax. According to the geneticists, epigenetic prion regulation of telomeres was at the heart of the treatment. The word "prion" made her mouth go dry. It still brought to mind the outbreaks of Mad Cow Disease in her youth, and the jerky gaits and blank-eyed stares of its victims. She shivered and tried to think about something else.

Lilith waited until Seth had his injection, then gave him a parting hug. "See you on the other side," she said.

He leaned over and kissed her. "I'll check with you later online."

Lilith nodded and walked down the hall to the efficiency apartment she'd been assigned. She knew they needed to avoid outside contamination because of their suppressed immune systems, but Lilith didn't understand why the researchers also wanted to keep the twelve of them apart.

"The changes in your bodies will be massive," one of the doctors had explained. "We don't want you to have any other pressures."

What "other pressures," she wondered. Sex? Arguments? Snoring? In the end, it hadn't seemed worth making a fuss over, so she and Seth—the only married couple—had gone along with their plan.

Lilith's room had a queen-size bed, a closet with built-in drawers, and a tiny galley kitchen that opened to a breakfast bar with two cane-bottom wooden stools. The adjoining living room had a three-cushion sofa upholstered in blue microfiber fabric, one blue-and-green striped chair, and a green ottoman that served double-duty as a cocktail table and footrest.

In addition to a pantry she'd stocked with her favorite comfort foods, a gourmet chef was available to fill their orders around the clock. A dumb waiter provided automated delivery from the kitchen to her apartment.

Lilith settled in with an audiobook—the first in a mystery series she'd been saving as a special treat—and a crossword puzzle. She wanted to focus on anything except what was going on in her body.

After a few minutes, her skin felt flushed. She went to the bathroom and got a cool compress for her head. She barely sat back down before a chill set in. Lilith searched through the linen closet for the warmest blanket and wrapped herself in it. The nausea started a few hours later, then the vomiting. She didn't notice Seth hadn't called until the next morning when her laptop chimed. Lilith accepted the call, and the holo projected into the room.

"Sorry I didn't call," he began. "Holy shit, Lilith, you look worse than I feel!"

Lilith grimaced, cataloguing her latest visible symptoms—flaking skin, itchy rashes on the backs of her hands and tops of her feet. But Seth's gray hair was disheveled and dark circles ringed his slate-blue eyes. Behind him, the sheets were twisted on his unmade bed.

"You don't look so great yourself," she said.

"Yeah, until I saw you, I thought I had a hard night." He pulled a blanket tighter around him. "My body's burning hot one minute, then I'm freezing the next."

"No nausea?" she asked.

He shook his head.

"Well, don't be surprised." Lilith grabbed a glass of cold water and took a big gulp. She couldn't satisfy her thirst. She blinked her eyes, trying to focus. The holo blurred, drifting in and out of clarity. "Guess it's all normal—the side effects the doctors warned us about."

Seth pressed his lips together. "I know they're monitoring us around the clock, but I want you to promise to call for assistance if it gets any worse … I wish I was there with you."

Lilith wanted to respond, but instead clenched her jaws as another wave of nausea flooded her mouth with saliva. She covered her mouth with one hand and waved with the other, then disconnected. She made it to the toilet just in time.

The next few days passed in a blur. Lilith ran a low fever and felt achy and sluggish, like she had a mild case of the flu. Each day, a medical assistant in a hazmat suit came in to take photographs and log the results of blood and urine tests.

By day six, Lilith had so many symptoms, she couldn't list them. She didn't have the energy to get out of bed.

"Where does it hurt?" one of the staff doctors asked, his voice muffled by his mask.

She tried to focus on his eyes, but plastic protective glasses hid them.

"Everywhere," she said. "I had no idea how much skin I have—and it all hurts!"

When he examined her breasts with rubber-gloved hands, she cringed.

"Tender?" he asked.

She nodded.

"It's to be expected." He pressed on her ovaries. "Your hormones are working harder than they ever have."

"What hormones!" she scoffed.

"Oh, you definitely have them, now." He sounded awed. "It's amazing, really. Your bloodwork could be that of a healthy thirty-year-old."

"My prime!" Lilith quipped, then grew quiet. She was afraid to ask if the changes were merely superficial. "What of the..."

"...the cancer?" He patted her hand and replied with enthusiasm. "The treatment has performed every bit as well as we hoped, Lilith. Your pancreas is healthy, with no sign of cancer."

No cancer? Relief rose within, releasing tightness in her chest she hadn't even realized was there. Her eyes brimmed with tears. "It's really gone?"

"Some would say it's a miracle, but really it's just the result of restoring the body's natural ability to heal itself." Even through the plastic, she could see his eyes sparkled. "This is new territory—a rapid remission unlike anything seen before." Excited, he spoke quickly. "When we publish the findings, it will revolutionize treatment for terminal illnesses. And I think it's just the beginning."

Suddenly energized, Lilith could hardly wait to tell Seth. But he'd been sleeping more than she had, and she didn't want to disrupt his healing. When he finally called hours later, Lilith noted his sunken eyes and grayish skin. He looked worse than the day before, which worried her.

"Hey, baby." She forced cheer into her voice. "How are you feeling?

"Not good, but the doctor says I'm better," he said.

"I have some good news," she said.

"Yeah?"

"My cancer is gone!" Just saying the words thrilled Lilith all over again.

Seth straightened and smiled. "That's the best news I've had—ever! It really worked."

"Did he say anything about yours?" Lilith asked.

"No, my testing was delayed a day or two," he said.

"I see," Lilith said, but she really didn't. She couldn't keep the fear from rising. Why wasn't he better? She resolved to get some answers from the doctor at her next check-up.

Chapter 4

During the next week, Lilith had to agree the transformations had only just begun. Her health started to improve dramatically, and she clearly saw changes. The wrinkles on her face and the brown spots on her hands faded more each day. For the first time in years, she wasn't shocked by her appearance.

The difference between how she thought of herself and the image in the mirror had confounded her for decades. One of the hardest parts of getting old had been seeing her own face turn into her mother's. Now her reflection once again matched the way she felt inside. But how would Gemini react to having a mother who looked younger than she did?

Xrays, MRIs, and bloodwork confirmed the internal changes, including improved bone density and restored hormone levels. Lilith's waist shrank and breasts firmed. Her muscle mass increased, and renewed collagen restored youthful tightness to her skin. A half-inch of strawberry blonde roots gave a rosy cast to her white hair.

"How's your stamina?" the doctor asked during one of her exams.

"Better," she said. "Much better. I'm not worn out by mid-afternoon. I can even keep pace with the online instructor for a full hour's cardio."

"That's great," he said. "The exercise may help speed your recovery. Keep it up."

"What about the others?" Lilith asked.

"I can't say much—privacy laws." He put away his stethoscope.

"Seth isn't looking good," she pressed. "We signed releases, so you can tell me about him."

The doctor sat in the chair facing her. "The treatment affects everyone differently. That's one of the reasons we wanted to keep you apart during this phase."

Lilith had a sudden sense of dread. "But it's working for all of us, right?"

"It's a matter of timing," he said. "You've proved to be the most responsive to the serum, so your rejuvenation has been the quickest. Seth is on the other end of the spectrum. His recovery is proceeding at about half the rate as yours."

"But the cancer?" she asked

"His blood work is much improved," he said. "Based on your progress and that of the others, I'm confident he will overcome it."

Soon after the doctor left, chimes alerted Lilith to an incoming message. Noting Kameitha Banks' name on the display, she enabled the holo. But Kameitha's image didn't project into the room as it normally did.

"I seem to be having some technical difficulties," Lilith muttered as she accepted the call.

After a pause, Kameitha said, "it's on my end. I just wanted to see your image before I shared mine." The holo flicked on, giving Lilith a 3D view. She blinked in surprise.

Lilith had long admired Kameitha's flawless skin, unmarred by wrinkles or spots. At eighty-five, her ebony eyes betrayed a sharp and active intellect. The treatment had accentuated those assets and gone far beyond.

Awed, Lilith said, "You're beautiful." Kameitha's face glowed. If she hadn't known better, Lilith would've guessed her age at no more than forty.

Kameitha smiled. "And you look radiant! I'm so glad to see I'm not the only one who has transformed. The doctors have been pretty close-mouthed about everyone's progress."

"I know," Lilith said. "They were even reluctant to tell me about Seth, and we had signed release forms."

"How's he doing?" Kameitha asked.

Lilith bit her lip and gave a slight shake of her head. "He's not as far along as we are… not by a long shot."

"That must be hard for you," Kameitha said.

"I'm worried about him, but the doctor doesn't seem concerned," Lilith said.

"I'm sure he wouldn't give you false hope," Kameitha said.

Lilith nodded. She thought that was true, but it was good to hear someone else say it.

"When we finally get out of here, let's go over to the Meteor and celebrate," Kameitha said.

"That sounds like a plan," Lilith said. "Gemini will pick us up, so maybe a late lunch?"

"Works for me," Kameitha said. "You're awfully brave. Jeremy was already unhappy with me because I had been relying on traditional treatments. This was way outside his comfort zone."

Lilith sighed. "Yeah, the doctors say Gemini's called every day. Even though they tell her we're improving, she isn't accepting this as a valid alternative to 'real' medicine."

"Like that was working!" Kameitha scoffed.

"Exactly!" Lilith said. "But when it's the only game in town…"

"Thankfully, that may no longer be true." Kameitha waved. "Catch you later."

In the following days, Lilith noticed Seth's hair had a golden tinge, he spoke with more enthusiasm, and said he hadn't been sleeping as much. All in all, the doctor's prediction seemed accurate. She monitored Seth's steady improvement, while counting down the days until they could be together again.

Chapter 5

Lilith stopped just outside the door to the conference room, working up the nerve to enter. The Pioneers gathered around the table bore little resemblance to those who'd sat there a month ago. The serum was a time machine to younger versions of the friends she'd known and worked with for decades.

Seth walked over and took her in his arms. "You look even better in person." He leaned down and gave her a lingering kiss, pulling her close.

Surprised at how affectionate he was, she said, "I've missed you."

"I missed you, too." His touch left her light-headed as desire swept through her body. The holo didn't do justice to the vigor in his movements and the sparkle in his eyes. Seth stood straighter, and his firm embrace reminded her of their wedding day. To Lilith's surprise, her body flushed with warmth and lust. Her heart raced as Seth escorted her to seats near the head of the table.

Kate rose and clanked a spoon on a glass. "Our lead geneticist needs no introduction, so without further delay, I'll turn the meeting over to him. I know you want to know about the results." She gestured toward him. "Dr. J."

A middle-aged, dark-haired man, Albert Jaenisch served as lead geneticist. As he stood, he slipped a pen into the pocket of his white lab coat with the Renu insignia and took the podium. "The results were more than we dared to hope for. On average, the treatment cut your biological age in half."

Lilith joined the others in giving the doctor a round of applause.

"We've seen cancer, arthritis, heart disease, and diabetes eradicated, and any tendency toward dementia erased," Dr. J said. "We couldn't have made these strides as quickly, or possibly at all, without your help."

Lilith smiled at Seth.

"The treatment is complete," Dr. J said. "Everyone has a clean bill of health."

"Here, here!" Hector stood and clapped, and the other Pioneers joined him.

After they settled, Dr. J asked, "Are there any questions?"

"How long will the effects last?" Ralen asked.

"We have no way to know that," Dr. J said. "That's one reason your health will always be closely monitored. There's much we don't know about how and why the serum works. Only time—and additional research—will tell."

"Not to look a gift horse in the mouth, but isn't it unusual to have a one-hundred percent success rate on an experimental treatment like this," Kameitha asked.

A few of the Pioneers frowned at her remark, but the others sat straighter, looking eager to hear his response.

"Indeed." Dr. J nodded in her direction. He absent-mindedly rolled a pen back and forth on the table in front of him. "And even in this study, the treatment affected each of you differently. Some of you look younger than the others because the treatment worked better for you."

"So, to Ralen's question, some can expect to remain healthy longer than others?" she asked.

Dr. J shrugged. "As I said, I'd just be guessing at this point. We'll have to monitor all of you before I'd be comfortable with that conclusion."

"But this is as good as we'll get?" Seth asked.

"Ah," Dr. J said. "You want to know if the serum is still working? Yes, it is, but the rejuvenation process has stopped. Whatever length your telomeres are now is the longest they will be."

A few minutes later when they rose to leave, Kameitha brushed against Lilith and smiled. "Let's celebrate!"

"Absolutely!" Lilith linked arms—Kameitha on one side and

Seth on the other. As they left the conference room, she glanced back and saw the others were also grouping in animated threesomes and foursomes. The sexual energy was electric.

"Hey—Kami, Seth—wait up!" Ralen shouted, his running footsteps echoing down the hallway. "You're not getting away that easily."

"Wouldn't think of it," Seth said.

"What's the plan?" their tall, lanky friend said with a rakish grin.

"It's a little early to go to the club," Kameitha said.

"We're almost at my room," Lilith said, "and there's something I want to give Seth before we go out."

"I'll bet there is," Kameitha teased.

Lilith chuckled. "Stop it. That's not what I meant. But now that you've mentioned it…"

"Definitely, let's stop by your room." Seth steered them down the hallway.

They took seats in Lilith's compact living room while she went to the kitchen. She pulled a bottle from a countertop wine cooler and placed it on a tray with four chilled crystal flutes.

"Close your eyes," Lilith called out. She set the tray in front of Seth. "Let's see how good your memory is."

Seth took one look at the vintage yellow label Veuve Clicquot champagne and gasped. "But we lost the bid at the auction."

Lilith grinned. "It wasn't hard to track down the buyer."

"And you've kept it secret all this time?" He stood and hugged her.

"When we started the longevity project, I figured it could take more than a decade for us to see results," Lilith said. "Long enough for this bottle to age properly."

He removed the wire harness and loosened the cork, which released with an explosive pop. "Let's celebrate in style!" He poured, and they raised their glasses. "To my wonderful wife, and the next hundred years."

"To the next hundred years," the other three echoed.

Ralen put down his glass and moved from the only chair to the hassock in front of where Kameitha sat on the couch.

"Since we're celebrating, have you heard about my magic hands?" he asked.

Kameitha grinned. "That sounds suspiciously like a come-on."

"And if it is?" Ralen's eyebrows raised.

"Ha ha," she said. "You're such a tease."

"As you may recall, I'm a certified reflexologist." Ralen motioned for Kameitha to put her feet up on the hassock. "I guarantee your feet will fall in love with me."

He pulled off her shoes and began massaging her feet. Kameitha moaned like she was in ecstasy. After a few minutes, he moved to Lilith.

"I see how you are—so fickle," Kameitha quipped.

He winked at her.

"But seriously, that was wonderful," Kameitha added.

Lilith leaned back and closed her eyes, letting his skillful massage relax her whole body. As her thoughts drifted, she imagined it was Kameitha touching her. Her skin tingled. Startled by her reaction, she jerked upright.

"Is everything okay?" Ralen asked, looking puzzled.

"Oh yes, just ticklish," she lied.

Ralen patted her feet and moved on to Seth.

Lilith leaned back again and tried to relax. Kameitha moved closer to her so their bodies touched from shoulder to knee. Was Kameitha coming on to her? She chided herself. Obviously, she had just forgotten what it was like to have a younger person's libido.

"Ah, excuse me." She rose to her feet, gathered the empty glasses, and walked to the adjoining kitchen. Maybe with a little distance, she could think straight. What was going on? She'd never been physically attracted to women before, but now she could barely keep her eyes off the petite African American.

What would Seth think if he knew? Feeling guilty, she looked over at him. Ralen's hand was sliding up the inside seam of Seth's pants. Seth's unfocused eyes and the tightness of his jeans betrayed his arousal.

Ralen caught her glance and pulled his hand back, his lips quivering with an embarrassed smile. She thought about confronting them, but that would be too hypocritical. She spun around and announced loudly, "Time to go to the club!"

They jumped to their feet to follow her.

Chapter 6

Back in her room after dancing until the club closed, Lilith nestled in bed beside Seth. They'd just finished making love, but her thoughts kept going back to earlier in the evening.

"What was going on with Ralen before we left for the club?"

Seth pulled her closer and kissed her forehead. "You saw?"

"Yep."

He groaned. "I've been asking myself the same thing all night. It was the strangest thing—I didn't want Ralen to stop, which makes no sense. Obviously, I want you, and I'd never do anything to hurt you. Can you forgive me?"

Lilith put her hand on his bare chest and felt his heartbeat. "Actually, I kind of understand."

"You do?"

"Because of Kameitha," she said. "I'm attracted to her."

"What?" he propped up on one arm to look at her. In the dim light, she could barely make out his features, but his slight smile made her think he was open to talking about it without getting angry.

"Nothing really happened, but I definitely wanted it to," she said.

"It's so strange that we'd all four be having these feelings," he said. "At least, I've always thought Ralen and Kameitha were straight."

"Well, I know they have kids, too." She paused. "I hadn't thought much about what the treatment might mean in terms of renewed sexual energy, had you?"

"I had a few fantasies—mostly about us making love with as much passion as we did tonight," he said.

She reached over and kissed him. "It was nice, wasn't it? Like when we started dating."

"But I never imagined anything like this—whatever it is—with Ralen," he said.

"Maybe our newfound attraction is a side effect."

"Of the treatment?" Seth said.

"What else could it be?" she asked.

"Maybe it's just the first time we've felt decent in decades?" he said.

"That could explain increased libido, but I don't think that would cause us to change our sexual preferences, do you?" She looked at him doubtfully.

"Maybe not, but it seems far-fetched to think of it as a side effect." He chuckled. "I can just imagine the ads, with the fast-talking announcer burying that in a long list of potential side effects."

Chapter 7

The next morning, Seth went back to his apartment to gather his belongings while Lilith packed. She knew it wouldn't take him long to fill two suitcases, but she wasn't expecting the door to chime right after he left.

"What did you forget?" Lilith asked, laughing, as she opened the door. Instead of Seth, however, Kameitha was at the door.

"May I come in?" she asked.

Lilith swallowed hard, her pulse suddenly racing. "Of course," she said. "But I thought we were going to meet later at the cafe."

Kameitha paused next to Lilith as she closed the door. "I thought this conversation would be better in private." She met Lilith's eyes. "About last night..."

"Yes?" Lilith stepped back and motioned to the couch. She sat on the chair facing Kameitha.

"You probably didn't even notice, but it was all I could do to keep from touching you," she said.

Lilith looked away, wondering how best to respond. "It's okay."

Kameitha sighed. "It's just not like me."

"I think we're both still adjusting to the hormones," Lilith said.

"Maybe so. Then you weren't offended?" Kameitha stood.

"No," Lilith shrugged. "Even though I tell myself it's crazy, I can't stop thinking about you, either."

"Really?" Kameitha paused by the door. She placed her hands

on both sides of Lilith's face, guiding their lips together in a gentle kiss.

Lilith considered pulling away, but only for a moment. Kameitha smelled of lilacs, and her touch ignited Lilith's desire. Lilith rested her hands lightly on Kameitha's thin waist. She drew her closer, and their kiss lengthened.

When the kiss ended, Kameitha stroked Lilith's hair with one hand, cradling her neck with the other. Then she cleared her throat and pulled away. Looking into Lilith's eyes, she said, "I better go before I do something really stupid. See you at the Meteor?"

Lilith paused. Before the treatment, she would've avoided anything that might endanger what she had with Seth. But even if it turned out to be a side effect, this new attraction excited every cell within her. She didn't want to run away from it. "Okay. Around one?"

Kameitha nodded.

She opened the door. Across the hallway, Seth and Ralen stood together outside his room, arms entwined, mirroring the intimate embrace she and Kameitha had shared moments before. From the way they looked into each other's eyes, Lilith knew they must have also connected. A quick jolt of jealousy quickly gave way to relief that she didn't have to hide her feelings for Kameitha.

"Ahem," she said.

Seth jumped and looked at her and Kameitha. He squeezed Ralen's shoulder and mumbled, "Later?"

"Sure," Ralen said.

Lilith smiled at Kameitha, then took Seth's hand as she closed the door behind him. "You and Ralen?" she asked.

He tilted his head. "You and Kameitha?"

Lilith nodded. As they walked back into her room, she struggled to reconcile her long-standing beliefs with what had just happened.

She had never considered how much her sexual preferences had been tied to her sense of self. Until now. What did it mean if she wasn't simply heterosexual, or monogamous, or faithful? All the labels tumbled around in her head. How would she define herself if she wasn't those things? Did the labels really matter? At the end of the day, she wanted to be happy, and she wanted that for Seth, Kameitha, and Ralen, too.

Usually her beliefs guided her behavior instead of the other way around. Now, though, she felt her actions with Kameitha were leading her down a different path and toward a new way of perceiving herself.

She and Seth sat side-by-side on the couch. After a pause, Lilith said, "This is a mess."

"Yeah."

"We have thirty years together, and I want at least that many more," she said.

"I feel the same," Seth said, the tension making his voice thin. "I would never want to do anything to jeopardize what we share."

"Neither would I, especially now that we have a future again."

Seth gave her hand a squeeze.

"But…" She took a deep breath.

"Yep, there is a 'but,'" Seth added with a nervous chuckle.

"…ninety-two years of experience says to be grateful when you receive an unexpected gift. And this new attraction feels like that," she said. "A gift."

"It does," he agreed.

"I don't want to start off our new life by limiting something that could bring us both joy, do you?" she asked.

"When you put it that way, it doesn't seem so crazy." Seth smiled.

Lilith snorted. "I'm glad you think so. I think we should be open to our feelings—be fearless. I never thought I would want to be with a woman, or that I would feel okay about you being with someone else. Yet there it is."

Seth nodded. "You and me—we're okay, then?"

"Yes, I think we are," she said, meaning it. "Kameitha and I are meeting for lunch. Why don't you and Ralen join us?"

Seth texted Ralen, then turned to her. "It's all set."

Chapter 8

"Did you call Gemini?" Lilith asked.

"Yes, she should be here soon," he said.

"Great." Lilith paced nervously across the lobby. "Keeping the good news from her has been hard to do."

"We didn't have a choice—that was what we all agreed to do," Seth said.

"She's been calling every day."

"She'll be fine."

Lilith sighed.

Gemini pulled up, stopping Seth's car in the circular driveway adjoining the lobby. When she spotted them, Gemini did a double take. Her mouth still gaped when Lilith opened the door and slid into the passenger seat.

"Mom?" Gemini turned toward the backseat. "Dad?"

Lilith smiled.

Seth chuckled. "Who else?"

"Oh my god!" Gemini gave Lilith a huge hug. "You look wonderful. Both of you look so... young! Seriously, you look like you've had total reconstruction surgery."

"No surgery at all," Seth said.

"But..." Gemini said.

"The longevity serum changes the way your body ages," Lilith said. "And yes, it re-sets your physical clock to when it was younger and healthy."

"I had no idea," Gemini said. "Why didn't you tell me before you went in? I hardly slept; I've been so worried about you."

"The research team didn't want us to talk with anyone until they felt comfortable with the results," Lilith said. "I'm really sorry."

"I've been frantic." Gemini started the car and drove. "I've called the center dozens of times, but no one would tell me anything except you were both doing well."

An hour later, Gemini pulled into their driveway in Park City. She carried one of Lilith's bags, and Seth brought his in.

"It's good to be home." Lilith said. They left the bags in the foyer and went into the den. Morning light filled the room, bringing out the room's warm orange-and-brown tones.

Seth sat next to Lilith on the couch. Sitting across from them, Gemini placed her hands on her knees and shook her head. "I just can't get over how wonderful you look. The kids won't know what to think about having grandparents who look as young as them. Which is great, but... tell me." Gemini's voice softened, with a hint of dread. "What did you decide about the cancer treatment? You've delayed it for a month, Mom, which is a very long time with your condition."

Lilith looked at Seth, who took Gemini's hand.

"We have good news, my girl," Seth told Gemini. "Your mother's cancer—and mine—are gone."

"Gone?" Gemini said.

"The treatment eradicated all traces of the cancer," Lilith said. "As he said, we're cured."

Gemini rose and walked to the window. When she turned around, tears streaked her face.

"I was so angry with you for not doing the radiation or other treatment," Gemini told Lilith. "I thought your longevity center was robbing me of my last days with you."

Lilith went to Gemini and wrapped her arms around her. "It's all right now." She smoothed Gemini's hair back from her face. "You don't have to worry about us anymore."

Gemini sniffed and brushed a tear from her cheek. "You're really cured?"

Seth joined them. "It's what we've been working on all these years. The earlier trials were promising, but no one really knew how the treatment would work on humans."

"I thought your remote viewing told you all the answers," Gemini said.

"We could only get answers to questions we asked," Lilith said, "and we didn't know enough to ask all the right questions."

"But you knew this—cure—was a possibility?" Gemini asked.

"We told you as much," Lilith said.

"I didn't think you meant it literally—that it could actually cure diseases like cancer," Gemini said.

"It's like I've always told you, Gem. It's better to under-promise and over-deliver," Seth said. "There was always the chance the serum could kill us or have side effects we didn't anticipate."

Lilith turned away, smiling at the thought of Kameitha and Ralen. That would be a conversation for another day.

Chapter 9

HUNTSVILLE, UTAH—After Gemini left, Lilith and Seth put away their bags and drove to Huntsville.

Ralen and Kameitha waited outside the Meteor. Kameitha greeted them with a kiss to both cheeks, and Ralen wrapped an arm around each of their shoulders as they followed Kameitha inside.

A waitress escorted them to a booth. Kameitha scooted onto the red vinyl-clad bench seat, and Lilith sat beside her.

"I'm starving for a Meteor burger," Ralen said.

"Sounds good to me, too," Seth said, putting down the menu. Lilith and Kameitha each ordered cheeseburgers.

As always, Lilith cringed at the decor. What had the original owner been thinking? She stared, appalled, at the stuffed head of his Saint Bernard on the wall, alongside jackelopes and moose heads.

Billed as the state's oldest continuously operating saloon, the Meteor had rough-hewn timber walls and signed dollar bills pinned to the ceiling. Reviewers described it as the "go-to" place for burgers in northern Utah.

"Don't you think it's odd that Dr. J didn't give us a diet or maybe an exercise plan?" Kameitha took a bite from her burger. She eyed Ralen as he struggled to get his mouth around the two beef patties, bratwurst, and fixings that made the Meteor burger famous.

"Maybe the serum is so powerful it gives us protection against artery-clogging fat," Lilith quipped.

Kameitha snorted and tilted her head toward the men. "They better hope so. This cheeseburger is bad enough, but a Meteor burger is tempting fate."

Mouths full, Seth and Ralen both shrugged.

Kameitha chuckled. "So, Lilith, I have to ask—how did your daughter react when she saw how fabulous you look?"

Lilith blushed. "Hmmm, I don't know quite how to answer that —happy we're cured of cancer but peeved we didn't let her know earlier. Did you connect with your son?"

"Ah, yes," Kameitha said. "Jeremy finally called back when I told him I was home. I haven't seen him yet—he's still fuming because I let him worry for a month. Maybe I'll get out of the doghouse eventually. At least he seemed pleased I'm going to live."

"But what if things had gone the other way?" Ralen said. "At least this way, it was a good surprise—no expectations to dash."

"I don't know how the rest of the family will react to the way we look," Lilith said. "It's beginning to worry me."

Seth reached across for her hand. "You look younger than Gemini now."

"And I feel younger than when I was her age," she added.

Kameitha cleared her throat. "Yes, what about that zing!"

The others chuckled. "I know the kids are not ready to hear about that!" Ralen said.

Kameitha brushed some crumbs off the table into her hand and dumped them on her plate. "All joking aside, I think it's time we got to know each other better."

Lilith nodded. "I was thinking the same thing—I mean, I've considered you my friends for years, but whenever we got together, all we discussed was remote viewing."

"Not that it's a bad thing," Seth said, "but Lilith is right— it's high time we got better acquainted."

Ralen raised his beer. "I'll drink to that!"

"I remember when we met," Lilith told Ralen. "You helped set up our first online investment club that used the Kelly Wagering method."

"Right," Ralen said. "It was the first time we made a consolidated effort to maximize the profits."

Lilith laughed. "And boy, did it tank!"

Ralen shook his head. "Even now, I can't explain why the first nine months were so bad—the groups had never had such low hit rates, and they never did again."

"If it hadn't been for your positive attitude, I don't know if we would've kept going," Seth told Kameitha. "But you wouldn't let us quit, and by midway through the second year, we were glad we stayed the course."

"Yeah, our first million—that was a trip!" Kameitha said.

"Who would've thought it would lead to this?" Lilith gestured at the four of them. "We would've been facing the end of our lives instead of what feels like a new beginning."

"Ah," Ralen cleared his throat. "You realize we're doing it again."

"What? Oh!" Lilith laughed. "I guess we are. Back in the rut of 'shop talk.'"

"Well, remote viewing is what we've shared all these years," Seth said.

"Old habits," Kameitha added with a shrug. "But at least Lilith and I have done a few things together—shopping, lunch."

"And shared a few stories about our families," Lilith said.

"Now we all have this treatment in common, too," Ralen said. "I don't know about you, but I'm shocked it really worked. I'd already made my peace with death."

Seth nodded. "Lilith and I had, too. We thought our time had run out."

"But now we have a future," Lilith said.

"It's going to be different for those who come after us," Kameitha said. "They'll know we survived."

"I know Kate doesn't want us to talk about the treatment as a cure for life-threatening illnesses, but even without that, people are going to go crazy," Lilith said. She held her breath as stroking fingers inched higher up her leggings. "Just look at what's spent on cosmetics and plastic surgery for results far inferior to this." Distracted, Lilith's voice trailed off.

She glanced at Kameitha, whose eyes remained on Ralen and Seth, but whose secretive smile betrayed her. Lilith clasped Kameitha's roaming hand as it reached the crease of her thigh, but Kameitha didn't pull away as she expected. Instead, her fingers continued to stroke Lilith's thigh, reaching forward, pulling Lilith's hand along, too.

After several more minutes, Kameitha gave Lilith's thigh a

squeeze, drew her hand away, and addressed Ralen. Lilith was finally able to breathe.

"I think that's a good approach, don't you?" Seth asked Lilith.

"Um, sorry?" Lilith said.

Seth frowned. "Continuing with the treatments for others with cancer. I think it makes sense to save as many terminal patients as we can—there's strength in numbers."

"Oh yes," Lilith said, still distracted.

The waitress returned with Ralen's card. "Have a nice day." She winked at Kameitha and Lilith as she walked away. Kameitha giggled, and Lilith joined in as they followed the men to the parking lot.

"What's got you all bubbly?" Seth asked.

Lilith pointed at Kameitha, who answered by leaning over and kissing the back of Lilith's neck.

"Let's go to my place," she breathed into Lilith's ear.

Suddenly speechless, Lilith quivered inside.

Seth looked from Lilith to Kameitha, then shrugged. "There'll be plenty of time for serious discussions about Renu… later." He smiled at Ralen. "Looks like I need a ride home. Care to join me for a drink? Happy hour's early today."

Chapter 10

PARK CITY, UTAH—"You've been kidnapped." Kameitha pulled Lilith toward the car, laughing. "But you still have to drive."

Lilith grinned. "That doesn't make any sense, but I like it." The door of her midnight blue Escalade clicked open as they approached, and Lilith slid inside. Were they really going to do this? Kameitha shut the passenger-side door. Without giving herself time to think, Lilith pushed the starter and waved to Seth.

He smiled at her from the passenger seat of Ralen's red Jaguar as both cars pulled out of the parking lot.

Park City was only an hour away, yet the trip lasted a year. She wanted to look at Kameitha but forced herself to focus on driving.

Kameitha slid her hand across the center console, resting her fingertips on Lilith's thigh. It made Lilith's thoughts replay the feel of Kameitha's touch against her bare skin. Lilith bit her bottom lip and sucked in a deep breath. She could hardly wait to be alone with her.

"This... attraction... is all new for me," Lilith said. Her hands were damp on the steering wheel, and the nervous churning of her stomach made her slightly nauseous. "And I've been with Seth so long, I don't even know where to begin."

"Me, too." Kameitha smiled at her. "Well, I mean, I haven't been with Seth..."

Lilith laughed. "Well, no."

"...but I'm pretty lost on where to begin, too," Kameitha said. "We'll be kind to each other, okay? No expectations—let's just do what comes naturally. Whatever *that* is."

"Yes, I'd like that," Lilith said, immediately feeling more at ease. If Kameitha was feeling the attraction as strongly as she was, that would be enough. Worst-case scenario, if things became uncomfortable between them, she had her car and could leave.

"Turn here," Kameitha said.

Lilith turned onto the road that went past Gwenlee Golf Club.

"Here." Kameitha motioned toward a driveway.

Lilith stopped the car under an overhang that spanned half the circular driveway. Before following Kameitha inside, she paused a moment, taking in the beauty of the mountains visible across a wooded valley—the same snow-capped peaks she could see from her home. The stone and timber construction of the few large houses dotted across the valley helped them blend with the natural scenery.

Floor-to-ceiling windows framed blue-green spruces visible through the south-facing glass wall. The beamed cathedral ceilings and river stone fireplace gave the great room a homey feel. Instead of the russet hues Seth favored, Kameitha's decor blended cool blue and gray with white accents.

She sat beside Kameitha on an overstuffed light-gray couch. As Lilith idly stroked the buttery-soft leather, Kameitha moved just close enough that their fingertips touched.

Then Kameitha placed her hand on Lilith's face. Their eyes met. Flecks of gold circled the pupils of Kameitha's dark brown eyes. Entranced, Lilith slid her hand into Kameitha's thick, curly hair and gently pulled her forward.

Their lips touched softly, timidly. A wave of dizziness left Lilith's head spinning. She pressed harder, hungrily. Her tongue slipped into Kameitha's mouth, probing as their bodies pressed together.

Lilith slid down, her back against the rear cushions, until they lay facing each other, their legs intertwined. She ran her hands along Kameitha's slender body, holding her so she wouldn't topple backward off the couch. Lilith slipped her hand beneath Kameitha's tunic. The feel of her soft skin sent a jolt of electricity through Lilith.

"You're killing me," Kameitha panted. "More, more."

Lilith helped Kameitha out of her tunic. She raised her hair and kissed the back of her neck. Kameitha shivered. Lilith inched Kameitha's pink lace bra aside with kisses.

Even through the heat of their lovemaking, Lilith was filled with wonder at how different she was. Unlike Seth's sturdy, solid frame, Kameitha's petite stature seemed fragile, yet strong.

Lilith's heart swelled, emotions balancing the passion. She wanted to make Kameitha happy, to please her in every way she could.

Lilith traced her side with a gentle caress. She slid her fingers beneath the band of Kameitha's leggings and slowly pulled them down, exposing the smooth skin of her hips and legs. She brushed her lips along the silky skin from Kameitha's waist to her feet, then repeated it on the other side.

She gently guided Kameitha onto her back and hovered over her. From head to toe—the lustre of her smooth, bronze skin, the firmness of her body—Kameitha was perfection. Lilith lowered to whisper breathily in Kameitha's ear, "You're so beautiful."

Kameitha drew her into a long kiss.

Eventually, Lilith pulled away and knelt at Kameitha's feet. She lifted one of Kameitha's ankles to kiss it, then her calves and inner thighs.

Kameitha arched toward her and moaned again. Lilith took her time, alternating between teasing and sating Kameitha's desires.

Then Kameitha slid onto the floor, pulling Lilith onto cushions beneath her. She unbuttoned Lilith's blouse and removed her leggings, peppering kisses all the while. Straddling Lilith, Kameitha reached for the stack of clothes she'd been wearing. "Got it." Kameitha held up her bright red silk scarf, then dragged it over Lilith's bare skin. Lilith sighed with pleasure.

Kameitha coiled it loosely around Lilith's wrists. "Is this okay?"

Lilith nodded.

"Just relax, my lovely."

Lilith could easily get free but letting Kameitha take control excited her. She surrendered, allowing herself to simply feel, and not think.

When their passion was finally spent, the room glowed yellowish orange in the waning sunlight. Lilith realized she had no idea how long they'd been there.

"Where did the day go?" Lilith said.

Kameitha reached on a chair behind her for a soft throw and

pulled it over them, drawing Lilith into her arms. "I don't want today to end."

"Me, neither." Lilith sighed. "But it's getting late. I have to get home soon."

Kameitha pressed her lips together as if she wanted to protest, then nodded. "Of course. How do you think Seth will handle this?"

"Since he's with Ralen, I don't think he'll be too concerned." Although that was a reasonable thing to assume, Lilith couldn't help but wonder. She pulled Kameitha close one more time, then rose to gather her clothes. As she put them on, she hoped Seth's afternoon had been as amazing as hers. Or did she? The idea of him with someone else sparked her possessiveness. She wasn't used to having competition. But the jealousy lasted only for a moment. She knew better. She knew it didn't have to be a choice—love didn't require that. Gratitude swept over her.

She glanced at Kameitha, who also had finished dressing. The red scarf around her neck made Lilith smile. Still, there was no way Seth could've found Ralen as bewitching as she found Kameitha.

"Catch you tomorrow?" Lilith said.

"Yes, I'd like that," Kameitha said. She stood in the doorway as Lilith drove off.

It only took Lilith a few minutes to drive the three miles to her home across the valley by another golf course. Ralen waved at Lilith as she pulled into the driveway. *Perfect timing.* She waved back. He got in his car and drove off.

Once inside, Lilith grabbed a sweater and walked onto the deck. Seth sat in one of the pumpkin-colored cushioned chairs, drink in hand. It was almost seven, and the sun neared the horizon. Purple and orange streaks reflected on the pond, which met the forest at their yard's boundary.

"Been out here long?" Lilith asked.

Seth looked up and motioned for her to join him. "Hey there."

She pulled over a chair so they were sitting with arms touching. He wrapped an arm around her, holding her close.

"What did we do to deserve all this?" he asked. "We have each other, our health, and our new partners. We are the luckiest people in the world."

She laid her head on his shoulder, breathing in the subtle musk of his scent, and the hint of unfamiliar cologne. Lilith wondered if she smelled like Kameitha.

Our new partners. Yes, that was how she thought of Kameitha and Ralen, too. "You know, I've never loved you more than I do right now." She leaned over to kiss him. "I can't remember being happier."

They sat for a few moments, watching the darkness settle and lights switch on at houses across the valley. Was one of those Kameitha's? An owl screeched.

"I've never tried to be intimate with more than one person at a time," he said. "I'm surprised it was so easy today."

"Ah, but you forget…" Lilith teased.

"What? I was always faithful!" Seth protested.

Lilith chuckled. "I know. It's just something I remembered earlier today when I had a moment of jealousy thinking about you and Ralen together. Do you remember when each new grandchild was born how we had to reassure the older children we still loved them just as much?"

Seth smiled. "You're right. This is a lot like that, isn't it? Not less love, but more."

"Maybe that's the benefit of age—of being confident enough to be honest about what you want and mature enough to not hurt others while you pursue your dreams. I'd hate to see how the grandkids would handle this, with no perspective to balance things."

"True," he said. "It's like we used to wish—that we could know all we know now when we were young."

Lilith stood and walked over to the railing. In the distance, a fish broke the water, sending ripples across the pond's surface. A breeze stirred the trees silhouetted against the sun's last rays, carrying the scent of spruce on the night air.

"That's true," she said. "We didn't know how wise we were when we said it, either."

Chapter 11

PARK CITY, UTAH—Lilith woke before Seth. Part of her wanted to analyze what had happened the previous day, while another part wanted to simply enjoy their newfound sexuality.

She had been amazed by the tenderness of her first time with Kameitha. It had been an expression of giving on both their parts that had touched her deeply. And she was grateful things between Ralen and Seth had worked so perfectly. She wanted to believe they could have it all, but only time would tell.

She sat upright in bed at the sound of her phone vibrating on the nightstand. As she grabbed it, the distinctive hunter's bugle of Seth's ringtone blared from another room.

Her caller ID said Renu. "Yes?" Lilith said.

"We're calling everyone in for more tests," the Renu rep said.

Lilith swallowed hard. "Is there a problem?" She kept her voice low as she walked toward the kitchen, trying to keep from waking Seth.

"No, nothing like that. Just an interesting... side effect."

After Lilith hung up, she poured water into the coffeemaker. If it wasn't a problem, what side effect did they mean? Could the others be experiencing the same sort of attractions?

"Who's calling so early in the morning?" Seth called out groggily.

Lilith checked the time—almost nine—and snorted. "It's not

45

exactly the crack of dawn." She returned to the bedroom and handed Seth his phone, then slipped on fresh leggings and a tunic.

He checked his voicemail.

"Renu?" Lilith asked.

"Yep." Seth pulled on jeans and shirt, and followed her into the living room.

"I don't know about you," she said, "but if the side effect is what I think it is, we should insist on keeping it!"

Seth laughed. "I'm for that!" He filled two travel mugs with coffee and handed her one as they headed toward the door.

"Do you think the others had similar... adventures?" she asked.

"Well, if it affected Hector like it did us, I'm sure he didn't waste any time letting Kate know," Seth said. "He's always on the lookout for anything that could land Renu in the funny papers."

"And Kate would've contacted Dr. J," Lilith said. "Yeah, I guess that could've happened."

As they sped down the highway, Lilith sipped her coffee and looked out the window, savoring images from the previous day that replayed in her thoughts. The playful look in Kameitha's eyes when she tied the red scarf around her wrists. Her clean, sweet scent. Her delicate caresses.

She couldn't help but contrast it with yesterday morning—how she'd awakened next to Seth at the Renu apartment, eager to join with him. He'd pulled her close, and they'd made love with more passion than she could remember in years.

It wasn't just because their bodies felt and looked better, although that certainly helped. No, it was something more—the sexuality, both familiar and new, spoke to her on a different level. It was challenging how she thought of herself.

She remembered how difficult it used to be to know who *she* was with so many demands on her to be a mother, a wife, a professional. It was easy for her true self to get lost, and for many years, it seemed like her life was overwhelmed by others' needs and wants.

After Gemini was grown, she'd had a decade of being single before she met Seth. It almost seemed like she reverted to the same core person she'd been as a teenager, with the same passions for learning, reading, writing, and art.

But her sexual identity had suffered. She wasn't young anymore —not even middle-aged. Her lessened desire was a blessing because she no longer attracted men as she once had. She struggled to redefine herself in new terms of desirability—nonsexual ones—not an easy task in a culture permeated by the culture of sex and youth.

In some ways, it was similar to the situation in which she now found herself, from the flip side. It was like she had returned to the sexuality of her younger years but now she attracted—and felt attracted to—women. Or, at least, one woman. But also one man. Well, maybe two.

It was confusing. So, who was she? Not straight or gay or even bisexual. None of those titles seemed to really describe how she felt... who she was.

"I hope this doesn't take too long," Seth said, breaking the silence as they pulled off the interstate onto the Ogden River Scenic Byway. "Ralen invited us to join him and Kameitha this afternoon at his house."

"Really?"

"He said they've been working on a new protocol," Seth said. "They're going to show it to the group, of course, but want our opinion first."

"Sounds interesting... let's do it."

When they arrived at Renu's front desk, Lilith and Seth joined the queue behind four of the international members—Xavier, Lorenz, Karla, and Yi. While almost half the group now called Utah home for at least part of the year, the others were still scattered across the globe.

"Any idea what this is all about?" Lilith asked Xavier, who stood at the end of the line with Lorenz. She had mentored Xavier—a Barcelona stockbroker—when he first joined the remote viewing group more than a decade ago.

"Not exactly." He smiled up at Lorenz, a reed-thin Dane who stood a head taller than him. "But judging from our experience and what I've been seeing around here since we arrived, I'd say there are some hormone issues."

In front of them, Karla and Yi stood so close Lilith couldn't see daylight between them. She gave Seth a knowing smile when they saw Hector in Kate's office with Dr. J and Boris Shevchenko, another of the Pioneers.

"Looks like our guess about Hector being behind this may have been on target," she said.

"Yeah, and it looks like he has a new friend." Seth grinned at Lilith as Boris put his arm around Hector's shoulders.

The barrage of tests proved relatively painless—a few vials of blood, a urine sample, and a scan. A medical doctor examined Lilith, and then a psychiatrist evaluated her.

She and Seth reconvened with the others in the conference room for an early lunch. Along one side of the room, a cold buffet of salads and fruit had been set up. Lilith filled her plate and sat next to Kameitha just as the marketing director entered. Kate's gaze swept the room, and she grinned. "Before we do anything else, we're going to get another picture."

After a few groans, the Pioneers put down their forks and followed Kate to the front of the building where the earlier image was taken. They milled around before lining up randomly.

"No." Kate grabbed Hector's arm and guided him to a spot between Ralen and Seth. "Line up in the same order as in the original photo."

After a few more adjustments—putting Monique on the front row and Xavier on the back—she took the picture. When they returned to the conference room, Kate displayed the new holo next to the earlier one.

Before the treatment, Lilith knew she looked young for a ninety-two-year-old woman, but no one would have mistaken her for a forty-year-old. Today's holo showed more than a different look—her hair's strawberry blonde hue and silky sheen had given her glowing vitality. Her large, angular, brown eyes proclaimed her Euro-Asian heritage with a fiery glint of sexuality.

Lilith tried to commit the images to memory. They caught the essence of their project—and the results—in a way no one could challenge.

The door slid open and Dr. J entered. Kate gestured for him to sit next to her.

"I'm sure you've already figured out why we wanted to do more tests right away." Dr. J grinned. "I hear things have been rather... exciting."

"How about sizzling," Kameitha said.

Lilith and the others laughed and nodded.

With a chuckle, Dr. J said, "Thanks, Kameitha. I'll add that clinical appraisal to everyone's charts—sizzling sexuality."

He stood and clicked off the room's overhead lights before starting his presentation. At the front of the room, a new holo shimmered into life. A complicated bar chart showed columns labeled homosexual and heterosexual, with a check mark next to each of their names. Lilith quickly determined the blue bars represented their original orientation, while the alternatives were orange and yellow.

Dr. J nodded. "We didn't predict the heightened attraction to the same sex for originally hetero individuals and to the opposite sex for those originally gay or lesbian. Yet the reverse attraction proved to be predominant after treatment. Without exception."

Why? Lilith wondered.

As if hearing her question, Dr. J said, "Not only had we not anticipated this, but it is unprecedented to document a dozen people simultaneously changing their preferred sexual orientation. Although, it was more of an expansion than a switch, since you maintained your previous preferences."

A murmur ran through the group. Seth reached over and squeezed Lilith's hand.

"What caused it?" Ralen asked.

"Our preliminary results indicate it's a byproduct of epigenetics," Dr. J said.

"What do you mean by that—epigenetics?" Kameitha asked.

"You don't have to change the DNA sequence to switch genes on and off," the geneticist said. "External or environmental factors —or in this case, the longevity treatment—can cause changes, too."

"So, the treatment flipped some sort of genetic switch?" Seth asked.

"It appears so." The doctor shrugged. "It will take time to really understand it, but our initial results uphold a study that had been discounted in the late Twentieth Century. It indicated stronger than average epimarks can convert sexual preference without altering sexual identity."

"Epimarks?" Kameitha asked.

"Temporary switches that influence such things as androgen signaling in the brain," he said.

Kate stood. "The doctors and I have already heard from several of you who see this as a positive outcome. Nonetheless, it could quickly become a political issue."

"How so?" Seth asked.

"Let's just say that certain segments of our society—very influential ones—have managed to prevent true equality for same-sex couples for decades," she said. "They won't welcome a treatment that removes sexuality barriers."

"So what?" Seth huffed. "Our research doesn't rely on public funding."

"Luckily, that's true," Kate said. "But they could lobby to outlaw the treatment, just like they've blocked benefits for same-sex couples and health care coverage for those with alternative lifestyles. We don't want to draw the zealots' attention. You know who I mean."

Lilith understood the reference. At the forefront was a corporate-backed lobbying group, Natural Order, which opposed anything other than government-approved pharmacology. They were particularly leery of anything that claimed to extend the lives of people whose lifestyles fell outside of what they considered "normal."

"You mean like the Natural Order's lobby against AIDS victims receiving government funding for anti-retroviral treatment?" she asked.

"Exactly," Kate said. "They blamed the gay lifestyle not only for the disease's transmission but also for posing a threat to family values. Because of thinking like that, Renu positioned the treatment as palliative care for cancer and other terminal illnesses."

Lilith wondered what the leaders of the Natural Order would do when they learned the treatment not only cured a variety of life-threatening maladies, but also affected sexual preferences.

Chapter 12

RENU CENTER, OGDEN RIVER SCENIC BYWAY—Dr. J cleared his throat, pulling their attention back to the holo projection. It showed a sequence of dividing and joining cells, with their corresponding epimarks labeled. He directed a laser pointer to one labeled "germ cell."

"During the first stages of embryonic development, epimarks direct sexual development. Afterward, if they are not erased correctly, a mother could pass to her son epimarks that activate female development. Similarly, a father could pass epimarks for male sexuality to his daughters."

Hector shrugged. "And what does that have to do with us?"

"We used germ cells—those are the eggs and sperm—to ensure that your unique genetic information was successfully passed to what is essentially your next generation. But the next generation is your own body, not a separate fetus."

"It sounds like we birthed ourselves," Hector said.

"It's a rough comparison, but close enough to the truth. Germ cells carry only half the DNA—for either male or female. The presence of telomeres protected the chromosomes throughout your transformation," Dr. J said. "At the same time, telomerase activity was minimized, just as it is in most embryonic activity."

"And that's important because?" Lilith asked.

"As you know, shortened telomeres are linked to aging," Dr. J said. "Of course, it's more complicated than that, but to the extent the telomeres and chromosomes remain intact, it's beneficial."

"But what brought us here today were the side effects—well, actually, this one side effect that didn't show up until you left the research center," Kate said. "Because of it, we need to decide whether to continue with the treatments."

Lilith and Seth exchanged a worried glance. She hadn't realized it was that serious.

"We can do a quick session here for some guidance," Lilith suggested. Since the group's early days, she had often acted as group manager when the twelve Pioneers viewed together. "It's a simple question, so let's use Associative Remote Viewing."

Always prepared, Kate handed out blank sheets of paper and pens to the Pioneers.

Lilith pulled out her phone and selected three tones from the Sounds Like app. She played an eagle's cry, a tinkling bell chime, and a siren's wail.

"Close your eyes and take three slow breaths." Lilith watched as the Pioneers followed her guidance. A few still fidgeted in their chairs after the first breath, but then they relaxed.

By the third breath, many bowed their heads and some slouched in their chairs, so relaxed they seemed on the verge of sleep.

"Go forward to three months in the future when we meet again in this room to provide feedback on the most appropriate path. Your intention is to hear whichever of those three sounds will be played, since it will be linked to the best outcome."

She paused, allowing time for them to accept the information at the subconscious level. "Now you will connect with your future self, your higher self, or however you perceive your connection with the future. Write down the first sound that comes to mind—the eagle's cry, the bell's chime or the siren."

Within minutes, the first ones picked up their pens and wrote on the paper. In less than five minutes, all had completed the task and faced her.

She placed three slips of paper with "yes," "no," and "other" written on them into a paper cup and held it out to Dr. J. "The first slip he draws will be linked to the eagle, the second to the chime, and the third to the siren."

Dr. J selected "other" first, then "yes," and finally "no."

Lilith nodded at him.

"Now, let's go around the table and share what sound what you heard," she said. The tally was seven chimes and four eagles. "The majority favors moving ahead with the treatments, although four indicate other options may need to be explored. Did anyone receive guidance on what those options might be?"

When no one offered ideas, Kate suggested, "Perhaps those four would brainstorm some possibilities and report back to us?"

The four Pioneers nodded, and Hector volunteered to lead the group.

"Seth has also brought an issue up for consideration—whether to keep the initial pace of a dozen treatments per month or to accelerate the schedule." Kate gestured to Seth.

"My concern is twofold," Seth said. "First, and most important, some of our current subscribers may die before their turn comes up if we keep to the proposed pace."

"That's definitely a problem," Dr. J said. "And while we've made every effort to prioritize treatments for those who already suffer from terminal illnesses, more people are diagnosed every day."

"This facility is equipped to safely triple the number treated if we cut the isolation time down to two weeks," Kate said.

"With the first group's astounding one-hundred percent success rate, I see no problem with doing that," Dr. J said. "But even if we triple the treatment schedule, that will only accommodate those with the most pressing health concerns."

"We'd at least be able to treat all the current subscribers who have terminal cancer within a year," Kate said. "Larger numbers of those treated will also help prove the effectiveness of the treatment."

"A larger trial size definitely makes the data more reliable and, therefore, more viable to other scientists," Dr. J added.

"But speeding up the treatment schedule will increase visibility more quickly, too. Every person's treatment will have a ripple effect," Hector said. "We need to be prepared."

"You mean, like that movie—it was just remade a few years ago —about six degrees of separation?" Kate asked.

"Exactly," Hector said. "I loved that movie, but I love the research behind it even more."

Lilith shrugged. "What are you talking about?"

"It's all about how you can be connected to any other person on the planet through a chain of acquaintances with no more than five intermediaries," he said.

"Hasn't social media made that obsolete?" Ralen said.

Kate turned to Monique, who sat next to Hector. "Let's ask our resident anthropologist."

"A lot of people would agree with Ralen," she said. "The 'small world theory' claims we've essentially reduced the intermediaries to zero. But the personal interactions are the ones that matter most. For the average American, you're talking fewer than one hundred fifty people who fall into the 'friend' category, with an average of fifteen people considered really close friends or family."

"One hundred fifty is still a lot of people," Hector said. "Just for the twelve of us, that's eighteen hundred people within our circles."

"And you can expect, with news like this, all of those people will share at least something with their circle of friends," Monique said.

"To my point," Hector said. "The news will spread like wildfire."

"And that brings me to my second point," Seth said. "I believe there's safety in numbers if the Natural Order does decide to try and shut us down—the more terminally ill people Renu saves, the better."

"So, you believe accelerating our treatment schedule may attract the attention of Natural Order more quickly, but it also will build our army of supporters faster?" Kate said. "I agree with you on that, Seth."

Lilith nodded. "The more people who have experienced this life-saving treatment or personally know someone who did, the less likely they are to fall victim to whatever tricks Natural Order may attempt."

"And they always do find a way to make a good thing look bad," Kameitha said. "Remember how they claimed the women's clinics advocated abortions so they could make huge profits by selling body parts and stem cells from the fetuses?"

Seth nodded. "Even though the clinics followed the same guidelines for disposing of fetuses as leading hospitals. But Natural Order doesn't let the truth get in the way of sensationalism."

Kate sighed. "I'm sure we'll get a taste of their tactics, no matter how careful we are."

"Okay, Seth, it sounds like another quick session is needed," Lilith suggested. "This time, we'll randomly associate outcomes with primary colors to decide on the treatment schedule."

Lilith led them through the breathing exercise. "Now write down the first primary color that comes to mind."

When they finished, she placed a single word—"increase," "decrease," and "maintain"—on slips of paper and placed them into a paper cup. She held it out to Kate. "The first slip of paper you choose will be linked to red, the second to blue, and the third to yellow."

Kate selected "maintain" first, then "decrease," and "increase."

Tallying up the colors around the table, the results were ten yellow for increasing the treatments and one red to maintain the current schedule.

"When we meet in three months, the medical team will give us feedback on what they feel were the best decisions," she said.

Lilith knew it was impossible to know what could have happened if they'd made a different choice, but the Pioneers had seen good results trusting in the outcome of sessions like these. She returned to her seat, confident about their decision for Renu to continue the treatments at an accelerated pace.

Kate returned to the front of the room. "Hector, did you have anything else today?"

He shook his head.

"Then I suggest we reconvene after your checkups next week," Kate said. "I'll be in touch if anything changes."

Kameitha turned toward Lilith. "Seth told you about the new protocol?"

She nodded. "We're planning to come over now, if that works for you."

"Of course." Kameitha smiled. "It won't take long to discuss. Ralen and I just want to share it with you first."

"We're good with that." Lilith stood, and the four walked out of the conference room together.

Chapter 13

PARK CITY, UTAH—As they drove back to Park City, Lilith pondered what Hector and Monique said about the circle of friends. Did her life really touch one hundred fifty people? Could a tenth of that number be called close friends?

She started counting off the people currently in her life—the various groups where she met for book study, meditation, walking, or just coffee. Organizations she belonged to in support of various causes and shared interests. Family. Friendships, many from her work years, which she maintained on Facebook, by phone, and occasional visits to cities where she used to live. And, of course, the remote viewing community. They were mostly online, but some were certainly among her closest confidantes, even before the treatment.

Altogether, she found the number surprisingly close to one hundred fifty, but her best friends numbered only five. Those were friends she had always believed she could tell her darkest secrets and know they would support her. When she thought more about it, she wondered if fifteen close friends was an average. Maybe extroverts had twenty or more "best" friends, while introverts had fewer, but closer, ones.

Lilith imagined how all those in her circle would react when they next met, and she grew anxious. Before the treatment, Lilith thought she would be eager to face the world with news of their success. After all, it was good news—a miracle really—that she and Seth were not only cancer-free but physically rejuvenated. Now she wasn't so sure. Was it because she no longer faced the immediate threat of death? Or was it because she empathized with how her peers viewed forty-somethings?

Lilith shook her head, telling herself she was silly. Real friends would be happy for her, even thrilled that she was healthy again.

"What is it?" Seth asked. "You seem upset."

"How do you feel about today's discussion?" Lilith asked.

"Funny you should ask," Seth said, signaling to merge onto I-15. "I was just thinking about that. Returning to our lives may be trickier than we thought."

"That's what I'm thinking, too," Lilith agreed. "My alumni group meets next month, and I'm almost afraid to go. I know they'll be happy for us, but there's no way anyone who's not already on the subscriber list will be able to get the treatment any time soon."

"I have the same situation," Seth said. "Some of the guys I used to work with are very ill. And, as Kate and Dr. J pointed out, even tripling the treatment rate, those not currently subscribers will have to wait at least a year. They won't all make it that long."

"I had thought we'd be beacons of hope, symbols of what is possible," she said. "I still think that. But, in the short term, it's not going to be that way, is it?"

"I think we need to come up with options," Seth said. "There has to be a way to get those who most need the treatment to the head of the line."

"True, but then there's the expense," Lilith said. "Experimental treatments aren't covered by insurance, and except for the Pioneers, most people we know don't have the kind of resources we do."

"That's where we would've been without remote viewing," Seth said as they merged onto I-80. "But Renu's price will come down."

"I know, but probably not in time for most of our friends," she said.

She stared out the window, her eyes unfocused. The vague shapes of snow-capped mountains morphed into her friend's face as she recalled the time they'd spent at Deer Valley resort.

"Do you remember Margie?" she asked.

"Your friend from D.C. who visited us a few years ago—the one who liked karaoke?"

"Yeah, that's her. She just turned ninety," Lilith said. "Last month, she found out she has inoperable melanoma in her eye."

Seth reached over and patted her hand. "I'm sorry, Lilith."

Tears brimmed in her eyes. Why couldn't this be easier? Lilith knew she should be celebrating her own recovery, but instead she kept thinking how many of her friends would die without the treatment. Her phone buzzed—another text from her best friend, Julie. Since they were released from Renu, Lilith had been texting Julie and her other close friends, assuring them everything was fine. She had avoided meeting with any of them.

"We don't know the long-term effects of the treatment," Seth continued. "We may experience accelerated aging over the next few years, or the cancer may return. We just don't know."

"I guess you're right," Lilith bit her lower lip. "It is experimental." She closed her eyes, asking for guidance, then texted Julie a time and place to meet.

"Then there's the population issue," Seth said.

Lilith squinted at Seth, puzzled. "What do you mean?"

"You know—too many people on the planet to feed, and all that," he said.

"Ha," she said. "I'd be worried about that if the population trends weren't going the other way."

"Really?" Doubt filled his voice. "What about all those world hunger pictures?"

"I'm not saying there aren't food and water shortages, or that people don't go hungry," Lilith said. "But that's more about economics and distribution. When it comes to population, some forecast that dropping fertility rates could lead to decreasing population levels by 2100."

"But that's based on the current death rate, right?" Seth said.

"True," Lilith said. "By the turn of the century, the median age will be forty-two, compared to thirty now. If the treatment means people survive, would that be so bad if those over sixty remain as healthy and productive as they were in their forties?"

"I think it will be a long time before the treatment becomes that common," Seth said.

"I thought so, too, but today's discussion made me wonder. We're all so connected through the internet, this won't be a secret for long."

Seth was quiet for several minutes. "You might be right. I remember seeing stats about how it took only four years for more than forty percent of American households to get smartphones, compared with about forty-five years for landlines."

"Well, we're not talking about a new gadget, but that's exactly the point I was making. This treatment meets a need for millions of people." Lilith chuckled when her phone vibrated. "Speak of the devil." She pulled the phone out of her purse and placed the call on speaker. "Hi, Gemini."

"Hi, Mom," she replied. "Are you busy this evening?"

Lilith glanced at Seth, who shrugged. "No, we don't have plans."

"Why don't you come over for dinner? The kids want to celebrate your recovery," Gemini said.

Lilith smiled. "Of course, we'd love that. What time?"

"Six?" Gemini said.

"Six it is." Lilith ended the call and took a deep breath. "This should be interesting." Butterflies flitted in her stomach as she considered how the rest of the family would react.

Seth turned onto Highway 224.

"I didn't realize Ralen lived so close," Lilith said. "And Kameitha's home is less than a mile from here."

"Yeah, looks like we all had the same idea when it came to buying houses. It doesn't get much better than Park City." Seth pulled off Empire Club Drive in front of a sprawling complex of high-end condos, then turned into a triple-wide driveway and parked.

Seth knocked on the massive wooden doors. Moments later, Ralen invited them in. A fire danced in the two-story stone fireplace, giving the room a flickering glow. Windows on both sides of it gave views of the mountains to the west. Across the room, a long granite countertop with bar seating opened to the kitchen, where Kameitha placed a pitcher and frosted glasses onto a tray.

"Your timing's perfect," she said. "Hope you like sangria."

"One of my favorites," Lilith said.

"Great," Seth added as Lilith joined him on the brown leather sectional facing the fireplace. Kameitha poured, then Ralen handed each a glass.

Lilith took a sip. "I understand you've been working on a new remote-viewing protocol."

Ralen glanced at Kameitha, then nodded. "Yes, we've done a few sets of twenty to test it. So far, we've had a pretty good hit rate."

"Nothing too astounding, but a solid seventy percent success rate," Kameitha said.

"That's not too shabby," Seth said, raising his glass in a toast. "I look at every point above sixty as like a point on the Richter Scale — each worth about ten times the previous rating."

They clinked glasses as Kameitha shared their spreadsheets. "Only the two of us viewed and self-judged each set, which had its own issues, but the data stayed more consistent."

"I can see that," Lilith said. "A trade-off of breadth for depth."

"It looks like you had some variation, though," Seth said after scrutinizing the data for a few minutes. "Here, for instance, you had a set of twenty that reached a seventy-five percent hit rate."

Kameitha leaned over to see where he was pointing. "Oh yes," she said. "That was the love sequence."

"The love sequence? Sounds like a cheesy song from the '80s. This I've got to hear."

Kameitha grinned. "Sure, let me tell you about the *love* vibe."

Lilith laughed.

Ralen gazed over his tented fingers, looking every bit the cranky professor. "It's really all vibrational, like it always is, except this time we focused on achieving a specific level."

Kameitha cleared her throat. "I call it the love vibration because it's tied to the heart, and to what some say is the vibration of the Earth itself."

"I've heard of that," Lilith said. "It has to do with magnetic waves?"

"Yeah. It was a big movement a couple of decades ago, but not so much lately," Kameitha said. "Although I don't know why. The science is solid."

"At one time, it was part of what they called the Global Coherence Initiative," Ralen said.

"There are even biofeedback apps to help monitor your own vibration," Kameitha said. "That's what we used to get in the right mindset to do that particular group of viewings. We tried to get our heart waves to equal 0.1 hertz, which is the frequency of your heart rhythm when you're in a coherent state with the Earth."

"How did you do that?" Lilith said.

"Just by visualizing things that made me feel love or happiness or peace," Ralen said. "That's all it took. The monitor made it clear when my vibration was in sync."

"Interesting," Lilith said. "So, the protocol is more about the prep work than the actual tasking or viewing?"

"You could say that," Kameitha said.

"After you focus on the heart until you're in sync, then you do a viewing as you normally would?" Seth asked.

"That's right," Ralen said.

"We only changed one variable at a time, and the love sequence was our most successful run," Kameitha said. "It worked best when the viewer had a coherent heart rhythm and used Associative Remote Viewing in a double-blind setting."

"We want to do a bigger trial with the whole group—just run through all the variables to confirm our initial findings," Ralen said.

"Sounds like a good plan," Seth said. "How can we help?"

"Just supporting us when we propose it would be wonderful," Kameitha said.

Lilith and Seth both nodded.

"Of course," Lilith said.

"Sure," Seth added. "Anything that helps us get more accurate data is always good."

A buzz drew Lilith's attention to her phone. "Looks like we need to go." She shut off the alarm. "We're expected at a family get-together."

They stood. Ralen draped an arm around Seth's shoulders as they walked toward the door.

"We'll be waiting to hear from you," Seth said.

Kameitha followed Lilith to the car, giving her a hug before Lilith slid in on the passenger side. By the time they turned onto Highway 224, Lilith was already missing her. From Seth's silence, she figured his thoughts were on Ralen.

"I don't know if I'm ready to face the kids," she said.

"Yeah, I know what you mean," Seth said. "I feel kind of like a mixed-up teenager myself."

Lilith chuckled. "Exactly what I was thinking! What do you think we should do about it?"

Seth shrugged. "Play it out, I guess, and see where we land."

Lilith thought about what that could mean—trying to work out everyone's schedules, guessing about feelings. It was everything she had hated about dating.

When she and Seth had gotten together, it was so easy. They were already online friends and met a few times privately before the

Pioneers formed a real group. Their vision for the Pioneers had brought them together more and more often, as they both slipped into leadership roles. Eventually, it just seemed natural to move in together.

While she shared a similar camaraderie with Kameitha and Ralen, the sexual tension brought back memories of Gemini's biological father. Their summer together more than sixty years ago still shone brightly in her memories—some of the best and worst times of Lilith's life.

Now she would describe her attraction to the handsome, dark-haired college professor as obsession, rather than love. When he'd broken up with her, she didn't think she could live without him. Boz Scaggs wailed "Look what you've done to me" on the radio and in her heart. Finally, the summer ended, and he called to make amends. In the heat of the make-up, they'd conceived Gemini, but Lilith soon realized lust wasn't a solid foundation for a lifetime together. She'd raised their beautiful daughter alone.

Lilith's body now responded to the constant sexual pull with urgency reminiscent of that time. It terrified and thrilled her in equal measure. Was she any wiser now? She had to wonder, because of the overwhelming impulse to follow her instincts. Every fiber in her body wanted to be with Kameitha.

She looked out the window but found herself distracted by Seth's image reflected in the glass. "Do you think it would be reckless for us all to try living together?" she said.

He glanced at her with a slight smile. "Just like that?"

"I know, it seems awfully fast." She sighed and turned toward him. "But the treatment has given us this new future. We're different now, and I think we should be bold and try a different living arrangement."

"Let's see if we can use their new protocol to test out some scenarios," Seth said. "We'll each come up with ideas and keep them to ourselves, then randomize the selections so we don't even know which one is being considered."

She thought about it a moment. "Yes, I like that. We could even bring the Pioneers together to have more input."

"It's what we do." Seth reached out and squeezed her hand briefly before returning it to the steering wheel. "I'm here for you, Lilith. We'll find a way to make this work for all of us."

Chapter 14

MIDWAY, UTAH—Seth and Lilith drove the half hour to Gemini's home in Midway. A carved wooden sign reading "Seven Oaks" marked the winding private drive. Just before six, they pulled in and parked in front of the four-car garage. Its doors were open, and every space was filled.

Silently noting Derek's silver Sienna and Lacy's black Outback, Lilith said, "Looks like the whole gang's here."

Lilith wasn't too surprised. Not long after Gemini's husband died five years ago, her children—both single parents—had moved back into the spacious, four-bedroom home where they'd been raised. To make room for them, Gemini had moved into the two-bedroom bunkhouse. A wood-shingled breezeway connected it to the main house and provided access to a natural hot spring soaking pool.

Every time Lilith visited the buff-brick home, it struck her anew what a wise decision Gemini and her children made. Instead of struggling to maintain separate households, Derek and Lacy shared responsibility for making the mortgage payments so their mother could stay in the home she loved, and their kids could attend top-ranked schools. Both had about an hour's commute—him to the outskirts of Ogden and her to Salt Lake City. Gemini was home with the kids before and after school.

Seconds after Seth's car door slammed shut, the front door

inched open. Wide eyes watched Lilith and Seth as they walked up the sidewalk.

"Gran?" Sixteen-year-old Rachel's voice quivered as she opened the door the rest of the way.

"Pops?" Faye poked her head from behind her younger cousin and squinted at him.

Lilith chuckled at their serious expressions. "It's really us, girls. Your Grandma Gem told you we'd look different, didn't she?"

They nodded.

"Come here." Lilith held her arms wide.

They took a few steps forward. Lilith wrapped an arm around each girl and gave her a hug. "See, same old Gran, with just a little more pep to help me keep up with you two." She playfully swatted their bums, earning a groan from Rachel and a sigh from Faye. "Now lead the way to the festivities."

Faye dropped back a step and gave Seth a long stare. "Your hair is changing color," she said. "And your face is… *so* different."

"You just didn't know me when I was younger," he said. "To me, I look more like myself. You'll see what I mean when you get older."

"Yeah, right." She grabbed his hand. "Come on, Pops"

They walked across the great room and onto to the Brazilian tiger wood deck that wrapped around the back of the house.

"They're here," Rachel announced cheerily.

Derek looked up from the grill. Lacy switched her gaze between her mother, who was setting the patio table, and Lilith.

"I don't believe this." Lacy threw her hands up. "You look my age, Gran."

Gemini chuckled at her daughter's reaction and shrugged. "Told you she didn't look much over forty."

Lilith laughed. "I'm still your grandmother, Lacy, and don't you forget it." She looked around. "Where are the boys?"

"They should've already been home," Gemini said. Just then, the front door opened.

Faye elbowed Rachel. "The guys are going to freak out!"

Rachel chortled. "So true!"

Lilith smiled at their banter as the girls ran to break the news to their younger brothers.

Lacy frowned at Lilith. "Mom's been really upset. She was so worried about you both."

Lilith sucked in her breath and nodded. Lacy's typical directness shouldn't have caught her off-guard, but it did. "I really am sorry we couldn't tell you earlier, honey," Lilith told Gemini as she took the seat next to her. "To be truthful, I wasn't sure I would make it through." She shook her head, remembering the pain. "It was pretty awful at first. Your body breaks down before it gets better."

"But you did… we did… get better." Seth walked over and stood with his hands on Lilith's shoulders.

"And thank goodness for that!" Gemini said.

"Actually, your Mom reacted to the serum faster than any of us. You can see how well the treatment worked for her."

"The cancer's really gone?" Lacy took a seat across from Lilith as she put a platter of steaming asparagus spears on the table.

"The doctors say the treatment restores cellular health, so there simply isn't a way for the cancer to thrive anymore," Seth explained.

"How does that even work?" Derek said. "It's mind-boggling."

"It is," Lilith said. "They say it's kind of like birthing yourself, or maybe cloning. Pretty complicated."

"And the Pioneers were responsible for figuring it out?" Lacy asked.

"Well, it couldn't have happened without our medical team," Lilith conceded. "But yes, we asked the right questions and viewed the answers needed for the breakthroughs to occur."

"Evan, Sam—you, too, girls—get in here. Dinner's served," Gemini called out. A few minutes later, the teens filed in, with the youngest lagging behind.

"What's up, my boy?" Seth asked.

The lanky fourteen-year-old gave Seth a puzzled look as he took the seat across from him. "Pops?"

Seth smiled and nodded. "Of course, it's me."

"The girls said you were a lot younger now." Sam looked over to Evan for support.

"Yeah, how is that even possible?" Evan asked, glancing between Seth and Lilith with a frown line between his eyebrows.

"It has to do with telomeres—you'll learn about that in biology," Seth said.

Rachel and Faye nodded, but Evan still looked puzzled.

"But this is so new even the doctors can't really explain how it works yet," Seth continued.

"Are you younger than Mom?" Sam asked Lilith.

Lacy choked on her drink.

"Of course not," Lilith replied. "My age hasn't changed, just how I look." Now that she'd said it, Lilith wasn't sure that was entirely truthful, but she couldn't explain it any better.

Derek snorted and elbowed Lacy. "Yeah, Sis, remember that. She just *looks* younger than you."

Lacy glared at him. "Hey bud, you need to look in the mirror. Seth could pass for your better-looking brother."

Derek shrugged and placed a hefty stack of steaks and grilled shrimp in front of Seth, who didn't waste any time spearing his share before passing the plate. "It's true. Everyone over fifty is going to want to look as good as you do."

"And then there are millions with cancer who will want the cure," Lacy said.

The teenagers bolted down their food. Rachel and Faye picked up their dishes and deposited them in the sink on the way out the door. Their laughter faded as they neared the bunkhouse, where they shared a room in the loft.

Evan made it halfway to the door before his dad noticed.

"Get back here, young man," Derek called out. "You know better than to leave your dishes on the table."

Evan sighed and picked up his empty plate. Sam joined him in the kitchen, and then they noisily made their way upstairs to their rooms.

Lilith hated that the great-grandchildren had left, but at least they'd made an appearance. Since they'd become teens, it was hard enough to get a "hello," much less have a conversation.

"I wouldn't be surprised to see Renu centers on every street corner, just like Starbucks," Derek said.

"Really? Like Starbucks?" Lilith sat back, letting herself actually imagine small, storefront treatment centers. In all the excitement about getting the first research center running and perfecting a treatment that worked on people, she had never envisioned anything like that. Her excitement quickly faded as she remembered their earlier discussion with Kate and Hector.

"You've actually hit on one of the problems," Lilith said. "Even if we cut the isolation time in half, as they plan to do, we have to figure out how to prioritize those who receive treatment."

"And if the FDA gets more involved, we'd pretty much have to start the testing phase from scratch," Seth added. "If that happens, it could be decades before the treatment is widely available."

Derek shook his head. "What are you going to do—take it overseas? That doesn't seem fair to folks here."

Lilith speared a piece of asparagus and swallowed it before answering. "There are a lot of factors to consider. But we've decided to treat as many people with terminal illness as we can in the next three months, then re-evaluate."

Lacy toyed with the last piece of steak on her plate. "How do you think our friends—and Mom's—are going to react?"

"What do you mean?" Lilith asked.

"Well, for one thing, it's kind of awkward to have a grandmother who looks my age. I can just imagine how it is for Mom," she said.

Stunned, Lilith looked at Gemini. Was Lacy right?

"Lacy, you don't have to be so negative," Gemini said. "The treatment saved your grandparents' lives. That's what matters."

"I know," Lacy said defensively. "And I am grateful for that— really. I'm simply pointing out what everyone else is thinking."

"No doubt about it. This fountain-of-youth cure is going to be all that's talked about by anyone who knows what you've been through with the cancer," Derek said.

"That's true, Mom, and a lot of desperate people are going to be knocking on your door," Gemini said.

Chapter 15

PARK CITY, UTAH—The next morning at ten, Ralen and Kameitha arrived at Seth and Lilith's home for brunch, responding to texts from the previous night.

"You have a project in mind for us? That didn't take long," Ralen said.

"We decided it couldn't wait," Lilith said. "But we want to keep the tasking blind, so we really can't tell you much about it."

"I see." Kameitha sat next to Ralen at the dining table after filling her plate at the breakfast bar.

"We would like to bring the other Pioneers in, too, to get more robust feedback," Seth added.

"Sounds perfect," Kameitha said.

"You brought biofeedback apps for everyone?" Lilith asked.

"Sure did," Kameitha said.

"We're ready to put the protocol to use," Ralen added.

After they finished eating, Seth and Ralen cleared the table, while Kameitha sat next to Lilith on the couch to draft an email requesting the rest of the Pioneers to join them around four that afternoon. That left plenty of time for Kameitha and Ralen to figure out how to set up the room so each person could monitor their heart resonance. It also gave Lilith and Seth time to refine their questions.

Scuffling noises from the kitchen drew Lilith's attention,

followed by the splatter of spraying water. "Stop!" Seth screeched and running footsteps ended with a thud and Ralen's grunt.

"Man!" Ralen laughed. "What's wrong? Afraid you'll melt like sugar?"

Another spray of water preceded Seth's roar. "I'm really going to get you now!"

Kameitha looked up at Lilith, obviously amused at the laughter and scuffling noises coming from the adjoining room. "Are they having a water fight?"

"They can't be! They're grown men." They finished composing the message and clicked "send," and then Lilith slid the laptop onto the counter. "But let's check it out." She and Kameitha stealthily approached the door, staying out of sight. They peeked around the doorway just as Ralen used the spray arm from the sink to squirt Seth, but he dodged to the side. Water arced across the room and hit Kameitha's chest.

"What!" She laughed and spluttered. Then she rushed at him, grabbing Ralen's hand and turning the spray arm so the water drenched his face. In surprise, Ralen released the spray arm and, lightning quick, Kameitha turned the water on Lilith.

Covering her face, Lilith ran a few steps and slid into Kameitha. They struggled good-naturedly, until Lilith reached over and slapped the handle down, shutting off the water. Her hair dripped into her face. Looking around, Lilith saw the others had fared no better. "You guys are crazy!"

"Crazy like a fox!" Kameitha grinned slyly. "Our very own wet T-shirt contest." She pulled Lilith over. "You look darn good wet."

"Umm, so do you." Lilith pressed Kameitha's back against the wall and kissed her. A few minutes later, Lilith opened her eyes slightly to see Seth and Ralen slip out of the room.

"Come on. I wouldn't want you to catch cold." Lilith took Kameitha's hand and led her down the hallway, past the closed door of the master bedroom to a guest bedroom. She pulled the door closed. "Let me help you out of those wet clothes."

———

BEFORE THE OTHERS arrived that afternoon, Lilith and Seth placed each question in an unmarked, sealed envelope, which they gave to

Kameitha. She shuffled them and handed the sealed envelopes to Ralen, who mixed them up more.

It surprised Lilith when all eight of the remaining Pioneers showed up. She hadn't realized those from outside Utah had not yet returned home.

"I couldn't leave," Yi said, pulling Karla close. "We wanted to spend more time together."

"And you're together, too?" Lilith asked Xavier and Lorenz, who were sitting together on the couch.

They nodded.

"For now, Monique is letting us stay with her," Xavier said.

"I see," Lilith said. She was beginning to wonder if they needed to seek guidance regarding alternative arrangements if people had already begun living together. Apparently, when the option was to be separated by hundreds or thousands of miles or to live together, it clarified their thinking.

Kameitha situated the viewers in a circle facing outward. Ralen gave each an older-model cell phone with the biofeedback app, which linked to a pressure cuff fitted over their pointer finger.

Lilith opened with a cool-down session.

"Clear your mind," she said. "Relax. Imagine a golden orb spinning above your head, sending its light around you. Surrounding you."

After several minutes of silence, she said, "Now write down the coordinates." She gave a six-digit number to one group of four, and a different six-digit number to another group of four. She turned up the volume on a recording of Hemi-Sync music. The binaural beats helped the viewers to reach a coherent brain-wave pattern by increasing interaction between the brain's two hemispheres. As Lilith walked around the room, she saw the monitors shift to green, indicating their hearts had reached the desired 0.1 hertz level. As that happened, they began writing and drawing as instructed.

Within five minutes, the first viewers put down their pens to indicate their completion. Within another ten minutes, all were done.

Kameitha and Lilith took half the transcripts to judge, and Seth and Ralen took the others. The sealed envelopes each bore one of the coordinate numbers the viewers had been given. Using the rating criteria developed at Stanford Research Institute, they compared each of the transcripts to the two computer-generated photos for each coordinate, then gave each photo a confidence ranking between one and seven.

Everyone gathered in the dining room.

"My team had a strong preference for what I'll call Side 1," Kameitha said, "with three of the four transcripts having confidence rankings between four and six for this coordinate. All had rankings of less than 3.5 for the other option, or Side 2, indicating no psychic connection was made with that target."

She used a projector app on her laptop to show the computer-generated photos on the wall—one was a steam locomotive and the other was a waterfall. Kameitha then pulled up the files showing the transcripts, which were filled with images of water.

"Side 1 was randomly linked to this statement." She opened the sealed envelope, reading it for the first time. "It is in the best interest of all concerned for the Pioneers to explore non-traditional living arrangements."

Lilith looked at Seth and smiled. She hadn't seen the tasking questions he formulated until now. They were surprisingly similar to her own.

"And Side 2 advocated 'maintaining the living arrangements Pioneers had prior to the treatment,'" Kameitha continued.

Around the table, couples grasped hands and exchanged smiles. Kameitha looked quizzically at Lilith. "Your question?" she asked.

Lilith shook her head.

Seth stepped over to the laptop and clicked the next set of photos. "Again, the computer randomly linked the two photos to coordinates," he explained. He showed the Side 1 photo of a person eating an ice cream cone; the Side 2 photo was of a shark. The rankings he and Ralen had given the transcripts were highest for Side 1. Many of the viewers had drawn people and cone-shaped objects.

"Side 1 was randomly linked to this outcome." He opened the sealed envelope for the coordinate and read, "Pursuing alternative living arrangements sooner rather than later is advisable for those who have undergone Renu treatment."

Another murmur rose from those sitting at the table. "That was mine," Lilith told Kameitha. "Obviously, Seth was on the same wavelength, although we developed our questions independently."

"I'd say this is clear-cut," Hector said. "For those of us who've been feeling drawn to do something different, this validates following our instinct."

"The question is, 'How different?'" Lilith said. "I haven't had a chance to talk with Seth about this yet, but earlier today, I envisioned something I'd like to share with all of you."

She cleared her throat and continued. "Many of us have beautiful homes in Park City and elsewhere that we bought soon after our early successes in the stock market. But now we find ourselves more than an hour from the research center. We could easily build a home with separate living suites and common areas that would give us the best of independent and communal living."

"Making it easy for us to enjoy our new relationships without interference or unwanted social pressures," Monique said.

"I like it." Kameitha's face lit up. She reached for Lilith's hand.

"It's very... civilized," Yi said, her gaze fixed on Karla. "Singapore is definitely too far away for me."

Karla nodded in agreement. "I can sell my condo in Brazil."

By the time the meeting came to an end several hours later, they'd leveraged their contacts to hire a real estate agent and an architect. Hector had arranged for the legal issues to be thoroughly vetted over the next few days, to ensure their financial interests would be individually and jointly protected.

As Seth closed the door behind the last person, he turned to Lilith. "That went remarkably well! And it wouldn't have happened if you hadn't shared your vision with us." Lilith laid her head against his shoulder as he held her in his arms. "The future is looking bright for all of us, my love," he said.

"It is, isn't it?" She looked up at Seth, studying his strong jawline stubbled with the day's growth, and couldn't help but wonder what the next months would bring. Things were moving fast, which she wanted, but it was also unnerving.

She looked around their spacious home, with its beamed cathedral ceilings, gleaming oak floors, and granite countertops. "Remember when we bought this place? I thought it was the most magnificent home I'd ever seen."

Seth laughed. "Sure, I remember. You said it wasn't a dream home, it was a rock star haven."

"Those were high times," she said. "We've become so used to making big money from our viewing, we forget how revolutionary it was."

"And it still is, so far as most people are concerned," he said. "I just can't understand why more people—even our own family and friends—don't try it."

Lilith shrugged. "Most people give up too soon. We almost did. Remember how that first trial bombed? Our forty-thousand-dollar investment was gone in a month."

Seth shivered. "How could I forget? Well, I'm glad we kept at it. But without you by my side, I don't know if I would've."

"Same here," Lilith said. "We have shared some amazing things, haven't we?"

"Yeah, but the treatment is in a class of its own," Seth said. "It's still hard to believe we're cured."

"It is, isn't it?" she said. "You know, I'll hate leaving this place, but I'm ready to move forward, aren't you?"

Seth nodded. "For years, these are the people who've shared our dreams—they stayed through the wagering trials, the research, the treatment. Now we're taking the next steps—together."

"When you look at it that way, all of us sharing a home doesn't seem so impetuous." Lilith pulled his arm and took a few steps down the hall toward the bedroom. "C'mon, I could use some rest."

He slid his hand down to her waist and pulled her close. "But I'm not sleepy."

She laughed. "Guess I'll have to tell you a bedtime story.

Chapter 16

Snugly cocooned in the bed covers the next morning, Lilith thought about just letting the phone ring. But maybe it was Renu again. What if this time it was a real problem? She grabbed the phone and read Kameitha's name on the caller ID. *Stop borrowing trouble,* she told herself.

Lilith pressed the speaker button. "Hey girl, this is getting to be a habit."

"Hmmm," Kameitha said. "With any luck, soon I won't have to call to wake you up."

Warmth spread through Lilith. "That's a nice thought." Propped on one arm, she turned to face Seth. "Don't you agree?"

He grunted, then sat up and stretched. "I think I need coffee."

Both women laughed.

Kameitha cleared her throat. "Not to name names, lazy bones, but some of us have been up for a couple of hours."

Amused, Lilith said, "Look, Seth. It's eight o'clock—half the day is gone!"

He shook his head and slipped on a robe. "You're both crazy."

"Well, that's true," Kameitha said. "But this time I have a real reason for calling so early. We have an appointment with the real estate agent at ten."

"What?" Lilith sputtered and sat upright.

"And it takes an hour to get there," Kameitha said.

"But we just hired her yesterday." Lilith kicked off the covers.

"Oh, Suzanne and I go way back. She was my son's friend in college," Kameitha said. "We've been texting since the group decided to use her. She's already got a half dozen sites for us to check out

Lilith jumped out of bed, opened the closet door and sorted through her clothes. "All right." She pulled out a pair of tan chinos and a white blouse. "It'll take me at least thirty minutes to shower and dress."

"I'll pick you up," Kameitha said. "Fair warning—I'll harass Seth if you're not ready."

Lilith chuckled. "You do that. Fair warning back to you—he's a slow riser. He doesn't usually say much before ten or until he's had at least two cups of coffee."

Showered and dressed, Lilith stood at the top of the stairs and listened to Seth's familiar laughter from below as she slipped on her favorite turquoise earrings. Once again, she thought how easily Kameitha and Ralen fit into their lives.

Lilith joined them in the kitchen. Kameitha sat at the breakfast bar, a steaming cup of coffee in hand. She wore jeans, a long-sleeved yellow top, and a rust-colored puff jacket. Seth, still in his robe, pointed to the holographic map projected from his laptop.

"No, even if we do end up in Eden, we're not going to call our place The Garden." He tilted his chin up in mock disdain.

Kameitha gave him a playful pout. "What do you think, Lil?"

"I'm not getting in the middle of that!"

"You're no fun," Kameitha said. "I tried to get Seth to come with us today, but Ralen beat me to the punch."

"Oh?" Lilith said.

"It's like Grand Central Station around here." Seth grabbed the coffee pot, poured Lilith a cup, and topped off Kameitha's. "He called just after I came downstairs to see if I wanted to meet the architect at the Club for lunch."

"Good idea." Lilith nodded and sipped her coffee.

"I think so, too," Seth said. "The architect can't do much until we decide on the land, but at least we can start talking about requirements."

She gave him a quick kiss and grabbed her jean jacket from the coat closet in the foyer. "We'll compare notes tonight."

Kameitha linked arms with Lilith and practically skipped to the car. "This is going to be great! I have a feeling we're going to find the perfect place today."

As she walked to the car, Lilith gave silent thanks for the gift of being alive. The sun lit a robin's egg-blue sky, promising a pleasant day. They buckled up and settled into a comfortable silence for several miles. Lilith cracked a window, and cool, crisp, fall air wafted through the car. "Too much?"

"No, it's perfect," Kameitha said. "I love the fresh air."

"So, tell me about Suzanne," Lilith said.

"As I mentioned, she's Jeremy's age, maybe a little younger, and a real go-getter," Kameitha said. "She's been Ogden's Realtor of the Year several times."

"Sounds impressive," Lilith said.

"I forwarded you my favorite links of the ones she sent," Kameitha said. "It's pretty hard to tell much about land without being there."

Lilith opened her email and clicked the first one: Eighty acres with limited access on a mountaintop.

"Great potential for small off-grid resort development," she read out loud. "That sounds perfect to me. I'd love to be off the grid."

"Me, too," Kameitha said, "but you'd have to really know what you're doing."

Lilith nodded. "It's been done before, my friend. We can do this! And compared to property values in Park City, this one's a steal at about five thousand an acre."

"I like the privacy," Kameitha said. "If I recall, it's surrounded by thousand-acre properties."

"You're right." Lilith checked the location map. "Looks like Powder Ridge Road connects to Highway 158, so it's less than thirty minutes to get to Ogden and probably only ten to the Renu Center."

"Of course, it's a different matter when it snows," Kameitha said. "It looks pretty inaccessible."

Lilith clicked the next link. "Oh, this one's next to the Snowflake Inn on Highway 158. I know where that is. And it overlooks Pineview Reservoir. Let's see—it's about ten times as much per acre as the other property."

"You'd have the option of not going completely off-grid," Kameitha said.

Lilith nodded as she pulled up the map. "And it's closer in." While it was only eleven miles from Ogden, the property was about the same distance as the other one to the Renu Center. She gave a low whistle when she clicked the next link. "Two million dollars for fifty-five acres... I see. It's adjacent to the Nordic Valley Ski Resort."

"Suzanne said they've already completed improvements to water lines and easements, as well as engineering and geotech studies," Kameitha said. "It's out Highway 162 between Eden and Liberty, so it's the farthest from the Renu Center and Ogden."

As they neared Suzanne's office in Ogden, Kameitha frowned slightly and her shoulders stiffened.

"You okay?" Lilith asked, puzzled by her sudden mood change.

"Hmm?" Kameitha said. "Yeah, fine."

"You seem preoccupied."

"The church we just passed reminded me of my meeting with Jeremy yesterday." Kameitha brushed a strand of hair back from her face. "It didn't go well."

"Oh?"

"He dropped by the house," Kameitha said. "We'd talked a few times, and he seemed genuinely happy about my recovery. But he hadn't mentioned coming by, and I hadn't told him how I looked."

"I guess that was a bit of a shock," Lilith said.

"He didn't take it well. He called me a jezebel." Kameitha gave a resigned grimace. "Have I mentioned that he's evangelical—a born-again Christian? He converted as a teenager while we were stationed at Fort Benning."

"What does that even mean—a jezebel?"

"Jezebel was a seductress in the Bible," Kameitha said. "After seeing me, he automatically assumed the treatment was all about vanity or sex."

"Did you get a chance to talk with him about it?" Lilith said.

"Are you kidding? He was in no mood to listen to anything I had to say," Kameitha said.

"I'm so sorry to hear that."

Kameitha huffed. "I can only imagine how he would've reacted if he'd realized we're in a relationship."

Lilith thought back to the dinner with Gemini and the kids. Lacy had openly expressed her concerns, but it was obviously an adjustment for all of them. How would they react when they learned about their relationship with Kameitha and Ralen? Would she and Seth have to choose between family and a promising future with their new partners? The thought stabbed her heart.

Chapter 17

SALT LAKE CITY, UTAH—Jeremy Banks sat on a wrought-iron bench in the mega church's courtyard, watching the faithful coming and going. A young woman chasing after her two toddlers. An elderly man with a cane, struggling up the three stone steps to reach the ornate, massive wooden doors.

Jeremy had gone directly there after leaving his mother's house to try and find some peace. His mother. An inferno of anger blazed through him at the thought of her. For years, he'd tried to show his mother the way to salvation. He'd redoubled his efforts when he learned she had cancer. Now he had to concede his failure and acknowledge the weight of her sins.

Jeremy found himself knocking on the pastor's door.

"Yes," Rev. Danny Day called out.

"Reverend, I apologize for interrupting," Jeremy stuttered as he entered the spacious office and took a seat. "But I don't know where else to turn."

"What is it, my son?" Rev. Day put down his pen and gave Jeremy his full attention.

Jeremy took a deep breath to steel his nerves. "It's my mother." He looked at the floor, ashamed to meet the pastor's eyes. "I fear she is a modern-day Jezebel, who will turn believers away from the word of God."

The white-haired preacher chuckled softly. "Surely, it can't be that bad."

Jeremy shuddered, reliving the moment she'd opened the door. "My mother belongs to a cult that uses divination to guide scientific research. I saw the results today." He closed his eyes to better picture her. "She's eighty-five, but now she looks how I remember her from when I was only knee-high. She looks twenty years younger than me!"

Rev. Day shook his head and gestured, palms up. "I share your sorrow at seeing your mother, or any elderly woman, succumb to the vices of pride and vanity rather than following God's plan for her. But you need not fear for the faithful."

"No!"

The preacher jerked back in his chair and away from him.

Jeremy shook his head. "I apologize for yelling, Reverend. But no." Jeremy put a sheaf of wrinkled papers on the pastor's immaculate oak desk. "This serum is like nothing you've ever seen. It defies the natural order. She was dying of cancer, but she's been cured."

Rev. Day picked up the papers and carefully reviewed what Jeremy had learned about the Renu Center and the dozen remote viewers who called themselves Methuselah's Pioneers since his mother called days ago with news of her recovery. When the preacher finally looked up at Jeremy, his lips pressed into a thin smile and his blue eyes sparkled. "This puts things in a different light, my boy. A different light, indeed."

Chapter 18

OGDEN, UTAH—A bell rang as Kameitha pushed opened the door to a realty office in a high-end strip mall. The forty-something woman looked up from her computer with a smile. Her face transformed the next second, with her mouth forming an "O."

"Ms. Kameitha? That's really you?" She stood as they approached.

Kameitha extended her hand. "So good to see you again, Suzanne. It's been a long time."

"Probably thirty years. Maybe more," Suzanne stuttered as she slowly lifted her hand. Before their hands touched, she pulled away, her dark eyes wide. She whispered, "Are you… a vampire?"

Lilith burst out laughing. Kameitha lowered her hand and stared at the real estate agent.

"You think she's a vampire?" Lilith choked out between guffaws. "But it's daylight."

Kameitha rolled her eyes and jabbed Lilith's shoulder. "You're not helping matters." She turned back to Suzanne, who'd backed away from them. "Don't be frightened," Kameitha said soothingly. "I should've mentioned that I've had a lot of work done. Really, I'm very flattered."

Lilith finally caught her breath. Her lips still twitched, but she fought the urge to laugh.

Suzanne tilted her head to the left as she examined Kameitha more closely. "A facelift?"

"Not exactly," Kameitha said. "An experimental treatment, very risky and, of course, ridiculously expensive."

The real estate agent's shoulders relaxed. "But worth every penny!" She took a deep breath and stepped forward with her hand outstretched and her professional smile plastered back in place. "I was just joking about the vampire thing, of course, but you do look fabulous. It's wonderful to see you again."

Minutes later, they sped up Highway 158 in Suzanne's silver Escalade toward the first place on their list. She parked at the Snowflake Inn, which adjoined undeveloped land with a "for sale" sign.

Lilith, glad she'd worn her boots, followed the two as they reminisced while trudging through knee-high brown grass and dodging scruffy bushes.

Settling into her pitch, Suzanne said, "You have to get to the ridge to fully appreciate this property." She stopped at the top of a rise. Below, Lilith's eyes traced the path of a stream as it followed the rolling hills. In the distance, higher peaks—some snow-capped—rose around the valley, and the Pineview Reservoir glinted in the sunlight.

"It's very peaceful," Kameitha said.

"And conveniently located," Lilith added.

Suzanne checked her tablet. "This is eleven acres. The boundary lines are marked." She pointed to wooden stakes with red flags barely visible in the four directions.

Back in the car, Kameitha checked the specs on their next stop. About twenty minutes later, they pulled onto a dirt road that wove up a steep hill. Suzanne parked in a clearing just big enough for her to turn around.

"This is the eighty-acre tract?" Kameitha said.

Suzanne nodded. "As you can see, it's much more rustic. This road actually cuts through the neighbor's acreage, but it's a dedicated easement so there's no problem with access."

Lilith followed as they walked side-by-side up a winding, narrow footpath. Ten minutes later, they stood on the rocky ledge of a clearing that looked large enough for their community compound. Blue and yellow wildflowers sprinkled the overgrown grasses that bowed to the constant wind. She walked to the far side and sucked in her breath. The ground fell away, exposing a cliffside of jagged granite boulders and sharp shale outcroppings. A waterfall trickled into a small pool below. It was much steeper than she'd realized.

"Any development here would have to be off the grid," Suzanne said. "But that is why it's considerably cheaper than anything else you'll find. In fact, it's quite the steal."

On their way back to the car, when they reached a wider part of the path, Kameitha dropped back to walk next to Lilith. She handed her a tiny blue flower.

"For me?" Lilith smiled. "How thoughtful."

"I love this place," Kameitha said, "but I can't figure how we'd get a road back to the clearing."

"That's just the kind of challenge Seth loves," Lilith said. "I like that it's not as accessible. It would give us more privacy."

When they reached the car, Suzanne finished applying lipstick and finger-combed her windblown hair. She drove about ten minutes before turning onto Highway 162. Along the way, Lilith noticed the signs for Nordic Valley Ski Resort. Suzanne pulled onto a street by a large sign that promoted lots with ski-in, ski-out access.

"Looks like this is quite the planned development," Lilith said.

"It was," Suzanne agreed, "until the bookkeeper embezzled the original investors' downpayment. The development went bankrupt, and now the bank is trying to unload it."

"Fifty-five acres," Kameitha said, turning a full circle to take in the surrounding peaks. "It's beautiful, too."

Lilith knew they would face the fewest obstacles to building here since most of the preliminary work had already been completed, but she didn't like it as well as the previous property.

"Ladies, what do you think? Did we find something you love, or should I keep on looking?" Suzanne asked.

"Give us a moment?" Kameitha said. She guided Lilith far enough down the path so Suzanne couldn't hear them talk. "I think any of these would work, but I prefer the eighty acres. How about you?"

"Well, this is lovely, and the first place would be very convenient," she said.

"The mountaintop off Powder Ridge Road just feels more like home," Kameitha said, "but it would be more of a challenge to build there."

Lilith grinned. "Challenges make for unique solutions."

"You really think Seth could make it work?"

"I do," Lilith said. "I can't imagine finding anyplace I'd like better, but we definitely need to get everyone's input. Among the twelve of us, we can be sure someone will spot any problems that aren't readily apparent to us."

They took their seats in the car, where Suzanne waited. "We'd like to put a contract on the eighty acres on the mountaintop," Kameitha said.

"Of course," Suzanne said, starting the car. "They're asking four hundred thousand. Do you want to counter-offer?"

Lilith and Kameitha exchanged looks, then shrugged. "The price is more than reasonable," Lilith said, "but we need to make the offer contingent on approval by our partners."

"We'll put down five thousand earnest money, but we need a week before finalizing the deal," Kameitha said.

Suzanne pressed the console to activate her phone and gave her assistant the details. By the time they reached her office, the contract was ready. Kameitha and Lilith signed the document.

"I'll present the offer to the owners," Suzanne said. "We'll look forward to hearing back from you within the week. And look, I apologize for my reaction when you arrived. You must think I'm a lunatic."

Kameitha shook Suzanne's hand. "Not to worry. I was quite flattered."

As they walked out of the office, Lilith grinned at Kameitha. "We're doing it. We're really doing it!"

Kameitha reached around Lilith's waist and pulled her close. "It's going to be fantastic!"

"We can't go back without photos," Lilith said.

"You're right," Kameitha said.

They backtracked to the property. Cell phones in hand, they wandered toward the clearing, taking photos from every vantage point. They paused at the top to admire the view. The breeze ruffled Kameitha's thick, curly hair, and her dark skin glowed warmly in the sunlight. "You take my breath away," Lilith said.

Kameitha turned toward her and snapped a picture. "I had to do that," she laughed, but quickly grew serious. She put her phone away and reached for Lilith. Their lips met, and their bodies pressed together.

"I want to remember this forever," she said.

Lilith caressed Kameitha's face. "For us, that could be a very long time."

Spotting a trail leading down to the pond, Lilith said, "C'mon. Let's go exploring." She led the way down an overgrown, rocky path.

"Here, take my hand." Lilith helped Kameitha down from a large boulder. A few steps later, Lilith skidded on loose gravel, but Kameitha grabbed her arm before she fell.

"I hope it's easier going up." Lilith shaded her eyes and looked at the twisting course they'd just come down. The cliff seemed higher from below.

"It's not much farther," Kameitha said cheerfully, taking the lead. The land leveled out as they neared the bottom.

"Whew!" Lilith said. "I wish we'd brought water."

"At least there's some in the car," Kameitha said, taking a seat on a large, flat-topped boulder bordering the six-foot-wide pool. Ferns and tufts of brown grass sprung up between the smaller rocks that made a roughly circular border. She sniffed, wrinkling her nose. "What is that smell?"

"Sulphur? Looks like there's a lot of mineral content in the water," Lilith said. "That's probably why the water is so murky."

"I wonder how deep it is." Kameitha knelt down and dipped her hand in the water. "Oh my!"

"What?" Lilith asked, alarmed.

"The water—it's hot!" Kameitha said.

"A hot spring?" Lilith crouched beside her and swept her fingers through the water. "I wonder why they didn't mention that in the property description?"

"Maybe they didn't want to attract skinny-dippers."

"You think?" Lilith laughed.

"I know it was a big problem at the Ogden Hot Springs," Kameitha said. "Even though they were on private land, people kept going there."

"Really? How do you know that?"

Kameitha laughed. "I was one of those people. There's nothing like star-gazing from a hot pot with snow on the ground."

"Sounds like fun. With the right person." Lilith squeezed Kameitha's hand.

"I'll star-gaze with you anytime."

"I'm going to take you up on that." Lilith sat down, pulled off her boots, and rolled her pant legs up to her knees. "Let's see if it's very deep."

Kameitha took off her shoes and joined Lilith, who stood about a foot from the pond's edge in ankle-deep water.

"This is really nice."

Lilith felt the way forward with her toes. "A little squishy, but firm enough." She continued forward about two more feet, then halted. "Whoa!" She slung her arm in front of Kameitha. "It's deeper here."

Lilith dipped her toes down, then crouched and reached her right foot further down while Kameitha held her by the left hand and elbow. The water was up to Lilith's knee, but she couldn't touch the bottom. "It really dropped off. It's more than three feet here."

They waded back to the bank and lay next to each other on the boulder, letting the sun dry their legs. Wind rustled the trees on the cliff above, and water trickled into the pond.

"It's really peaceful."

"Yeah, I think we're going to love it here." Kameitha rolled onto her side, sliding her hand under Lilith's jean jacket and blouse to rest it on her waist. Lilith shivered at the touch. Kameitha's other hand cradled Lilith's head.

Lilith caught her breath, intoxicated by Kameitha's closeness. She reveled at the contrasts—Kameitha's sweet scent against the backdrop of the pond's bitter aroma, and the warmth of her body as the chill fall air caressed their bodies. She closed her eyes and pressed her lips against Kameitha's in a lingering kiss.

"Mmmm," Kameitha purred. "What did I do to deserve that?"

Lilith brushed Kameitha's windblown hair back from her face. "Just being you is plenty enough for me."

"I'm glad, because that's how I feel about you," Kameitha said. "This is all such an adventure, isn't it?"

"Yes," Lilith said. "Who would've thought we'd feel this way at our age? It seems too good to be true."

"Guess we're going to have to rethink what it means to be old," Kameitha said.

"That's us—longevity pioneers," Lilith quipped.

Kameitha snorted, then looked up at the sound of voices. Two women, one holding a clipboard, and a man stood at the top of the cliff. She and Lilith sat up, brushing dust off their clothes and straightening their shirts. One of the women gave a timid wave, which Kameitha returned, before the group wandered out of sight.

"Looks like it's a good thing we put money down," Lilith said, as she rolled her pant legs down and slipped her feet back into her socks and boots.

"Good thing they didn't come a few minutes later." Kameitha pulled Lilith over, lifted her hair and kissed her neck. "I was thinking of all sorts of ways to devour you."

A thrill ran through Lilith, leaving her breathless.

Kameitha slipped on her shoes and stood, offering Lilith a hand up. Taking it, she stood. With bodies touching and hands entwined, electric energy pulsed around them.

Again, voices carried down from above. Kameitha shook her body like a wet dog's and stepped away from Lilith. "We'd better go."

Lilith nodded and followed her up the steep trail.

Chapter 19

NEAR EDEN, UTAH—Jeremy Banks slammed the door on his battered blue Chevy. He didn't know what model it was, and he didn't care. Rev. Day had given it to him after Jeremy donated to the church the brand new, cherry red Corvette his mother had gifted him on his fiftieth birthday. Whenever he saw the white-haired preacher pulling up to the church in it, Jeremy knew he'd done the right thing. The Corvette had softened Jeremy's resolve to stand up against the temptations of the flesh. Only a man of God could be strong enough to resist.

Opening his backpack, Jeremy pulled out the matte gray quadracopter. He leaned against the car trunk as he ran through the usual checklist, slipped on his virtual vision goggles, and sent the drone skyward at seventy-two miles per hour toward the realty office where his friend Suzanne worked. He spotted his mom's car turning off Highway 158 onto a gravel road.

Jeremy circled the drone until they got out of the car, then enabled tracking to follow the two women inching down the steep incline. The drone avoided the rocky cliff that blocked his sight and hovered on the other side, giving a clear shot of their faces even from a constant height of three hundred feet.

His drone followed them to the side of a steaming pond. Autofocus on the zoom lens kept the images so crisp, he felt they should have turned around when he gasped.

"No!" he yelled and pounded on the car trunk. Shame and anger flashed through him, blinding him to all else. His mother was kissing another woman!

His thoughts turned to his childhood and the memory of her kind face hovering above him, smiling. What had happened to that woman? Where was the mother he loved?

When the power warning beeped and pulled his attention back to the drone, it had tracked their movements back up the rocky pathway. He toggled the lever, calling the drone back to him.

Rev. Day had been right. His mother had been lying to Jeremy about the serum all along. It wasn't about saving lives. Now he had proof.

Chapter 20

PARK CITY, UTAH—When Lilith and Kameitha arrived at her house, Ralen's car was in the driveway. "They're back from the club," Lilith said.

From the foyer, she looked through the French doors and spotted Seth and Ralen on the deck. "I'll join you in a second. First, I'll get us something to eat," she told Kameitha. "Is salad okay?"

"Sure, but don't you want help?" Kameitha wiggled her eyebrows.

Lilith grinned and gave Kameitha's hand a squeeze. "I'd love your company, but they'll want to hear about the land."

A few minutes later, Lilith placed a trayful of food and drinks on the table. Seth sat next to Ralen, with Kameitha's phone between them so both could see the photos she'd taken.

"I have a few more." Lilith went back inside and returned with her phone. When she handed it to Seth, he recoiled from her. "Whew! What's that smell?"

At first, Lilith didn't know what he meant. Then she looked at Kameitha and laughed. "Sulphur."

"We checked out a pond on the property. It's fed by a hot spring," Kameitha said. "I guess we just got used to the smell."

Ralen pinched his nose. "Hard to believe you could get used to that."

"But a hot spring?" Seth grinned and gave them a thumbs-up.

"That's great." Ralen pointed to the pictures. "It's beautiful land, but pretty rugged."

"We'll make it work." Seth's voice rose with excitement.

Lilith laughed. "I told her you'd love the challenge."

"Apparently the neighbors mostly rely on snowmobiles to get to their homes in the winter," Kameitha said. "That seems pretty inconvenient. You think we can do better?"

"We have the capital to do whatever we want," Seth said. "It's just a matter of finding the best solution—whether a lift of some sort is better than tunneling, or even rail. The architect has a staff with diverse talents, and he's excited about the concept of combining independent and shared space."

"What did he say?" Lilith asked.

"He suggested a three-story house," Ralen said. "Each floor will have four adjoining master suites, with a full kitchen and living and dining areas in a central hub."

"Let's send the pictures over to get his input," Seth said.

"The rest of the gang should be arriving in an hour or two, and we'll be able to get a decision on whether to proceed with this site," Ralen said. "But I think it looks perfect."

"I like that it's different, and that it's not right in the middle of everything," Seth added. "We don't need people watching us every minute. Particularly once the word gets out, it will be good to have a retreat where we can have privacy."

"And where people won't be afraid they're living next to vampires," Lilith said.

"Vampires?" Ralen asked, his eyes wide in surprise.

Kameitha punched Lilith's shoulder. "It's nothing," she told Ralen.

"Oh, it was something." Lilith grinned. "The real estate agent thought she was a vampire because Kameitha looks like she did thirty years ago."

"Really!" Seth said. "Sounds like the agent watches too much TV."

"Guess it just goes to show what we're up against," Ralen said. "People aren't going to know what to think of us."

"Vat you talking 'bout." Lilith bared her teeth and playfully nipped at Ralen's neck. "I vant to drink your blood."

———

HECTOR WAS the first of the Pioneers to arrive. "I hear we have a pending contract?" He frowned at Lilith and Kameitha.

"Nothing is final, of course, Hector," Lilith said soothingly. "So, don't get all worked up."

"We just gave the real estate agent the earnest money to ensure we had the property tied up until everyone could weigh-in," Kameitha added.

He huffed. "Then no harm done." He settled in, beer in hand, and began reading the document.

By the time the others arrived, Lilith and Kameitha had consolidated the photos and projected the images onto the screen in the theatre room. Blown up to lifesize, they gave the impression of actually being there.

"The view's breathtaking," Yi said.

"I'm impressed you were able to find suitable land so quickly," Karla added.

"We sent the photos over to the architects, and they don't foresee any problems," Seth said.

"We could keep looking, but there's not a lot of property for sale that's close to the Renu Center," Lilith said. "And most of it is more conventional—suburban, planned communities."

"You mean we'd have nosey neighbors," Carlos said.

"I think we should avoid that," Xavier said.

"I agree," Monique said. "The more distance we can put between our home and the others, the better."

Lorenz stood, frowning. "I don't want to hide anything. I'm proud to be with Xavier."

"But it's not about just you and Xavier." Monique spoke quietly, but intently. "You know how I feel about it, or I wouldn't have asked you both to stay with me. The twelve of us are going against the patterns of accepted behavior, and as more people get the treatment, the number will grow. Our living arrangements will challenge some people's beliefs and values."

"You mean folks are going to get ticked off?" Ralen said.

Monique stared at him. "That's one way of saying it. Yes, some people will be angry."

"Not flaunting our communal living arrangement is good for everyone," Seth said.

"I'd agree with that," Hector said. "No use stirring the pot until it starts smoking."

Lilith squinted at him. "I guess that makes sense, but I don't think I want to go to your house for dinner. So, is everyone in favor of moving ahead with the purchase of the mountaintop property?"

Most nodded, and some gave a thumbs-up.

"Then it's unanimous," Hector said. "I'll finalize the contract with Suzanne. We should be able to close the deal within a couple of weeks."

"The architects can get started on the design immediately," Ralen said. "By springtime, we'll be ready to start construction."

"We need requirements for the architects," Seth said. "I'll send out a survey to gather your input."

"We want to incorporate all the best features of where you live now, so don't hold back," Ralen added. "Remember—it's always better and easier to build what you want than to add it later."

"Okay, then," Hector said. "We'll meet again next week after our checkups. By then, my group of viewers should have its findings."

As she turned off the porch light after the last car pulled away, Lilith turned to Seth. "Do you have any second thoughts about this?"

"About us all living together?" Seth replied from down the hall. She joined him in the bedroom. He sat on the edge of the bed, removing his shoes. "Actually, the more we talk about it, the more I think it's the right thing to do. Why? Do you have concerns?"

"It's definitely what I want," Lilith said, removing her top and reaching for her nightshirt. "I just wonder how our families are going to react. And our friends."

He patted the bed and put his arm around her as she sat beside him. "Our living together doesn't hurt anyone, so why shouldn't we pursue what makes us happy?"

Lilith nodded and leaned her head against his shoulder. "You're right, of course. You can't please everyone."

"Look, you've been my best friend for more than thirty years. As long as we're taking care of each other, the rest will sort itself out." He lifted her chin and kissed the tip of her nose. "Now go to sleep and quit worrying."

Easier said than done. Replaying the real estate agent's reaction, she grinned. Still, it bothered her that the woman had been scared. Even after Kameitha's explanation, Suzanne had continued giving them puzzled looks when she thought no one saw. And Lacy was concerned not only about Gemini, but about how all their friends would react. None of this was what Lilith had expected before the treatment.

Seth was right—their actions didn't hurt anyone. But they did affect others, and Lilith cared about that. Perhaps if the serum only rid them of disease, others would be more accepting. But at what cost? The potential was so great, but unexpected obstacles were quickly becoming real to her. Hours later, Lilith still lay awake while Seth snored.

Chapter 21

RENU CENTER, OGDEN RIVER SCENIC BYWAY—Hector stood at the head of the conference table, drumming his pen against its glass surface. "Okay, it's not like you haven't seen each other in years." Slowly, the Pioneers quit chatting with each other and took their seats around the table.

"Don't be cranky," Karla said. "It's not a courtroom, you know."

Hector nodded. "You're right, Karla. If it were, you'd all be held in contempt by now."

She rolled her eyes. After a few snickers, the others gave him their attention.

"Last week we decided Renu should resume the treatment schedule," Hector said. "But our viewing results weren't unanimous, so Nan, Boris, Yi and I met to look into what that might mean. Nan and Boris will discuss our findings."

Smoothing her long, tan skirt as she stood, Nan addressed the group. "We used a series of questions to narrow the options. First, we tried to determine if there was a medical reason to not resume treatments. Thankfully, that wasn't the case, so we moved on."

"We viewed several other options—funding, side effects, religion, political issues, the effect on family and friends," Boris said. "But it turned out to not be just one thing."

"It's how they overlap," Nan said. "The treatments—or those

who undergo the treatments—affect many facets of society. We are disrupting the norm."

"Let's see a show of hands if you've had a rough encounter with a family member or friend," Yi said. Hands went up around the table. "Just as I suspected—all of us. For me, it was my best friend. Or I should say, my former best friend. She doesn't want to have anything to do with me because I'm no longer sick and dying, and she is."

"The point is," Hector said, "we need to find ways to mitigate the friction between the ill and aging past, and the healthy, youthful future."

"That makes no sense." Xavier scowled, his tone belligerent. "If someone needs a cure for cancer and we have it, why should it matter what anyone else thinks?"

"It's a cultural thing," Monique said. "It wouldn't be the first time that a cure was sidetracked because of public opinion and antiquated laws. I know you all remember how marijuana was banned for years, despite its long history of health benefits for treating everything from malaria to rheumatism."

"But we're talking life and death," Xavier insisted.

Monique shrugged. "The culture changes, or it doesn't."

"We touched on this already when we discussed the circle of friends," Yi added. "We want to think our friends will be happy for us. Yet it's human nature to think, 'What about me?' And as more people are treated, the disparity will grow."

"We didn't come up with solutions, so much as paths in the right direction," Boris said. "The first thing we suggest is that Renu establish a foundation to give access to those with terminal illnesses who can't afford the treatment."

"What did you have in mind—offering a free treatment each month?" Kate asked.

Yi pulled up a file on her phone. "Fifty-three million people died last year, Kate. Fewer than two million were killed in accidents. Twelve free treatments would hardly make a difference."

"I see your point." Kate fidgeted in her chair, not meeting Yi's gaze. "But at least it's a place to start." A stony silence settled between them. "I don't know what more we can do. Renu offers people a real cure from terminal illnesses, but the investors expect to make substantial profits. It's not a nonprofit."

"The Pioneers are stockholders, too," Hector said. "We've also played a key role in guiding this endeavor, and that's what we're doing now. Renu's Board of Directors, which you represent, Kate, would be foolish to stop listening to us now."

"How many free treatments do you recommend?" she said, her voice tense.

"It needs to be proportional to the total number of paid treatments," Hector said. "Ten percent."

"One free treatment for every ten—you can't be serious?" Kate glared at him.

"Really?" Yi threw her hands up. "This is a no-brainer, Kate. If we fail to bring some equanimity to the process, the backlash may grow so strong that no one will be able to get the treatment."

Kate blanched. "You can't believe the government would outlaw a treatment that restores youth and vigor. It saved your lives!"

"And because of that, it will accentuate the disparity between the haves and the have-nots to a degree never before seen," Hector said. "It's not just about money or things. It's about life and death, and the quality of life."

"You could liken it to the French Revolution," Karla added. "We're like Marie Antoinette saying, 'Let them eat cake.' But in this case, it's 'Let them grow old and die.'"

A familiar, uneasy feeling arose as Lilith listened to the interchange and watched Kate pace at the back of the room with her face contorted in frustration—or was that anger? Since the project began, something had nagged at the back of Lilith's mind, but she hadn't been able to pinpoint it. Maybe this was it—they'd been too focused on the treatment's benefits. During the research phase, they'd only given occasional lip-service to how others would view it. If the treatment failed, public opinion wouldn't matter because they'd be dead. The treatment's positive results had been beyond comprehension until they'd actually experienced the physical changes and had their health restored.

The territory they'd entered had no precedent, but human nature should've given them a clue. In hindsight, she wondered why the magnitude of a potential backlash hadn't been apparent from the start.

And that was without considering the sexuality issues. She glanced at Kameitha, who was deep in conversation with Nan. The changes would've been monumental on their own—the reversal of the Stage Four cancer, the rejuvenation of her body—but all that had become a backdrop to their newfound desires. Nothing like that had been anticipated.

If it had been, perhaps she would've realized how her perceptions would change without the threat of imminent death. It was Abraham Maslow's Hierarchy of Needs in action, just as she'd learned in college so many years ago. Once the treatment restored her basic physical needs, the next rung on the ladder—love and belonging—became the focus.

Now their group had begun moving toward a collective living arrangement to enable their new relationships to thrive. As more people took the treatment and found their sexuality changed, many would have a similar drive to protect their new relationships. How would it play out on a larger scale—with hundreds, even thousands, of people who'd taken the treatment? Conversely, how many would find their new sexuality repugnant and try to repress it?

As Lilith grappled with the possibilities, Kate took her seat. Everyone grew quiet around the table. "I will take your recommendation to the Board, with my support, but I can't guarantee they'll approve it."

Hector nodded. "That's all we ask, Kate. Thanks."

"But you have to realize, while your contributions have been significant—both monetarily and otherwise—we have other investors," she continued.

The comment rankled Hector, as Lilith could clearly see from his flushed cheeks.

"Research and development costs of new drugs have more than doubled in the last decade, but with our guidance, Renu avoided many false leads," Hector countered.

"Even so, it took fifteen years of research and more than $1.5 billion to get to this point," Kate said. "A substantial return on investment in the first years is critical."

Steel tinged Hector's voice. "Yes, but that was half the average developmental cost for a new drug. It would have taken who-knows-how-long without us."

"No one is arguing that." Kate raised her hands defensively.

Hector slammed his pen down on the table and glared at her. "Well, don't let the rest of the Board forget it when you talk about the foundation."

In the silence that followed, Yi spoke softly. "Kate, I'd ask you to also call the Board's attention to how many of the big pharmaceutical companies work with people who can't afford their drugs, particularly the new cancer drugs that are $10,000 or more per month. We've all seen the ads. They offer discounts or even provide their drugs for free."

"We'll look into that, as well," Kate told Yi, avoiding Hector's gaze. "And it's another reason why we believe Renu's treatment is a bargain at $1 million. When you look at the cost of drugs and paying at least $25,000 for surgical treatment of cancer with far less effective results, Renu is a steal."

Again, Yi pulled up data on her phone. "And don't forget, if you're doing comparative costs, the average facelift costs $10,000."

Kate grinned. "You have a point. And even better, Renu's treatment is not just a superficial fix to one part of the body."

Seeking to bolster the calmer dialogue, Lilith agreed. "There's definitely a need for the foundation, but it's obvious that no other treatment offers the benefits Renu does. It literally turns back a person's biological clock and eradicates terminal disease."

"That touches on some of the other issues our group looked at." Hector's voice had resumed its formal, lawyerly tone. "As we've already seen, the age reversal challenges how we relate to our friends and family. It's hard to predict how that will play out in terms of religion and politics but allowing ourselves separation from others with our new living arrangements is a good move."

Boris raised a finger to catch Hector's attention. "Our sessions make it clear that keeping a low profile and enhancing personal safety will be important to Renu's success, at least in the near-term."

"What does that mean?" Kate asked. "It's not like we planned to advertise during the Super Bowl."

"Just that word of mouth will bring more than enough people to Renu's door," Boris said.

"Did you get any specific data on that?" Kate asked.

"It wasn't easy, but yes," Boris said. "Wording the questions was the hardest part, but that's what drives the session. We followed the usual guidelines—using neutral words, focusing on one target at a time, keeping the tasker and viewer both blind to the target."

"How did you do that?" Seth asked. "All four of you obviously at least knew the issues, which would have made double-blind sessions impossible."

The team members grinned, their heads bobbing in agreement.

"Of course, you're right," Hector said. "Nan, Yi and Boris all manage groups, so after we worded the taskings, they turned the actual viewing over to their groups."

"Then we analyzed the sessions and came up with recommendations," Nan said. "Although numbers are very hard to get through remote viewing, our viewers got indicators we thought clearly showed growth, Kate."

"One had a drawing of one person, then an arrow pointing to a crowd of people," Yi said. "And another showed it as a single branch growing into a large vine with many branches and flowers."

"Their descriptors included words such as 'natural,' 'effortless,' and 'person-to-person,'" Nan added.

Familiar with the symbolic language of the subconscious, Lilith could easily see why the team made their recommendations.

"The problem will be meeting the demand when so many are desperate for help," Hector said.

Gemini's words echoed in Lilith's mind: "A lot of desperate people are going to be knocking on your door.

Chapter 22

"Hey, wait up!" Kameitha called, as they left the research center. Already halfway across the parking lot, Lilith and Seth turned and stopped. Ralen also hurried to join them.

"Want to go over to the Meteor for a drink?" Kameitha said.

"That's where we were headed," Seth said. "C'mon. The SUV's got plenty of room."

"Shotgun!" Ralen said, opening the front passenger-side door.

"Seriously?" Lilith smiled at him. "You sound like my pesky little brother. I haven't heard that since we were teenagers. You know, it's still annoying."

Ralen gave her a sheepish grin as he slid into the front seat. "Long legs, you know?"

"Right!" Kameitha laughed.

"Oh, go on!" Lilith punched Ralen playfully in the shoulder as she slid into the seat by Kameitha. "I know you just want to be next to Seth. Or were you and Kameitha in cahoots to get us together."

"Oops, found out!" Kameitha said.

"I thought as much." Lilith smiled and leaned back in the seat as Seth started the car. She closed her eyes and willed herself to relax. Except for the past few minutes of playfulness, the morning had been stressful, with all the issues said and unsaid. Who knew what tomorrow would bring, but for now, she had her health and the partners she loved surrounding her. In more than ninety years of living, Lilith had learned at least one thing—happiness came one moment at a time, and this was one of those moments.

When Lilith opened her eyes, Kameitha was watching her. "A penny for your thoughts."

"Oh, just thinking about how happy I am." Lilith smiled at her.

"Me, too," Kameitha said. "Even Hector couldn't bring me down for long."

Seth snorted. "You can depend on him to focus on the dark side."

"Still, I think his group brought up good points," Ralen said. "I hope the Board implements the foundation."

At the Meteor, they took a booth at the back and ordered Bloody Marys all around. Following Seth's lead, they lifted frosted glasses and clanked them in a toast. "To friends."

After the waitress left with their food order, Seth met Lilith's eyes. She grinned and gave him a slight nod of encouragement. "Last night, Lilith and I decided we'd like to propose something to you," he said.

Lilith reached for Kameitha's hand. "Would you want to move in with us now?"

Kameitha's head snapped up, and she gave an excited squeal. "You mean it?"

Ralen didn't say anything, but Lilith thought he was holding back a smile.

With worry etched on his wrinkled brow, Seth reached over and put a hand on Ralen's shoulder. "Maybe you think it's not worth the effort since we'll all be moving as soon as the new compound is completed? But that will be at least nine or ten months."

Ralen remained quiet, intently studying his nails, but winked at Lilith and Kameitha when Seth turned away.

Seth rushed to add, "In case you're worried about privacy, we have plenty of room, so you could have your own bedrooms."

"Oh, I do like that," Kameitha quipped. "I get first dibs!"

Still waiting for Ralen's reaction, Seth's voice dropped to almost a whisper. "We could spend more time together."

It was all Lilith could do to not laugh.

Ralen elbowed Seth in the side. "Just pulling your chain a bit." He grinned and ruffled Seth's hair. "I think it's a great idea."

"Really?" Seth sighed with relief.

Lilith shook her head, amazed at how clueless Seth could be at times, and Kameitha rolled her eyes.

"When you didn't say anything, I thought I'd blown it," Seth said. "You really want to move in now?"

"I've been wondering why it took you so long to ask," Ralen said.

Kameitha hugged Lilith. "We've been discussing the same thing, but your home is the only place big enough for all of us. We didn't want to be presumptuous."

"Now we really do have something to toast." Seth raised his glass again, and the others, smiling, joined.

"To us!" Ralen said.

"To us!" the others echoed, clanking their glasses together, then taking hearty sips.

Although she smiled with the rest of them, Lilith wondered again at the wisdom of what they were doing. In her heart, she knew it was right for the four of them to be together. That wasn't the problem. But their relationships with family and the world at large gave her pause. And she couldn't help but wonder if the treatment would change them in other ways, if not now, then later. What were they overlooking?

"Pardon me, but I have to ask. Are you related to Lilith Davidson?" The familiar voice broke her reverie. She looked up into the hazel eyes of Elizabeth Jenkins, her former co-worker at the Tribune. She'd been an auburn-haired professional with attitude, but was now gray-haired and stooped, with wrinkles creasing her soft face. "You just look so much like she did when we first met."

"Elizabeth?" Lilith mentally sucked in her breath as she stood. She gave the woman's hand a gentle squeeze. "It's so good to see you. It's been too long."

Confusion clouded Elizabeth's eyes as she withdrew her hand. "You know my name?"

"Of course." Lilith chuckled nervously. "I've, ah, had a lot of work done, as you can see." She gestured to her face. "How long has it been—twenty-five, thirty years?"

"But...." Elizabeth moved back a step. Wide-eyed and slack-mouthed, she stuttered, "You haven't changed at all. That's just... not possible."

Concerned about her pallor, Lilith said, "Please, have a seat, and I'll explain."

Elizabeth shook her head. "I just can't believe this. Look at you... and at me." She covered her mouth with one hand and waved her cane with the other. "How can that be?"

"It's a new drug," Lilith said, searching for the right words.

"I've never heard of any kind of drug that could do that," Elizabeth said flatly.

"It's still experimental, but it has remarkable restorative properties. Won't you sit?" Lilith took a step toward her, but Elizabeth backed toward a younger woman, who waited in the aisle.

"Mother, is everything all right?" the woman asked.

Elizabeth shook her head and gaped at Lilith. Then a different expression crossed her face. "Would the drug make it to where I could walk again?"

Lilith cleared her throat. "As I said, it's experimental. Right now, the tests are extremely limited, and the subjects have already been chosen."

"I see," Elizabeth's tone was bitter. "Well, then, good for you." She turned and her daughter helped her walk to the door.

Lilith followed her a few steps before Kameitha gently clasped Lilith's arm and guided her back to the booth. "It will be okay."

Lilith bit her lip and sighed. "I couldn't explain it."

"Yeah, we all have some awkward moments ahead," Seth said.

"I just feel so bad. She has to use a cane to walk, and here I am, getting around like a forty-year-old."

"Don't beat yourself up." Seth took both of her hands in his and gave them a reassuring squeeze. "We took a chance—a big chance —on a risky new procedure. We can't allow ourselves to get overwhelmed by survivor's guilt. That's what it is, you know. We're surviving and thriving, but others are not, and there's not anything we can do about it."

"Maybe for now." Lilith took a deep breath to calm her nerves. "But that has to change, and soon." Still shaken, she pulled out her phone and checked her calendar. Though tempted to change her meeting tomorrow with her best friend Julie, Lilith sighed and put her phone away. She'd already delayed their meeting once. Whatever would be, would be.

———

LILITH SPOTTED Julie's cobalt blue Subaru in the parking lot when she drove up to PC Roasters, their favorite coffeeshop. Lilith took a deep breath before she entered, mentally bracing for her friend's reaction. They'd known each other since college, yet even after all that time, Lilith couldn't predict how this conversation would go. They were in uncharted territory.

Julie had just raised her latte to take a sip when Lilith arrived. "Lilith?" She slowly lowered the mug, then she shook her head. "I don't believe it! Come over here." Julie used the table for support as she stood, then wrapped her arms around Lilith. "My goddess, don't you look amazing!"

"Oh, Julie!" Tears spilled onto Lilith's cheeks as she hugged Julie back. "I was afraid you'd be angry with me."

Julie held her at arm's length. "Pish posh. What have I got to be angry about when my best friend is obviously healthy and happy? Now come." She patted the booth next to her. "I want to know all about what's been happening. Last I heard, they'd locked you up for a couple of weeks to get that experimental treatment you've been working on with your woo woo friends. Ever since then, you've been ducking my calls."

Lilith wiped her face dry and looked down, avoiding Julie's gaze. "Yeah, I'm sorry about that. I just didn't know what to say to you."

"Since when has that been a problem between us?" Julie tilted her head and smoothed back her curly white hair with one hand. "In all the years we've known each other, you have always been the one person I knew I could depend on. And you know I'm always here for you, too."

"I don't know where to start."

"How about with the obvious—are you as healthy as you appear to be? And where did you get the makeover? You've been holding out on me."

Lilith smiled. "It's all from the longevity treatment. It worked so much better than we ever hoped it would."

"Are you…" Julie met her eyes.

"Yes, I'm cured. The cancer's gone."

Julie sighed with relief. "Praise the goddess. That's what I wanted to hear."

"I know! And yet, that kind of gets lost because of all this," she motioned to herself. "The treatment really turned back the clock."

Julie nodded. "If I didn't know better, I'd say you were closer to forty than ninety. And you say that's from the same longevity treatment that cured the cancer?"

"It is," Lilith said. "I won't lie—it wasn't a picnic. At one point, I felt so bad I knew I was going to die."

"But you didn't. And now you're here to show what is possible," Julie said. "If I were to guess, you didn't want to flaunt it because you know my kidneys aren't getting any better."

Lilith bit her lip and gave a single nod.

"Oh, and I look old enough to be your grandmother."

Lilith laughed and shook her head.

Julie took a deep breath. "You've always been too empathetic for your own good, Lil. Sure, I'd love a miracle cure, too, but I'm not blaming you if I can't get it. I remember how expensive you said it is, and how the Renu supporters get preference."

"You're amazing, Julie," Lilith said quietly. "I can't tell you how much I want to be able to get you into the program for treatment, but right now, it's just not possible."

Julie shook her head. "Are you listening to me, girl? You and I go way back, and over the years, we've both had a lot of friends who died, right?"

Lilith nodded.

"Just remember—you are no more to blame today when someone is sick or if they die than you were before you had the treatment. And that includes me." Julie reached out and took Lilith's hand. "What you're doing is important because it gives hope to the otherwise hopeless. And one day, this treatment is going to change everything."

23

December 2029

RENU CENTER, OGDEN RIVER SCENIC BYWAY—When the Pioneers gathered in early December to see the preliminary design plans, they were in such high spirits it felt to Lilith like Christmas had come early. Karla, Yi, Boris and Hector drove in together—as new roommates at Hector's sprawling home in Ogden —and Nan, Xavier and Lorenz came with Monique from her Park City estate where they all now lived together. Lilith mused to herself how simple the process of deciding who would live together on each level of their new home had become now that those selections had occurred naturally.

"Is there anything we've overlooked?" the architect asked as the presentation ended.

The Pioneers exchanged looks around the table. Receiving smiles, nods, and thumbs up, Seth replied, "I think I can speak for us all—you've done an amazing job at incorporating our many requirements into an elegant design. How soon can construction begin?"

"We'll begin ordering many of the fixtures and materials immediately," the architect said. "Let's hope for an early spring so we can begin work on the road, geothermal generator, and wind turbines. There's a lot to be done before we start on the house itself. Getting power and water on site is critical."

After the architects left, Dr. J and Kate gave a quick review of Renu's progress since the Pioneers' treatment.

"Based on your recommendations, we not only continued the treatments, but increased the schedule," Kate said.

"Over the past ninety days, we completed eight more trials," Dr. J said. "Your findings proved sound—all the patients made a complete recovery from their terminal illnesses and are doing well."

"With your guidance, we were able to save more people than we would've following our original plan." Kate looked at Hector. "We also established a foundation, although the Board approved a five percent rate of free treatments instead of ten percent. In a show of good faith, however, the next trial will be comprised of a dozen terminal patients, chosen randomly from those who've contacted us since the project began, and it will be completely free for all twelve of them."

Hector bowed his head appreciatively to Kate. He applauded, and the others joined in.

Kate dipped her head. "I accept your accolades on behalf of the Board."

"Did the ninety-six you treated all have the same... side effect?" Lilith asked.

"If you mean did their sexual preferences expand, the answer is yes," Dr. J said. "And each group is very cohesive. Of course, as subscribers to the Renu group, they had prior history together. At the very least, they shared an interest in this project. Unlike your group, those receiving subsequent treatments weren't kept isolated within the Center and could visit with each other during their two-week quarantine from outsiders."

"How did that work out?" Lilith asked.

"They started forming partnership bonds sooner," Dr. J said. "As soon as they were well enough to interact, the expanded sexuality was evident."

Lilith thought about that for a few moments. Apparently the change was an integral part of the process, perhaps linked to the transformation itself.

"You said the success rate is still one hundred percent?" Seth asked.

"Yes," Dr. J said. "It is remarkable. Although, as I explained previously, not everyone recovers at the same pace or has the same level of regeneration. Even so, the treatment has completely eradicated the cancer, heart disease, or other terminal illness every patient suffered."

"We're getting inquiries regularly from the press, but we've continued to issue only a broad statement citing promising preliminary results from our revolutionary palliative treatment," Kate said.

"That's not going to hold them off forever," Karla said. "A few reporters have already tracked me down."

"Same here," Boris said. "Word about the treatment is definitely spreading."

"And not all the reactions are good." Kameitha kept her eyes downcast and twisted her hands together. "I hate to tell you, but my son's church is planning to protest the treatments."

Surprised faces turned toward her.

"Thankfully, Jeremy's not a Mormon." A palpable sigh carried through the room at that point of clarification. None of them wanted to confront the Latter-Day Saints, who comprised two-thirds of Utah's population.

Lilith smiled at Kameitha, encouraging her to continue. "Although his church is relatively small, it's a very vocal group, and, based on what I see online, the preacher's weekly televised show has a sizable following. Their back-to-the-Bible philosophy opposes so-called 'unnatural healing practices.' They specifically object to such things as vaccinations and surgery, so the process, as well as the results, make this treatment offensive to them."

"It sounds a lot like the Natural Order, although they support Big Pharma," Kate said.

"Jeremy and many of his friends belong to both," Kameitha said.

"What about the sexuality issues?" Hector said.

"They haven't picked up on that yet." Kameitha bit her lip. "I'm sure it's only a matter of time, though, since we've all started living with our new partners."

"That won't be as apparent when we move into our new home in Eden," Hector said.

"Well, that's still several months away," Kameitha said. "Even then, it will be obvious that our lifestyle has changed since the treatment. For some, it will only raise more questions."

THE CONVERSATION STAYED with Lilith throughout the week. She didn't sleep well, and during the day, she found her mind drifting toward "what ifs." When she tried to think of something else, the next thing she knew, her thoughts circled around to how the treatment affected everyone touched by their lives.

"What if" Jeremy's church focused on the sexuality issues? If things became too heated, how could she go back to living without Kameitha? The past few months with the four of them living together had been the happiest she could recall. Sure, Ralen's pranks occasionally upset Seth and Kameitha was moody at times, but overall, the transition had been smooth.

Lilith checked the messages on her phone and smiled. Finally, Gemini had accepted her invitation to lunch. Despite several attempts, they hadn't gotten together since the family dinner right after their treatment. Jeremy's reaction had raised Lilith's anxiety. Did Gemini feel like he did?

Taking advantage of an unseasonably warm day, Lilith served lunch on the patio. "I'm glad you could make it. I was beginning to think you were avoiding me."

Gemini sighed and took a sip of tea. "At least you're consistent. You still don't beat around the bush."

Lilith shrugged.

"It's just awkward for all of us, but I think especially for the grandkids," Gemini said. "For all the talk of being individuals, teens are really just pack animals. Being different makes you a target, and that includes having family members who are different."

Lilith took a deep breath, trying to steady herself before plunging in. "I do understand, and it was never our intent to make anyone uncomfortable. We raised you to be understanding of others' differences, and I think you taught your children that, as well."

"Of course, Mom," she said. "I'm just trying to explain why I haven't been as responsive as you may have wanted. Sometimes there's just a lag between what we think and what we feel. You know that."

"True." Lilith nodded. "Seth and I have been dealing with that very issue since the treatment."

Gemini toyed with her food, moving a cherry tomato around on the plate. "Is everything okay with you two?"

"Actually, our relationship has never been better. We're feeling great on so many levels," Lilith said. "It's just that since the treatment, we've desired a different lifestyle than before."

"Don't tell me Seth wants a harem!" Gemini said.

"Why would you say that?" Lilith asked.

"Relax, Mom, I was just kidding. It is Utah, after all. He wouldn't be the first man with a bunch of wives. Of course, that was years ago, and I know you would never go for that."

Lilith wanted to tell Gemini about her feelings for Kameitha and Ralen, but the words stuck in her throat. One step at a time. "No, it's not like that, but we are making changes. For one thing, we're planning to move soon so the twelve of us can live together."

Gemini looked up. "A commune? That doesn't sound like you at all."

"I wouldn't call it a commune."

"You're giving up your home?" Gemini said. "I thought you loved it."

"I do, but the weekly trips to the clinic are getting to be a chore. Plus, it's important for me to be around others who've shared this journey. They understand Seth and me. Other people don't."

Gemini avoided her gaze. "I'm sure Lacy will get over it, if that's what you mean. She's just very protective of me."

"It's not just Lacy or the kids. It's our other friends, too. For us, it's much different than just recovering from illness or having a more youthful appearance."

"I can see that, Mom," Gemini said flatly.

"And the good thing is, we have the resources to build a truly magnificent home."

Gemini leaned forward, frowning. "You're already to that point? I thought it was still at the discussion phase."

"We bought eighty acres on a mountaintop between Eden and the research center. Construction will begin when the weather breaks."

"That's a lot to take in." Gemini brushed her hair back from her face. "I guess I've gotten used to you being a few minutes away, even if we don't get together that often."

"I'll miss that, too," Lilith agreed. "It will be different, but it's only an hour away."

Gemini laughed. "You're right. Around here, that's a short commute. I'm glad it's not farther."

"Me, too." Lilith paused and took a sip of tea. "Related to the move—I know you've heard me talk about Kameitha. She and Ralen, another friend from our group, have moved in here."

"They're living with you?" Gemini tilted her head and squinted her eyes. Lilith recognized the look from Gemini's childhood, from times when she was trying to make sense of what someone said.

"Right. The quicker all of our current homes are sold, the easier it will be to fund construction of the new one."

"Isn't Kameitha's home in Park City, too?" Gemini asked.

Lilith nodded. "Ralen and Monique live here, too. A lot of us bought in Park City with the proceeds from our remote viewing investment club."

Gemini whistled softly. "If you're all giving up your homes here, I can't wait to see what you build."

"It's going to be amazing," Lilith agreed. Although she'd eaten only a few bites of her salad, she put her napkin on the table and pushed the plate away. "The move isn't the only thing I wanted to talk with you about. I don't know if you ever met Kameitha's son, Jeremy?"

"No, I don't think so." Gemini finished her salad and took a sip of water.

"He belongs to one of the evangelical groups that oppose medical intervention. Kameitha says he and his group are planning to protest Renu. They'll probably get a lot of media attention, so I wanted to tell you in advance.

"Oh, Mom, I'm sorry to hear that." Gemini reached over and squeezed her hand.

"Thanks. I thought you might want to warn the kids."

"I will." Gemini's phone alarm buzzed. "Sorry to rush, but I have a two o'clock appointment." She scooted her chair back.

"I love you, honey." Lilith walked over and gave her a hug.

"I love you, too." Gemini frowned as she pulled away. "Be careful, Mom. Sometimes these things get out of control."

"Yeah, I know," Lilith said as they walked toward the door. "That's one reason we want to move to a less populated area. We've quickly learned there's no going back."

"That sounds kind of paranoid," Gemini said.

"Not really. It's just that we're so different now, our old lives don't fit. We're a reminder to our friends who haven't had the treatment that they're no longer young or healthy."

Gemini grimaced and gestured at the brown age spots on her hands as she reached for the doorknob.

Lilith sighed. "Yes, I know that includes you and all of our families. But our ties are stronger. It's just too much for most of our friends to handle."

"So, you decided to isolate yourselves?" Gemini shielded her eyes from the sun as she stood on the front porch, squinting back at Lilith in the doorway.

"It's not that way," Lilith said. "It's more like insulating ourselves from those who may not be open-minded."

"If you say so, Mom." She reached over and kissed Lilith's cheek.

Watching Gemini walk toward her car, Lilith wondered if she might be right. Frustrated at not having an answer, she pushed the door closed and wished it was that easy to shut out the voices inside. What was the truth? Were they following their hearts or hiding from the world?

Chapter 24

OGDEN RIVER SCENIC BYWAY, UTAH—Their four phones buzzed simultaneously a few miles before they arrived at the private driveway leading to the Renu Research Center.

"It's from Kate," Ralen said.

"Protesters!" Kameitha added.

"It's too late to turn around," Seth said.

As they topped the next hill, a dozen protesters came into view. They attempted to block the driveway, waving signs at traffic passing in both directions on the Ogden River Scenic Byway. Seth slowed, inching the car forward until the protesters parted so he could turn onto the curving lane.

On either side of the car, they chanted slogans echoed on the signs they carried: "Natural not Renu" and "Save your life, Lose your soul." Ralen flinched as one of the protesters spat on the passenger-side window; the four of them jumped in their seats when another protester banged his fist against the trunk as they passed.

"They must have just arrived or Kate would've postponed our checkups," Ralen said.

When they reached the circle drive, Kate and Hector stood in front of the building beside a man and two women, who carried signs.

"Oh no." Kameitha turned toward Lilith, pointing at a middle-aged man with his graying hair pulled to one side in three chin-length braids. "That's Jeremy."

Lilith squeezed her hand. "Everything will be okay." She tried to make her words convincing, even if it felt like a lie.

Kameitha grunted as she reached for the door handle. "It better be."

"You've been warned," Hector told the protesters as Lilith and the others approached. Kate pulled out her phone.

A woman's nasal voice droned through the speaker. "Wasatch County Sheriff's Department emergency line."

Kate paused and looked at Jeremy and the women. "This is your last chance." They didn't move. She held her phone up and told the dispatcher, "Yes, I'd like immediate assistance, please. Trespassers are protesting illegally on private property and threatening my clients."

While Kate gave the address, Kameitha approached Jeremy. He paced on the sidewalk with the women along the front of the building, chanting "RENU equals sin" and "Offense to God."

When she blocked his path, Jeremy tried to go around her, but Kameitha grabbed his arm. "What do you think you're doing here?"

"Let me go or I'll sue for harassment," Jeremy said.

Kameitha released him, but her mouth hardened and her ebony eyes flashed a warning. "It works both ways, son. You have no business here. You should be ashamed…"

"I should be ashamed? I'm not the one who allowed my body to be tainted."

"The treatment saved my life. I thought you understood, but apparently all you wanted when you called last week was to find out when we'd be here. You lied to me."

Jeremy sneered at her. "I owe you nothing. You're not my mother. You're a man-made abomination. An offense to God!"

Kameitha backed away with a shocked look on her face. Lilith stepped up and told Jeremy, "Someday you'll remember this and wish you'd acted differently." She took Kameitha's arm and guided her away. Seth held the door to the Center open for them.

"Hey, buddy." Ralen walked so close his face was only inches away from Jeremy's. "Whatever happened to 'honor thy father and mother?' Or do you just choose to ignore that part of the Bible?"

Jeremy stepped back.

"What? You don't want to pick on someone your own size?" Ralen grunted. "That's what I figured." He joined the others inside the Center.

Kameitha sat on a bench in the hallway. "I can't believe he'd talk to me like that." Tears streaked down her cheeks.

"In time, he'll see things differently," Lilith said soothingly.

Kameitha shook her head. "I've told myself that, all these years since we were in Georgia. But he only gets less tolerant."

———

A WHITE VAN with the Wolf TV logo pulled in front of the Center. A siren on the Byway grew steadily louder. Moments later, blue lights flashed as the Wasatch County Sheriff cars sped down the driveway.

While the reporter, cameraman and deputies were getting out of their vehicles, Monique's car pulled in. Hector motioned for Kate to escort her, Nan, Xavier, and Lorenz inside.

"So, the powder keg finally blew," Xavier said.

Kate nodded as they walked to the conference room. "It's that evangelical group Kameitha warned us about. They claim we're doing the devil's work."

"Great," Karla said. "That's all we need."

"Thankfully Hector and his group were the first to arrive," Kate said. "He's got everything under control."

About ten minutes later, Hector joined them inside. "All's quiet," he said. "The deputies issued warnings and said they'd arrest anyone who tries to block our driveway again."

"Are all the protesters gone?" Kameitha asked.

"Well, they moved to the other side of the Byway and off our property," Hector said. "That's the best we can ask for, legally."

"What about the reporter?" Kate asked.

"For now, I thought it was best not to comment," Hector said. "I want to see what the protesters come up with before we offer our side of the story."

When their check-ups were done, the Pioneers reconvened in the conference room to watch the evening news together.

"At least it wasn't the lead story," Kate said. Toward the end of the broadcast, the piece began with a shot of the Center's Tree of Life sculpture in the foreground. Protesters marched in front of the building, and the camera zoomed in on their signs as the reporter talked.

"Protesters took to the streets today at the Renu Research Center on the outskirts of Ogden. They want to shut it down, saying what Renu offers isn't hospice for the dying, but is more like the Fountain of Youth."

The scene shifted to picketers slowing traffic to a crawl along the Ogden River Scenic Byway, then to a close-up of a young female reporter. She held the microphone in front of a middle-aged man with thick, wiry white hair identified on the screen as Rev. Danny Day of Zion's Sword Church.

"First it was the abortionists—murderers of the unborn. Now these sinners would deny death." He pointed down the curving driveway leading to the Center.

"Are you saying that saving lives is a sin?" the reporter asked.

Rev. Day scowled at the camera. He thumped on a Bible, which he thrust at the reporter's face, causing her to jump back. "The Bible says, 'Cursed is the man who trusts in man and makes flesh his strength, whose heart departs from the Lord.'"

The camera switched to a close-up of a protester in front of the research center. "Why are you here today?" the off-camera reporter asked Jeremy Banks.

"My mother was among the first to step through these doors and into the gates of hell," he said.

Kameitha cringed, and Lilith put an arm around her.

"God had called her home, but she fell to temptations of the body and denied his mercy. Not only was her cancer cured, but her youth was restored." He held up two pictures showing Kameitha before and after the treatments.

"That's an amazing change," the reporter said, sounding intrigued.

Jeremy's face grew red. "Birth and death are sacred to the Almighty, and His alone to decide. As it says in Ecclesiastes: 'To everything there is a season... a time to be born, a time to die.'"

In a split-screen shot, the anchor told the reporter, "I think that's a first for our show—right-to-death protesters."

The young female reporter nodded. "Yes, Rev. Day and his followers oppose all medical intervention, but they claim this treatment is on a whole new level. We asked Renu's attorney Hector

Juarez about the claims that the serum not only cures disease but restores the body's youthfulness."

"It's too early to comment on the treatment since the human trials have just begun," he said. "The safety and privacy of our patients is our top concern."

"Is the example Mr. Banks showed typical of your Center's results?" When Hector didn't reply, the reporter asked, "Are you using gene therapy or stem cell treatment?"

"As I said, I have no comment at this time," Hector said. "Harassment by Rev. Day, his followers, or others will not be tolerated."

"Definitely a story we'll be following in the coming weeks," the anchor concluded.

Kate shut off the holo screen.

"I don't know how he got my picture," Kameitha said.

Ralen reached over and patted Kameitha's back. "With a telephoto lens, you don't have to be very close to get a good picture."

Distraught, Kameitha looked around the table. "I'm so sorry."

"You're not responsible for what he does," Karla barked.

"She's right." Yi pounded a fist on the table for emphasis. "And from the looks of Rev. Day, there's plenty more to come."

"I'm afraid that may be true." Hector's shoulders slumped. "Don't take any chances. We know how violent some abortion protesters have been, and these seem cut from the same cloth."

"We'll triple the security around the building," Kate said. "I'll ask Dr. J to start rotating the time for your weekly checkups so they're not predictable, but I think you all should come in together. We'll be sure to have even more security when you're here."

"Aren't people always here getting the treatment?" Lorenz asked.

She nodded. "Yes. We've been treating three dozen each month. But, at least for now, it looks like the protesters are focusing on your group. We won't take any chances, of course."

Chapter 25

RENU CENTER, OGDEN RIVER SCENIC BYWAY—Lilith's phone buzzed as they walked toward the parking lot. She looked at the screen and paused to let Kameitha and the men get a few feet ahead before she answered. "Hi, Gemini."

"Mom, where are you? Derek said the Center was on the news. Are you okay?" Her words rushed out.

"Hey, calm down," Lilith said. "I'm fine. We're all fine."

"But are you there?"

"At the Center?" she said. "Yes. We're just now leaving. We had our weekly checkup. Everything is fine."

"I don't like this," Gemini said. "I know you told us to expect protesters, but these guys sound wacko. That Rev. Day's a religious nut. I've seen him on TV before, protesting at abortion clinics. Scary stuff."

Kameitha looked back and Lilith waved her on. "Gem, let me call you back later, okay?"

"All right," she said. "Just be careful."

Kameitha looked away when Lilith got in the car.

"Hey, what's wrong?" Lilith asked.

Kameitha shook her head.

"Look, people are going to talk. It's okay." Lilith placed her hand on Kameitha's. "I'm just sorry you were the one singled out on the news. It could've been any of us, and it may still be. But most people won't pay attention to the likes of Rev. Day."

"You're a good friend to stand by me like this." Kameitha placed her hand on top of Lilith's. "I just feel responsible. After all, it's my son making trouble."

As the car pulled onto the Byway, Lilith watched the shadows flicker as they passed under streetlights, creating a rhythmic pattern of light and dark. The whirring crunch of the tires against the road added another level of distraction, which she welcomed. By the time they reached home an hour later, the adrenaline had worn off, leaving her exhausted. Kameitha had fallen asleep leaning against Lilith, and Ralen could barely keep his eyes open.

Kameitha headed toward her room, and Lilith followed. But when she reached the doorway, Kameitha stopped.

"Please don't take this wrong, but I could use some time alone tonight." Her hand lingered for a moment on Lilith's shoulder, then Kameitha tenderly kissed her cheek before disappearing inside the room.

Lilith stood in the hall for a moment, looking at the closed door. She wanted to comfort Kameitha or at least be there for her. Their relationship was new, but she wasn't in it just for the good times.

"Lil."

She hadn't heard Seth walk up behind her. He placed his arms around her in a gentle embrace and rested his face against hers.

"It will be all right," he murmured soothingly. "You don't need to be alone tonight." With his arm draped around her shoulders, they walked down the dim hallway to Ralen's room.

"Kami just needs time to figure things out," Ralen said, his eyes filled with kindness. "She doesn't mean to shut you out. It's just what she does when she gets stressed."

Lilith nodded. Although comforted by their attention, part of her wanted to bolt back to her own room in hopes that Kameitha would join her later.

Ralen took both her hands. "It's going to be all right." He drew her close and kissed her cheek. With Ralen on one side and Seth on the other, she entered the room, stealing a backward glance.

Seth pulled down the covers on the king-size bed and moved to the center. He patted the outer side of the bed, and Lilith climbed in. Ralen lay on Seth's other side. "Try to get some sleep." Seth kissed her, then rolled onto his back. Within minutes, Ralen's steady breathing and Seth's snores told her they were both asleep.

Seth had left the door open and Lilith gazed down the dimly lit hallway, wondering if Kameitha had settled in for the night or was still awake. She repeated the events of the day in her mind—arriving at the clinic, finding protesters there, Jeremy's hatefulness. As distressing as the protesters were, she found her thoughts returning to Kameitha's shutting her out. Everyone had different coping styles, but over the years, she and Seth had found it best to work things out together. Would Kameitha be there for her when she needed it, or expect her to handle things on her own?

Despite her churning thoughts, Seth's familiar musky smell and warmth eventually lulled her to sleep. Sometime later, Lilith woke to see a shadowy form beside the bed.

"Lilith?" Kameitha whispered. "Can I join you?"

"Of course!" Lilith held up the covers and moved closer to Seth to make room for her. Kameitha slipped into bed, wrapping her arms around Lilith. Kameitha's lips tasted salty as they pressed softly against hers.

"I didn't mean to push you away," Kameitha choked out in a broken, stuffy voice.

Lilith lightly brushed her hand over Kameitha's hair and tear-streaked cheek. "Shush. Shush. I'm just glad you're here now."

She reached for a tissue on the bedside table and handed it to Kameitha. "I'm sorry your son treated you that way. Kids can pull at your heartstrings no matter how old they are. You wouldn't be who you are if you didn't care." She slipped her arm around Kameitha, pulling her closer. "We'll get through this together," Lilith whispered. "Try to get some sleep. Things will be better in the morning."

"Thanks for understanding." Kameitha turned over, and Lilith moved so their bodies fit close together. Seth snored even more loudly than usual, ending with a snort. Then he threw his arm over them both.

Kameitha giggled. "How do you sleep through that?"

"Years of practice." Lilith smiled and closed her eyes. Maybe there was hope for their relationship after all.

———

GEMINI ANSWERED on the third ring.

"Is this a good time to talk?" Lilith asked. It was midmorning and Lilith sat on the patio, enjoying the sunlight.

"Just a minute." Gemini covered the phone to speak with someone, then returned, placing the call on visual. A hologram of Gemini's face hovered next to Lilith's phone. "Thanks for calling, Mom."

"I wanted to get back with you about yesterday," Lilith said.

"Yeah. What are you going to do? The more I think about this, the scarier it gets." Gemini frowned. "Like we talked about before, it's only a matter of time before the Natural Order gets involved."

"Right. Actually, that's one reason we're trying to get as many people treated as possible. Hopefully someone from Natural Order or a family member will go through the process. Then the organization's leaders may be more sympathetic."

Gemini looked down, silent for a moment, then shrugged. "You're probably right. It's just... well, the results are almost too good."

"What do you mean?" Lilith asked.

"Well, if the treatment only cured terminal illnesses, I think most people would think it's great," Gemini said.

Lilith cocked her head, considering the idea, and motioned for Gemini to proceed. "Please, go on."

"It's just the other stuff—the rejuvenation or however you describe it—that is so hard to accept," Gemini said. "The medical community tries to cure illness all the time, and when it works, it's great. But it doesn't roll back the clock and make the person younger. That's what I keep grappling with. Biologically, you're probably younger than me now. You definitely look younger. I don't know how to handle that—none of us do."

Lilith heard the concern in Gemini's voice and saw it in her squinting eyes and frown. "Sounds like it's more than just you, Gem. What's going on with the kids?"

"It's the grandkids. Somehow one of the class bullies found out you and Seth had the treatment. Now he's giving Rachel and Evan a hard time."

"I guess Lacy being against it from the first hasn't helped matters any," Lilith said.

Gemini sighed. "It's not that she's against it, per se. It's just that her best friend is dying."

"Oh, I didn't realize," Lilith said.

"It's Sadie. You may remember her."

Sadness made her chest ache as Lilith recalled the freckle-faced girl who'd spent summer sleepovers with Lacy at their home.

"She's been underfoot since they met in grade school," Gemini continued. "They've raised their kids and gone through divorces together."

"How old are her children?" Lilith remembered friends of hers who died young, leaving behind children to cope with the loss of a parent. That had always been the hardest part.

"One's Rachel's age, and the others are fourteen and ten," Gemini said.

"I'm so sorry to hear that, Gemini," Lilith said.

"Lacy isn't prepared for her best friend to die in a month or two." Gemini pressed her lips firmly together, as if biting back words. "To be brutally frank, she's having a hard time reconciling Sadie dying while you're living.

Lilith sighed and threw her hands up in frustration. "I can't die and make Sadie live. That horse has left the barn."

Gemini gave her a pained look. "Lacy's glad you found a cure— of course, we all are! But it's just natural to expect our parents and grandparents will die before people our own age."

Lilith wanted to argue with Gemini. But the truth was, Renu wouldn't save Sadie's life. Too many subscribers with terminal illnesses already waited for the treatment. She'd be dead by the time they could get to Sadie, unless Lilith intervened somehow. Should she try? And how would the serum work on a much younger person —would it simply make her healthy or would Sadie revert to a teen or even a child? Lilith had never asked, and perhaps Dr. J didn't know.

"I don't know what to say," Lilith said. "I believed in our work and put my life on the line to test it. The treatment worked much better than any of us dared to hope. Naively, we thought it would be hailed as a huge breakthrough, even better than penicillin or the polio vaccine."

"The physical transformation is just so jarring." Gemini motioned to Lilith's face. "And of course, that's what's got the bullies all riled up. With their usual lack of imagination, they call you vampires. As popular as the undead are these days, you wouldn't think that could stigmatize anyone, but it does."

"Vampires?" *Again.* "Well, it's not the first time we've come across that comparison. But I don't see how that would be bad."

"They heckle the kids and bait them with silver chains and wooden crosses. One doused Rachel with so-called 'holy water' to see if she would melt."

"Sounds like they confuse vampires with witches and werewolves," Lilith said, stifling a chuckle.

"Well, that's a different story. The more 'religious' kids shun her and Evan because their parents tell them you're devil-worshippers." Gemini stifled a grin. "It would be funny if they weren't so intense about it. Rachel came home crying."

Lilith shook her head, finding it hard to believe. "Do you think it would help if I talked with Lacy or the kids?"

"Not just yet," Gemini said. "We'll get together again in a couple of weeks. They need a little more time to get used to it."

Tilting her head, Lilith considered Gemini's suggestion. "But how will they get used to the changes without seeing us?"

"It's the idea of your transformation they need to accept," Gemini said. "In the meantime, though, I'd certainly feel better if you stayed away from the Center."

"I can't do that," Lilith said. "Since I was in the first trial, it's critical to have regular checkups. If there is a long-term problem with the serum, it should show up first with our group, so the doctors need to follow us closely."

"I worry about you, Mom," Gemini said.

Lilith smiled. "I appreciate that, more than you know. We'll keep working on ways to help more people like Sadie. I know what it's like to lose a friend, and when you're young, it is especially hard to accept."

When Lilith hung up, she found Seth watching her from the doorway. "I heard," he said.

Lilith bit her lower lip, fighting to hold back the tears welling up inside. "Do you remember Sadie? She stayed with us for a few days that summer the kids built the treehouse at the lake."

Seth nodded, moving over to her side. "Yeah, she was a cute kid. I know how hard this must be for Lacy."

"I feel guilty, Seth. It should've been Sadie who got the treatment, not me. Gemini's right—I've lived a long life."

Seth pulled her close. "Life's not fair. You know that. Besides, you can't save everyone, Lilith. What about your friend Margie in

D.C., and my friend from work? If the roles were reversed, I'm sure there's a sick child Sadie would want to save instead of herself if she could. Or if you just drove over to the hospital and walked through the pediatric ward, how many would you want to save?"

Lilith cringed. "I don't even want to think about that."

"You're just one person, but you're important to this project," he said. "Our job is to make the treatment available as soon as it can be to as many people as possible. We've been working on it for fifteen years, but it wouldn't have happened without you. We're all doing the best we can do."

"I hear what you're saying, but it still hurts."

Seth nodded. "I know."

Chapter 26

PARK CITY, UTAH—"Guess Renu really isn't taking any chances." Seth gestured toward the white stretch limo, which had pulled to a stop in front of them. "Looks like the real deal."

"The real what—real fancy?" Lilith said, puzzled.

"It's a beauty." Ralen ran his hand along the fender. "Armored body and military-grade runflat tires." He tapped on the smoke-tinted windows. "Yep, bullet-proof glass."

"Bullet-proof glass?" Kameitha opened the car door. "Cool! I could get used to this."

Lilith wasn't so sure. Did they really need an armored vehicle?

Lilith and Kameitha sat on the empty bench seat across from Monique, Xavier, Nan and Lorenz, who looked up at them as they entered.

"Ah, so we're the second stop," Ralen said, scooting in between Nan and Seth.

Xavier caressed the smooth leather seats. "It's like riding in a luxury tank."

Seth snorted. "The perfect combination."

"Yeah," Nan said. "But there's no sneaking around in this thing."

"If you mean we can't sneak into the Center, that was already out of the question. There's only one road in, which means we have to pass the protesters to get there," Ralen said.

"I know," Nan said. "But this just makes it look like we're expecting trouble."

Seth gave her a puzzled look. "We are. That's what protesters do —cause trouble."

Nan rolled her eyes. "I just meant… oh, never mind."

The next stop was at Hector's house to pick up the remaining Pioneers.

"This is a lively bunch," Hector quipped after a few minutes of quiet.

Lilith shrugged. "Just a lot for us to consider, I guess."

As they neared the driveway, they passed uniformed security in a face-off with dozens of protesters on the other side of the Byway. After the limo turned and approached the building, Lilith counted four more armed guards, also dressed in black riot gear, patrolling the entrance.

The Pioneers walked behind a row of guards and entered the building. Six desks had been added in the lobby. Phones buzzed and multiple voices assaulted her ears.

"What's going on?" Lilith asked.

"Since last week's newscast, calls have been coming in nonstop about the Fountain of Youth and our miracle cancer cure, not to mention the social media hits. We still can't keep up with the traffic, but this allows us to respond to some of it." She gestured at the energetic cadre of young men and women answering multi-line phones with flashing red lights and tapping their keyboards while scanning monitors.

"How are you responding?" Lilith asked.

Kate tilted her head at Hector. "Counsel advised us to remain as vague as possible."

"Mainly, we're signing people up to receive an email newsletter so we can send out information once it becomes available," Hector said.

"Is that helping?" Kameitha asked.

"It seems to be," Kate said. "At the very least, we're listening to them, which calms most of them down."

"Are you getting a lot of nuts?" Xavier asked.

She shrugged. "A fair share. But many of the callers or their loved ones have a terminal illness. What they want is hope, and we can give them that. The question is, will the treatment be in time?"

A nurse entering the room broke an uneasy silence that had settled over the group. "Lilith Davidson."

Lilith stood as the nurse motioned toward the hall.

Kate put her hand on Lilith's arm as she passed. "We need to discuss a few things after your check-up."

———

THE CONFERENCE ROOM was empty when Lilith arrived, but Kate had left six sealed manila envelopes on the table. Each had the name of a remote viewing group manager. Lilith toyed with her packet. Should she open it? Once she knew what was inside, she would be front-loaded. Being informed about a "target" often made it harder to do a session, but someone needed to have the whole picture. Tearing open the envelope, Lilith decided to take on that responsibility. Seth could manage her group, as he often did.

As she opened the envelope, Kate walked in. "Good," she said. "I hoped you would decide to oversee this."

"I'm glad you want additional tasking," Lilith said. "I was just about to propose a few sessions, but it's better for Renu leadership to be involved. Plus, I'm curious what kinds of issues you want addressed."

Lilith read the list of questions to herself:

- Should the Ogden Research Center be enlarged to meet the growing demand?
- Should Renu move to another country to avoid the Natural Order?
- Would Renu fare any better elsewhere?
- What's the best way to handle spouses and other family members affected by their loved one's treatment and its side effects?
- What's the best way to prioritize those receiving treatment?

"Do you need anything else from me?" Kate asked when Lilith looked up.

"I may," she said. "I'll get back to you after we have a chance to set up the project."

Kate turned to leave as the other Pioneers straggled in. Lilith kept the packets to herself. When everyone was assembled, she asked, "Does anyone want to volunteer to help set up the taskings so we can keep them blind to the group managers? There's quite a lot of territory to cover. It will take all the groups to view these questions."

Lorenz stood. "I'll help."

"Great," she said, surprised. The tall Dane didn't usually volunteer, and it had been years since he'd managed a group. "Lorenz, let's start at my house, okay? The patio should be pleasant this afternoon."

"Sure," he said. "If we don't finish tonight, we can meet at our place tomorrow. Monique's home is close enough it won't be a problem. Either way, I think we'd be more comfortable away from the picket line."

"I agree." Lilith picked up the envelopes and looked around the room. "Group managers, we'll send you a text tonight when the tasking emails are ready for you to review. All of you—let us know of any questions or concerns."

When they reached the limo, Ralen said, "Looks like it's going to be a busy week."

"I'm excited about it," Lilith said. "It's work we definitely need to do."

Lilith looked out the window at the Renu facility as they drove away and smiled. Kate was asking the same questions she, Seth, Kameitha and Ralen had been discussing among themselves. But the conversation needed to shift to the larger group. Kate's request validated the time was right to move beyond talk and toward problem resolution. The Pioneers had come this far with the longevity project, so Lilith had faith they could overcome these obstacles, too.

The limo dropped them off at her home, and Lorenz and Lilith settled in the living room. He read through Kate's questions while Lilith gathered paper and pens. They both had their laptops, but Lilith liked to doodle. It helped her find unexpected connections and solutions.

"I'm not sure this is the way I would address the issues," Lorenz said, looking up from the contents of the envelope.

"I had the same thought," Lilith agreed. "What do you suggest?"

"It seems like the reaction to the treatment—whether it's from other family members, friends, or the Natural Order—may be one issue."

"I agree," Lilith said. "They may not have the same fix, but then again, they might."

Lorenz nodded. "The reaction to the side effect, however, may be a different focus."

Lilith looked over at a video cube on the mantle of Seth and her with Gemini, the grandchildren and their children. She tried to picture Kameitha and Ralen there, too, but couldn't quite imagine it. "I haven't told my family members or friends yet, have you?" Lilith asked.

"No, I'm so far away from home, no one I know outside our group has been around to comment on my relationship with Xavier," he said. "But it's the other changes—like our communal living arrangements—that make me think it's fundamental."

Lilith nodded. "That makes sense."

"The other major issue—the most pressing one—is prioritizing the treatments," he said.

"Yes," she replied. "I think all of us have been struggling with that one."

"My ex-wife—the mother of my children—is dying." Lorenz turned away, but not before Lilith saw the pain in his furrowed brow and slumped shoulders. "And there's nothing I can do to help her. To say my children don't understand is an understatement."

"I'm so sorry, Lorenz," Lilith said. "There must be a way for us to make the treatment available to more people who really need it."

"I like the foundation for that reason. But giving away even ten percent of the treatments wouldn't have been enough," he said.

"What makes you say that?" Lilith asked.

He drew overlapping circles until they filled a sheet of paper. "Remember that discussion we had about the circle of friends? The more of us who've had the treatment, the more people are affected through our friends, relatives, and their circle of friends."

"Right. And by now, more than a hundred people have been treated. I imagine the number of lives touched is into the hundreds of thousands," Lilith said.

"Even at the current rate of treatment, before long, a million people will be affected," Lorenz said. "Then a billion, until everyone on Earth is connected to a person who's undergone the treatment."

"That does make it clear why we need to have a better way to prioritize treatment of the terminally ill," Lilith said. "If we don't, things could easily spin out of control."

"But we can avoid that," Lorenz said. "We just have to get ahead of it. And that's what we do best."

Lilith nodded. "I guess we need to get down to preparing the taskings?"

Lorenz smiled. "Absolutely."

"Since each of the groups uses a slightly different approach, I think we should take advantage of that, while still providing them with the same issues," Lilith said.

"How can we do that?" Lorenz asked. "I've been out of project management for so long, it's pretty hard to envision."

"Well, for instance, Seth will want to keep blind to the target. In our Associative Remote Viewing (ARV) group, he acts as an independent judge for the other members. When they submit their sketches and transcripts to him, he will look at two photos and see which is the better match. Each photo is linked to a different outcome, but only one will be 'correct.' If he's blind to the choice, Seth can't be influenced by his personal bias."

"Of course," Lorenz said.

"Some of the other groups use ARV but the members judge their own transcripts," Lilith said. "Instead of using photographs, some—like Ralen's group—link the outcomes to sensory perceptions like sound or smell."

"But the question could still be the same?" Lorenz asked.

"Yes, with ARV, you're dealing with a set choice," she agreed. "Then we have groups—some using ARV and others using Controlled Remote Viewing for open-ended questions—that work best when they are front-loaded instead of blind to the target."

"I usually prefer that," Lorenz said. "CRV sessions can take hours anyway, so narrowing the focus helps. Of course, we'll have to be careful to keep the wording as neutral as possible."

"Right," Lilith said. "We can let them know something general, like whether the task is a location or procedure."

After trying different wording, they settled on multiple approaches for the same question. To address the optimum location for expansion, they chose both set-number and open-ended questions. For ARV's set-number tasks, they designated outcomes of "Ogden Research Center," "Other," or "Both." The CRV open-ended question with front-loading read "The target is a location.

Describe the optimum location." They reworded the other questions similarly.

"I think each of the six groups should address all the questions, then we'll pool the responses for analysis," Lilith suggested.

"That process has worked so far. It should provide accurate data."

Lilith nodded. "Yes, I think this will do nicely. But rather than use sealed envelopes, let's ask Kate to assign random numbers to each task."

"Using coordinates like that does seem a simpler way of doing things," Lorenz said. "Plus, it would save us another trip to the Center. That's getting to be stressful."

"I agree." Thoughts of the armed guards and protesters at Renu sent a chill up her spine.

After the cues were completed, they emailed the revised questions to Kate. As suggested, she assigned coordinates for each task and emailed them to the six group managers.

Chapter 27

It took a week for Lilith and Lorenz to gather and analyze the data from all six groups. Lilith approached Judging as more of an art form than a science. She found Lorenz' analytical style of interpreting the remote viewing transcripts complemented her more-intuitive method, which centered on symbols and analogies.

After the initial review, she and Lorenz had created additional taskings to determine such things as the locations for future Renu centers. Now they stood before the Pioneers in the conference room to share the results.

"We had three major questions and several follow-up topics," Lorenz began. "Each of the six groups addressed these, so we had lots of input."

"The answers were consistent—make the treatment available to everyone as quickly and inexpensively as possible," Lilith said. "That is our best avenue for softening the reaction of our family and friends, and for helping them deal with the enhanced sexuality aspects of the treatment."

"It's also the best short-term approach for the terminally ill," Lorenz said.

"So, you're saying the best way to smooth over everything—from our family's reaction to prioritizing who receives treatment—is just to do as many treatments as possible?" Hector sighed. "That's pretty much where we are now."

"No," Lilith said. "I'm talking a huge growth in a short period of time."

"In the follow-up sessions, we determined the tipping point was about seven thousand people," Lorenz said.

"What does that mean—tipping point?" Yi asked.

"When that many people have completed the treatment, support for the program should spread rapidly," Lorenz said.

"But it takes time to build new facilities and staff them," Xavier said. "Even if the current rate doubles again to one hundred treated per month, it will be years before we reach seven thousand people."

Around the room, groups of two and three leaned in and talked among themselves, or scribbled comments to share with their neighbors.

"There's more." Lorenz held up his hand, commanding their attention. "Many of you came up with a red "X" in your sessions." He projected a series of drawings of buildings showing large Xs and arrows pointing to the Renu insignia. "While we haven't yet been able to interpret what that means, from its prevalence, we think it may be the key to making this increase possible."

He and Lilith waited for the rumbling to subside before continuing.

"We also got a lot of comments about the treatment's timing," Lorenz said. "When we tasked you with follow-up questions, we got leads for additional research, notably to develop a version of the treatment that can be taken prior to the onset of terminal illness."

Dr. J stood. "We've already started researching that—modifying the serum to enhance the body's natural defenses much earlier, before life-threatening diseases arise. It's gratifying your sessions show we're on the right track."

"And we'll dedicate our resources to guide your research, just like we did to develop the current treatment," Lilith said. "Seth and Nan will coordinate that part of the project since their groups showed the most connection to that outcome."

"In the meantime, if anyone has an idea of what 'X' is— however far-fetched it may seem—be sure to share it with the group," Lorenz said.

Several of those seated around the conference table shrugged and looked toward each other. After several moments, Lilith gestured toward the doctor. "Dr. J also has feedback for the sessions we did three months ago."

"At your recommendation, we decreased the isolation time to two weeks, which allowed us to triple the number of people treated," he said. "Remarkably, with one hundred and fifty-eight treated, our perfect success rate for eradicating terminal illness continues. We've observed no long-term side effects other than the enhanced sexuality.

"Just to refresh your memory—three sound cues were tied to outcomes," Kate said. "Today you'll only hear the one for the accurate response. It was linked to decreasing the isolation time for those undergoing the treatment." She chimed a bell.

"We also had color cues," she said. "Here's the one linked to increasing the number of treatments." She showed a yellow sheet of paper.

"Based on our continued success rate, we're now reducing the isolation period to only one week," Dr. J said.

"Maybe by your next checkup, we'll have a better idea of what this 'X' means," Kate said.

As they made their way to the limo, Lilith overheard Monique joking with Nan. "Sounds like a treasure map—X marks the spot."

"But we need X-ray vision to find it," Nan quipped back.

"What if it *is* about X-rays," Monique said, her voice now serious. "We've certainly had enough of them lately. Perhaps Dr. J is missing something?"

"Maybe," Hector pulled out his phone and started tapping on the keys. "I'm asking Kate to have the medical team double-check all the test results. It certainly can't hurt anything."

"Didn't you say it was a red 'X?'" Xavier asked.

Lorenz nodded.

"A red X. Could it be a cross instead of an X?" Xavier asked. "Like Red Cross?"

"Or maybe it's the Swiss Cross—white on a red background. But everyone thinks it's a red cross," Lorenz said.

"Really?" Lilith said. "People think it's a red cross?"

Lorenz shrugged.

"Maybe we should explore putting clinics in Switzerland?" Monique suggested.

"Or, if it's a red cross, maybe we need to look at disasters," Seth said.

"Once we see what it is, I think we're all going to feel really stupid, like if we'd drawn yellow arches and couldn't figure it out."

"I wonder if it could be the new house we're building," Ralen suggested. "From the air, the three levels could look X-shaped."

"Not really," Seth said. "The drawings may give that impression, but they make more of a squared-off cloverleaf."

As Ralen followed Seth into the limo, he suggested, "Why don't we take a trip out there? I haven't been since right after we bought the land."

"Great idea!" Nan said.

Seth gave the driver directions. Ten minutes later, the limo pulled off the Ogden River Scenic Byway onto Powder Ridge Road, then turned on Highway 158. The car crawled up a winding gravel road that hadn't been there when Lilith and Kameitha visited a month before. The limo stopped at the top of a rise.

Lilith looked out over the rugged terrain with its varied shades of green from conifers and spruce, its gray granite outcroppings, and slick black shelves of shale. Patches of white lingered in the shadows from snowfall the previous week.

The road dipped, then curved around and up. Across a valley on the flat top of the highest ridge, Lilith counted three dump trucks, two bulldozers and other heavy machinery she couldn't name. Several men in yellow and red hard hats looked tiny as they gestured to the mammoth trucks. The limo driver carefully pulled into the weeds on the side of the narrow road to give a truck room to pass.

When they reached the worksite, a broad-shouldered man with a curly black beard put his hand up and gestured for them to stop. The driver lowered his window.

"This is private property," the worker barked.

Seth, who sat behind the driver, lowered his window.

"Oh, it's you, Mr. Davidson," the worker said.

"Just came to check on the progress."

The man nodded. "I'll tell the foreman. Park behind that truck." By the time they got out of the limo, a tall, slim man had joined the worker. He extended his hand.

"Good to see you again, Everett." Seth shook the man's hand. "Could you give us an update on how things are progressing?"

"Sure," he said. "You caught us at a good time. These are the last loads of the day." He motioned at the dump trucks. "It's a hard-hat area. You'll have to take turns wearing the hats we have on hand."

Seth gave a nod. "Of course."

Kameitha nudged Lilith and tilted her head toward the cliff.

"You can tell us about it later," Lilith told Seth. "We're going down to the pond."

They were halfway to the cliff's edge when Karla called after them. "Can we join you? We've never been down there."

"Sure. It's a lot more pleasant than trudging through the dust and noise up here." Kameitha motioned toward the dump trucks and dozers that crowded the ridge.

Karla and Yi followed Kameitha and Lilith down the narrow footpath between huge boulders. They were all out of breath by the time they reached the bottom.

"It's beautiful!" Yi exclaimed.

Lilith followed her gaze to the waterfall spilling over the towering veins of dark gray slate. Tufts of waist-high grasses— some golden and others green—bowed to the constant breeze, which swept ledges of pale stone that stairstepped to the top of the ridge.

Yi and Karla hurried over to the pond, kneeling to dip their hands in its murky water.

"And hot!" Karla said. "Just like you told us."

Following slowly behind them, Kameitha put her hand on Lilith's waist. "I haven't forgotten our first time here," she whispered in Lilith's ear.

"Me, neither." Lilith stopped and stood closer to Kameitha. "I think this place is enchanted, don't you?"

"Definitely a special place for lovers." Kameitha looked up at Lilith.

Their lips barely touched, but Lilith's pulse raced. She glanced toward the pond, but Karla and Yi were no longer there. "Come on." Lilith took Kameitha's hand and led her to a partially sheltered area beneath a stone outcropping at the base of the cliff. She deftly unfastened Kameitha's jeans and pulled her close. As they kissed, Lilith slipped her hand downward until Kameitha gasped with pleasure. Moments later, Kameitha shivered and dropped her head against Lilith's shoulder as her body relaxed.

"Mmmm," Lilith said. "Our enchanted place."

Kameitha gave her a lingering kiss. Then, gazing into her eyes, she whispered, "I love you, Lilith."

Lilith's breath caught. Although she'd thought it many times, neither of them had said the words. Her heart raced, and its warmth seemed to envelop them both. She drew Kameitha closer and whispered in her ear, "I love you, too."

Above, Seth's voice yelled out. "Lilith? Kameitha? Time to go."

Reluctant to move, Lilith said, "I wish we could stay here forever."

Kameitha grinned and gave Lilith's lips a quick brush with hers, then pulled away and fastened her jeans. "We have the rest of our lives to share." She clasped Lilith's hand. "And that's a very long time." They walked toward the footpath. Karla and Yi were already nearing the top of the cliff, where Seth and Ralen stood looking down.

Seth smiled and waved. "Thought we'd lost you."

Kameitha winked at Lilith and replied, "I wouldn't complain if you left us behind."

Lilith giggled and piled into the limo next to Karla and Yi, who were holding hands. They looked as flushed as Lilith felt. She wrapped an arm around Kameitha's shoulders, pulling her close.

"I especially like the geothermal system," Hector said as he took a seat.

"It's pretty slick, all right," Ralen said, before turning to Seth. "And the way you had the site oriented so the ski trails run parallel to the road makes a lot of sense."

The limo pulled back onto the highway, headed toward Hector's home in Ogden.

"I like the way the three wings will be positioned so all the bedrooms have views of the mountains," Boris said.

Nan chuckled. "The trick would be to arrange them so you didn't have mountain views. We're surrounded."

"So precise," Hector said. "I love it. A woman after my own heart."

"You would say that." Boris smirked.

"But it is nice how the rooms will be angled to give the maximum view," Nan said.

"I'd never seen bladeless wind turbines before," Xavier said.

"And the idea of using solar road panels for the driveway and walkways makes a lot of sense," Monique said. "There'll be no need to shovel snow!"

"Yeah, solar road panels would have been prohibitively expensive even a couple of years ago," Seth said. "Since other countries and more states have gotten on board, it's really brought the cost down. If they're as efficient as I've read, we may even be able to sell power back to the electric company."

"I doubt that," Ralen said. "We're going to need a lot of juice to keep a place this size running, especially with all the technical gadgets."

"You may be right," Seth conceded.

"So, they're on track to start building in February?" Lilith said.

"The foreman said they're ahead of schedule," Seth said. "And I believe it. If we continue to have a mild winter, I wouldn't be surprised if they start the foundation next month."

"Did you see anything X-shaped?" Kameitha asked.

"No." Ralen shook his head. "It's like Seth said—the shape is more like a cloverleaf, or even a spiral."

They pulled into Hector's driveway. "I know we'll find it," the lawyer said.

Chapter 28

PARK CITY, UTAH—That night, Lilith dreamt of Xs.

She saw T-shirts emblazoned with red Xs worn by skydivers, skateboarders, and bungee jumpers. The words "exciting" and "extreme" echoed in her thoughts.

One sequence featured a hospital. She was an emergency medic who X-rayed broken bones. White doors with red Xs swung open as EMTs wheeled people on gurneys into the treatment room from a long line of ambulances. When the doors swung shut, the Renu tree of life was on the other side.

Crowded streets filled another dreamscape. Dressed in dirty clothes, Lilith squatted on the curbside and held out her empty food bowl. She called out to those passing, but no one stopped.

Then the scene switched, and she was flying above sunflower fields. Stretching to the distant horizon, the flowers' yellow faces turned up toward the clear, blue sky.

She dreamed of logos with red Xs like Xtra and Xcellent but couldn't remember anything about the products when she awoke to Kameitha's gentle caress. "Are you having a bad dream?"

Groggily, Lilith rolled onto her side and faced Kameitha. "Um, kind of. Can't get that 'X' out of my head."

Kameitha smiled and brushed the hair back from Lilith's face. "Me, too, but at least I got a break while I was sleeping. Come up with anything?"

Lilith shared her dreams, then sighed. "I just keep thinking it's something we see everyday."

Kameitha rose, leaving Lilith staring at the ceiling. A beam of sunlight peaked through a small part in the curtains and cut across the foot of the bed, providing the only light in the dim room. Lilith repeated the dream images in her mind, trying to find any threads of connection.

When Lilith heard the shower running in the adjoining bathroom, she gave up and went in search of coffee.

"Here you go." Seth poured a cup and handed it to her. "From what Kameitha said, sounds like you need caffeine even more than usual."

"Thanks, babe." They kissed. Lilith took a sip from the cup and sat on the bar stool facing him. "Looks like you haven't been up long, either."

"Just too lazy to get dressed," he said. "So, you didn't get much rest?"

"Yeah, it was a crazy night." Lilith recounted her dreams. "The one where I was a beggar was really disturbing."

He finished capping a pint of strawberries and pushed the bowl in front of her. "No begging allowed." Seth grinned. "Eat up."

"What's the problem?" Ralen asked, giving Lilith a peck on the cheek before he took the stool next to her.

After Lilith told him about the dreams, he said, "Yeah, I get the one about the beggar."

"You do?" she said, taking another mouthful of berries.

"Ever since we got the feedback, I've been thinking about how expanding our treatment will affect things. And by that, I mean everything."

"But that doesn't have anything to do with beggars," Lilith said, confused.

"In a way, it does," he said. "I know we've talked about world population and food supplies. And I agree we have the ability to grow enough food for everyone, but even now, millions go to bed hungry because the food doesn't get to everyone who needs it."

"The empty bowls," Lilith said, nodding at the symbolism.

"When you compound the current problem by adding lots of people who would've died, what do you think will happen?" Ralen asked. "That's what keeps me awake at night."

"But the sessions show we should do as many treatments as possible," Seth said, spearing his last berry.

"That's right. It's the path our viewers suggested," Lilith said. "We have to trust the process."

"Oh, I certainly trust the process, but I realize its limitations." Ralen shrugged and gestured with his palms up. "It's like they used to say when computers first came out—garbage in, garbage out."

"You're concerned we haven't asked the right questions?" Seth asked.

"I think the information we have is good, as far as it goes." Ralen shifted his weight on the stool. "We just don't have enough knowledge about the many variables to ask all the right questions. Yet."

"It's a big cultural shift, and I can see changes happening rapidly as people live longer," Seth said. "But it's hard to predict exactly how things will change."

"Yeah, it's probably like with our treatment," Lilith said. "We didn't have any way to predict the side effect."

"One thing I don't think we've considered enough is the fear factor," Ralen said. "Even after seeing a friends' recovery, the treatment won't seem safe to some people."

"That's probably what Natural Order will play on—the fear," Lilith said. "It's always about fear."

Ralen nodded. "When you get to the bottom line, even Rev. Danny Day and Jeremy focus on the fear."

"Well, regarding your dreams, Lilith, initially Renu treatments will be offered in the more affluent places, so the food issue probably won't be immediate."

"But we are going to be stomping on the toes of influential people," Ralen said.

"What do you mean?" Seth asked.

"When we can offer many of the terminally ill a viable option, it will significantly impact the profits of hospitals, doctors, insurers, and pharmaceutical companies," Ralen said. "And they are major campaign contributors."

"Weren't you working on figures for that?" Seth said.

"Just a ballpark," Ralen said. "But if you add the amounts spent for treating heart disease, strokes, respiratory illness, and Alzheimers, that's more than $765 billion each year."

"Whew," Lilith said.

"We'll definitely be up against the big boys," Seth said.

"At some point, they'll quit fighting and want a cut of the action," Lilith said.

Ralen pointed at her. "That is *exactly* what we need to facilitate. Getting them on board so we're not fighting on every front."

"That would take the wind out of Natural Order's sails, too," Seth said.

"How so?" Lilith asked.

"For all their posturing about nature, when you look at who funds Natural Order, it's the big corporations," Seth said.

"Sad, but true." Ralen nodded.

Kameitha towel-dried her hair as she walked into the kitchen. "This is a pretty heavy discussion for so early in the morning."

"Ralen's been scheming on this for a while," Seth said.

"Yeah, we've had a few discussions about it, too." Kameitha hugged Ralen with a whispered "good morning," then pulled up a stool next to Seth. "Somehow we've got to get the medical industry to see us as a partner rather than a threat."

"Maybe that's where my group and Nan's come in," Seth suggested. "Our tasking is aimed at developing a form of the treatment that works before someone is terminally ill."

"And you think that will help with this problem?" Lilith tilted her head, considering the statement. "Seems like it would make things even worse... maybe even wipe out the entire medical industry as we now know it."

"I think he's on target," Ralen told Lilith. "I can see you might be able to focus on that as part of your session, Seth. Figuring out how to bring them into the process as soon as possible is the key."

"We haven't even gotten this part off the ground yet—treating the terminally ill," Kameitha said. "I can't begin to imagine what offering it as preventative treatment would look like."

"Same here," Lilith said. "It's a good thing we don't have to rely on imagination."

"Preventative treatment could help smooth the cultural shift you brought up earlier, Lilith," Seth said.

"How's that?"

"At this point, it's just conjecture." Seth stood and placed their empty bowls in the sink. "But if Renu could preserve a person's vitality and health, there'd be little difference between someone who's twenty or forty or ninety."

Lilith sat a moment, letting the words sink in. "I wonder how that would work. Would a thirty-year-old revert to how they looked and felt at twenty? Or would you give everyone a treatment at a certain age to keep them from aging?"

"Those are the kinds of questions Nan and I are exploring with our viewers." Seth returned with a cup of coffee in his hands. "Then we'll get into the 'how' of it, but I think it will go much quicker. We can adapt some of the taskings we used to develop this longevity serum."

Ralen stood. "I hate to leave in the middle of things, but we have an appointment with the architects."

"You're right." Seth rose to his feet. "I completely forgot. We're supposed to meet them at the construction site, then I'm meeting with Nan."

"Could I join you?" Kameitha asked. "I think I lost my sunglasses there yesterday."

"You wore them to the Center yesterday morning," Lilith said. "Maybe someone found them."

"No, I already called," Kameitha said. "I'm just going to run out to the site and look around. Besides, I did a little dowsing on it and got a 'yes' for the property."

"Why don't we all go?" Lilith said.

They climbed into her Escalade. By the time she pulled onto the road to the property, Lilith almost regretted talking about her dreams. Between Ralen's statistics on everything corporate to Seth's thoughts about how to task his new team, her mind was reeling.

Kameitha, on the other hand, had been quiet most of the way. Lilith figured she felt embarrassed about losing the sunglasses she'd given her.

Lilith parked behind the same pickup as the previous day. Everett saw them and walked over.

"Back again so soon?" He shook Seth's hand.

"We need to look for her lost sunglasses." Seth motioned toward Kameitha and then in the direction of the pond. "And the architects are meeting us here soon, too."

"Just remember to give those trucks plenty of room," Everett cautioned.

"Of course." Lilith squinted and sputtered as dust whipped up by a huge dump truck blew in her face.

When they got to the valley, Lilith and Kameitha headed toward the base of the cliff, checking the footpath along the way. Seth and Ralen walked along the edge of the pond.

They searched for more than twenty minutes, then regrouped where the footpath began at the bottom of the cliff.

"Well, this time I guess your dowsing was little off," Ralen told Kameitha. They all headed toward the top.

A few minutes later, Lilith pointed and called out, "Over there!" Sunlight reflected off something metallic about a foot to the right of the path,

"It's them!" Kameitha crawled over a boulder and reached for her glasses. The loose rocks on the path shifted, and she slipped.

Lilith grabbed for her, but Kameitha tumbled backward, falling a few feet and hitting the ground hard.

Lilith scrambled after her. "Are you okay?"

Kameitha propped herself up on her elbows, brushing the dust from her clothes. "Not so much." She grimaced. "My ankle really hurts."

"Do you think you can stand, leaning on us?" Ralen asked.

She nodded.

Lilith hurried up the hill. By the time Seth and Ralen reached the car with Kameitha, Lilith waited with Everett, who had filled a plastic sandwich bag with ice.

"Thanks," Kameitha told him. A moan escaped as she slid into the back seat. Ralen placed her foot on his knee and held the makeshift ice pack on her ankle.

Seth spoke briefly to the two architects who waited by the car, then climbed into the passenger seat. "Everett says the closest clinic's in Eden."

"I'll be okay," Kameitha protested. "You should go ahead with your meeting." Her face had paled to a dull, lusterless shade, and her eyes squinted in pain.

"They needed to check the progress at the site anyway," Seth said. "We can talk later."

Lilith slipped into the driver's seat and handed him her phone. "You navigate."

Chapter 29

EDEN, UTAH—"There it is. On the right." Seth pointed to an Xtreme Care Clinic sign a block ahead.

Lilith pulled into the strip mall's parking lot. After check-in, it took thirty minutes before Kameitha's name was called. Now another hour had passed.

"What's taking so long?" Frustrated, she absentmindedly picked at loose strands on the upholstered chair. "Think she's okay?"

"You know these places are slow," Seth said in a soothing tone.

Ralen looked up from his tablet. "I don't think her ankle's broken. But I'm sure they had to do X-rays. That takes time."

Lilith gazed out the window. Images from her dreams flooded back. The emergency room. The signs. She looked up. The sign! The clinic's logo, in bold red letters, read "Xtreme Care Clinic."

She made a choking sound that drew Seth's attention. "What is it?" He reached over and pounded her back twice. "Are you okay?"

She nodded and pointed to the sign. He looked out the window with a puzzled frown. Then his mouth fell open. "That's it!"

"Yeah!" she exclaimed.

"What?" Ralen moved closer.

"The sign," Seth said. "The X."

"These clinics are everywhere," Lilith said, her voice rising. "What was it our grandson said—that he could imagine one on every corner, like Starbucks?"

Seth nodded.

Lilith pulled up stats for Xtreme Care Clinics on her phone. With almost seven thousand locations, there were almost as prevalent as Walgreens, and in about half as many locations as Starbucks. But how could they get Xtreme Care Clinics to offer the longevity treatment? And how far could they lower the cost with more demand?

"Sorry it took so long."

Startled, Lilith looked up from her phone and saw Kameitha standing beside her. A black, open-toed boot held together with Velcro covered her foot and ankle.

Lilith jumped up and hugged her. "Your ankle—is it broken?"

"No, just a sprain, but the ligaments are partially torn," Kameitha said. "I have to be careful with it for about six weeks and do physical therapy, then I should be good as new."

"That's great news!" Lilith said.

"And I got pain meds in case it starts to hurt worse."

"That's smart… you always hurt more at night," Lilith said.

"What's all the excitement about?" Kameitha looked from Lilith to the two men. "You look like kids on Christmas morning."

Lilith smiled. "Come on. We'll tell you in the car."

Kameitha shrugged. When they reached the car, Ralen helped her in. Lilith sat behind the wheel, grinning at Kameitha as she called Kate.

"Guess where we are," Lilith said.

"Seriously? You want to play a guessing game?" Kate sighed. "Since you have the vid on, it's not much of a puzzle. Is everyone okay?"

"Better than you can imagine," Lilith said.

Seth glanced at Kameitha. "Although she might disagree."

Kameitha squinted her eyes at them. "I go in to get my ankle fixed and when I come out, you're all acting like you've been konked in the head. What's up?"

"My question exactly," Kate's tone changed from concerned to puzzled. "Why do you look so happy if you're at an urgent care center?"

Lilith laughed. "I need you to check into something for me, Kate. What can you find out about the owner of Xtreme Care Clinics?"

"Extreme Care Clinics?" she said, puzzled.

"Listen carefully. X-treme Care Clinics." Seth enunciated slowly and pointed to the sign.

"The 'X' in the sessions is for the urgent care franchise?" Kate's voice rose with excitement.

"Oh My God!" Kameitha pointed at the sign. "The X!"

Lilith laughed. "It's just a hunch, but it feels right to me."

"I agree!" Kate said. "What do you need to know about the owner?"

"I don't know exactly." Lilith shrugged. "Anything you can find —what his net worth is, his family situation, any stated plans for expansion or takeovers."

"And see if the Board thinks the centers can be converted and what it would cost," Seth suggested. "Looks like there are seven thousand of them."

"Ask Dr. J if the treatment is ready for mass implementation," Ralen said. "From our viewings, I'd say it is, but that's definitely his call."

"More than seven thousand clinics," Kate mused. "That would be a game-changer. Training that many doctors and getting them on board with our goals could be challenging."

"I have faith in you," Seth said.

When Kate hung up, they sat for a few more minutes in the parking lot. Lilith couldn't take her eyes off the sign with its huge red X.

"I guess it's true—there are no coincidences," Kameitha said. "I just wish I didn't have to sprain my ankle for us to figure out what X meant."

Ralen reached over and hugged her. "Thanks for taking one for the team."

"You're not welcome." She punched his arm and slipped on her sunglasses. "Just kidding. Let's go home and celebrate."

Chapter 30

PARK CITY, UTAH—"I'm not quite up to partying after all," Kameitha said when they got home. She swallowed one of the pain pills with a glass of water.

Ralen followed her down the hall toward his room. "I need to catch up on a few things, too."

Seth turned to Lilith. "How about you?"

Lilith grinned. "I think we should at least toast our discovery. How about an Irish coffee?"

Seth went to the bar and took two mugs from the glass shelves. Lilith grabbed the Bailey's.

"Do we know anyone who works for Xtreme Care Clinics?" Lilith asked. As Seth mixed the ingredients, the rich aromas of coffee and the sweet, creamy liqueur drifted her way.

He paused and scrunched his face in thought. "Maybe Lacy would have some ideas."

"You think?" Lilith considered it for a moment. "I guess an emergency room nurse might get patients urgent care centers can't handle. I was really thinking more on the business end, though."

"We should be able to find some of the corporate information online." Seth sat Lilith's mug in front of her and opened his laptop. She blew on the steaming concoction as he typed in a query.

"Here it is," he said. The screen read "Division of Corporations and Commercial Code, Business Search."

"We can find the executives and management team there?" Lilith asked.

Seth entered the company name. On the page that came up, he pressed the box titled, "View Management Team."

She held up her mug. "Cheers!"

"Cheers—to the red X." Seth tapped her mug with his.

Lilith returned her focus to the laptop. "What do you think is our best starting place—the executive name, management team, or filed documents?"

"Let's get them all and go from there." Seth filled out the online forms and pressed his thumb on the scanner to pay.

"From this list, looks like a lot are foreign-owned," she said. "It just shows the corporate name and address."

"Not much help, but at least it's a starting point." Seth printed out the documents they'd purchased, and they pressed closer together so both could see as Lilith traced her finger down the page.

Seth reached over, moving her hand aside as he pointed. "Jackpot! The owner's name and contact information for the headquarters." He pulled out his phone.

"Wait a second," Lilith said. "What are you going to say?"

"That I'd like to set up a meeting to discuss a business proposition."

"Don't you think you should wait for Kate and Dr. J to get back to us first?" Lilith said.

"I'm not going to actually talk with the exec." Seth shook his head and grinned. "That's not how things work. It will probably take a couple of weeks just to get on his calendar. By then, we should have the information we need." Seth punched the numbers into his phone.

Lilith frowned at him. For once, she wished he'd slow down and think things through. What if Dr. J wasn't ready to expand until he understood the side effect better? Or if the Board balked at the idea of converting existing centers?

"Anyway, we can always cancel the appointment if they have a problem with it," he said as the phone buzzed.

A woman answered. "Xtreme Care Clinics, corporate headquarters. Mr. Donaghey's office. How may I help you?"

"This is Seth Davidson. I'd like to make an appointment with Mr. Donaghey."

"What may I say is the nature of your business?"

Seth looked at Lilith and shrugged. "To discuss a potential joint venture."

"And what company do you represent, Mr. Davidson?"

"It's a new business—Renu Research Center," he said.

"R-E-N-E-W?"

"No, R-E-N-U," he replied.

"The earliest opening on his calendar is a week from today. From four to four-thirty."

"That will work." Seth winked at Lilith. "Thank you." When he hung up, he said, "What did I tell you? I knew we wouldn't get in for several days. At least now we're on his calendar."

"Well, you need to tell Kate what you did," Lilith said.

"That can wait until tomorrow." Seth grinned and pulled her close. "We've worked enough for one day. You know me—all work and no play make Seth a dull boy."

———

THE NEXT DAY, Lilith watched with amusement as Seth tried to calm Hector down over the vid phone. "Nothing's set in stone. I'll cancel if it's a problem."

"Of course, it's a problem." Hector's face turned red, and he waved his hands as he talked. "Now we have to rush to get prepared for the meeting."

"I didn't mean to make things more difficult, really. I knew it would take us several days to get prepared, and the director wasn't available until next week anyway."

"Don't do anything like this again," Hector commanded.

"I won't." Seth clicked the phone off and shook his head. "Kate turned me over to Hector."

"I saw." Lilith grinned. "He wasn't happy."

"Yeah, well, it's a control thing with Hector. It always has to be his idea, his timeline." Seth turned away. "He's just irritated that I thought of it first."

Lilith chuckled. "Maybe so."

"The bottom line is the meeting with Xtreme Care is still on," Seth said. "Kate said Dr. J gave the thumbs-up, and the Board is working on what it would cost to implement."

"So, it's a 'go'—everyone favors expansion?"

"It certainly seems that way," Seth said. "Even Hector didn't oppose the meeting. He was just miffed at me for contacting Donaghey."

Lilith laughed. "I would say 'I told you so,' but…"

———

LILITH ADJUSTED the strap on her slingback heels and followed Seth, Kate and Hector into the lobby of Xtreme Care Clinics' corporate headquarters. They'd driven to Salt Lake City and had a leisurely lunch, killing time until their four o'clock appointment.

The security desk guard smiled at them when he clicked off the phone. "Mr. Donaghey's assistant will be down to escort you. You can have a seat there." He motioned to a padded bench.

The two men stood on either end of the bench where Kate and Lilith sat. They'd barely opened their tablets when a twenty-something woman wearing a tight, blue pencil skirt, a fitted white blouse, and three-inch black heels headed their way. Extending her hand, she said, "I'm Carrie, Mr. Donaghey's assistant. Please, follow me."

They followed her to the elevator. The doors opened on the top floor to an expansive view of the mountains. They walked into a room twice as large as Lilith's great room. A stoop-shouldered, balding man with bushy white eyebrows sat behind an oak desk that stretched across one corner, facing the door. From the deep wrinkles etched into his leathery, tanned skin, Lilith guessed he was about seventy.

He stood as they entered and extended his hand. "I'm Peter Donaghey. Mr. Davidson?"

Seth shook his hand. "Pleasure to meet you. Please, call me Seth," he said.

"I'm Peter."

"And this is our attorney, Hector Juarez." He gestured at Hector, then turned slightly. "And Renu's spokesperson, Kate Flowers, and Lilith Davidson, one of our key executives."

"Davidson?" Peter said, eyebrows raised.

"Yes, I'm Seth's wife," Lilith explained.

Peter nodded at them and motioned toward four Danish modern chairs with white leather seats that faced the desk.

The assistant motioned toward the latest-model beverage center in polished steel. "May I get you something to drink—coffee, tea, water?"

"No, thanks," Seth said. The others shook their heads, as well, though Peter lifted his pointer finger and Carrie nodded. A moment later, she sat a tiny ceramic espresso cup in front of him.

"I thought there might be a mistake when I looked at my appointments for today and saw Renu listed." Peter looked down at his tablet. "You're a startup company specializing in palliative care research. Is that right?"

"Yes, that's us," Kate said. "We began our human trials a little over three months ago, and the results thus far have proven far better than we expected."

"I'm happy for you," Peter said. "But my assistant said you're interested in discussing a joint venture. I can't see what palliative care and my Xtreme Care Clinics have in common."

"Once you hear more about how our treatment works, I'm sure you'll understand," Hector said. "For the most part, we have been able to keep a low profile. But soon it will become common knowledge that Renu's treatment can reverse terminal ailments like cancer and heart disease."

"What do you mean—reverse?" Peter's brow furrowed.

"Cure," Hector said. "I was one of the first to receive the treatment, as were the Davidsons. We all had terminal cancer. Now it's gone."

"In remission?" Peter took a sip of his espresso.

"No," Hector said. "Gone."

Peter pursed his lips in thought. "That's quite a claim. And, it doesn't sound like palliative care at all."

Kate nodded. "It has proven much more effective than we imagined. In fact, it's pretty much the opposite of palliative care because we treat the underlying causes of terminal illnesses, not merely the symptoms."

"The protesters on the news a couple of weeks ago said something about it being a Fountain of Youth," Peter said. "What was that about?"

Lilith and Seth exchanged a glance, then she said, "Before the treatment, we looked our age." She turned to the assistant. "How old would you say we are?"

"And don't be kind," Hector added.

Carrie shrugged. "Probably late forties, early fifties at the most."

"I'm ninety-two." Lilith pointed to Hector and Seth. "And they're also over ninety."

The assistant's mouth dropped open. Peter looked from one to the other, squinting his eyes. "No offense, but that's pretty hard to believe."

Both Lilith and Seth handed him their passports, which Peter studied. "These certainly say you're both in your nineties, but as any bar-hopping teen knows, IDs can be faked."

"These are before and after images of the first group that took the treatment." Hector put a holo cube on his phone's projector and showed them side by side.

"Fascinating," Peter said. "A holo would definitely be harder to reproduce, but any image can be faked."

"We realize it's not easy to comprehend," Kate said.

"To reverse aging, you'd most likely have to lengthen telomeres." When Kate didn't contradict him, Peter continued. "Are you using a stem cell treatment?"

"As you can appreciate, that type of information won't be available to you until after the merger," Hector said.

"But we're prepared to do whatever it takes to prove the process works," Kate said.

"I can't imagine what you could say or do that would convince me of something that is obviously impossible," he said.

"I assure you, there is a way," Kate said. "If you're like most of us, someone you love is suffering from cancer or another terminal illness."

"That's a safe guess, given my age." He sounded bored.

"To show our good faith, we're prepared to offer Renu's treatment to you or someone you choose," Kate said. "At no cost."

Peter tilted his head as he considered her proposal. "Why would you do that?" He tapped his tablet. "According to my sources, the treatment costs $1 million, and so far, it has only been offered to a very select group."

"That's true," Hector said. "Those diagnosed as terminally ill who supported the research are being offered the treatment first."

"Then why me?" Peter asked.

"As you can imagine, when other terminally ill friends and family members see what Renu can do, they want the treatment, too," Kate said. "But right now, we have only one treatment center.

Even with a one-week treatment period, we can handle fewer than fifty people per month."

"To be blunt," Hector leaned toward Peter, "it would take years to establish a network of clinics like the one you already have with the Xtreme Care Clinics. But that is what we need to meet the demand that's already building to a dangerous level. As you noted, protesters are out in front of the Center twenty-four seven opposing our treatment. What you don't see are those who call and email us, clamoring for it. They outnumber the protesters ten to one."

Peter's eyes opened wide. "You want to take over my network of clinics? I've spent my lifetime building that."

"No, we want a joint venture—a partnership. Not a takeover," Hector said. "You'd provide the properties and the expertise of managing the clinics. We'd provide the training and whatever retooling is needed for the longevity treatments. We'd use your staff whenever possible and add other specialists as needed."

"We just need to move on this quickly," Lilith said. "One hundred fifty-eight people have already been treated, which means thousands of their friends and families already want help."

"And that number grows exponentially as more people are treated," Seth said. "The quicker we can expand, the better."

"But we have more than seven thousand centers," Peter protested. "Surely that's overkill."

"We'll work with your staff to determine how many are needed," Kate said. "But the demand is there already and will only continue to grow."

"It would be up to you whether to add this to your current treatment model or to convert some or all of the facilities solely to Renu Centers," Seth said.

Peter looked at Seth, then shook his head. "I don't know what I expected from this meeting, but this wasn't it."

"It's a lot to consider," Lilith said. "But once you see Renu's effect on someone you love, I know you'll want to be part of this."

"You can really cure cancer?" Peter asked.

"So far, the cure rate's been one hundred percent." Kate knocked on the wooden tabletop.

"That's unheard of." Peter turned toward Lilith with squinted eyes, as if trying to bring her into focus. "And you're really ninety-two? Unbelievable."

She grinned at him.

"We want you to see firsthand what we're talking about before making a commitment," Kate said. "Does someone in your family have a terminal illness?"

Peter glanced at his assistant. "I was just diagnosed with pancreatic cancer." Carrie's eyes widened, and she put her hand over her mouth. "I hadn't told you, or anyone, because I wanted to get things in order here first," he told her.

"I know we can help you, because I had pancreatic cancer, too," Lilith said.

He shook his head, his lips pressed tightly together. "It's Stage Four."

"The treatment *can* help you," Seth repeated.

"You'd need to be at Renu for a week," Kate said. "Total isolation from the outside is required—not even email or text. Our treatments always begin on Mondays, and we'd need to know at least a week in advance."

"I know you're not prepared to talk details," Hector said. "But in return for the treatment, I've prepared a statement declaring your intention to proceed with merger talks pending a successful outcome of the treatment."

"And if I die or simply decide not to go through with the merger?" Peter said, his tone challenging.

"The declaration will have no effect on your estate." He pushed the disc across the desk. "Have your attorneys review it. If you are comfortable with the terms, we'll send a courier to pick up the signed copy."

"I'll get back with you," Peter said. "I just need to think about this. It's a lot to take in."

"One thing to note," Hector said. "You'll find a medical release outlining an unusual side effect. Pay attention to it."

Peter had been smiling, but the light left his eyes. "I figured there was a catch."

Seth glanced at Carrie. "I don't want to assume anything, but I'd guess you're heterosexual."

Peter grimaced. "Not that it's any of your business, but yes."

"I was, too," Seth said. "Before the treatment. Now things are bit more complicated."

Peter's face turned chalky. "Are you saying the treatment made you homosexual? It must be a tendency you already had. No way would it change me."

Seth turned his palms up. "Think what you like. I'm just saying, we're all bisexual now and we weren't before."

Lilith walked over and wrapped her arm around Seth's waist. "It's not a bad thing. In fact, it's made having a longer time to live a lot more interesting."

"As I said, you need to think about it before you sign the release," Hector cautioned.

"So, I lose my identity or lose my life." Peter's voice rose with anger. "Heck of a choice."

"It's better than no choice at all," Lilith said sharply. "And that's exactly what you faced before we came in today."

Kate reached over and gave Peter's hand a quick squeeze. "The response to the side effect has been overwhelmingly positive, even by people like yourself who felt strongly about their identity as a heterosexual."

She and the others stood.

"Thank you for your time," Hector said.

"I hope we'll see you soon at Renu," Kate added.

They rode down the elevator in silence. When they got into the limo, Seth said, "What do you think?"

"I think he'll be at the Center next week," Lilith said. "With pancreatic cancer, there's not much of a choice for him, no matter how much he protests about the side effect."

"I'm not so sure," Seth said. "He may be one of those people who'd rather die than be associated with anything or anyone gay or bisexual."

"Let's hope that's not the case," Kate said. "We need his support."

"He may need a little time to get a private investigator to check us out more extensively, like we did him," Hector said. "But I agree, it won't take long."

Seth bumped Lilith's shoulder with his knuckles and grinned. "Looks like our viewing steered us in the right direction again."

Chapter 31

RENU CENTER, OGDEN RIVER SCENIC BYWAY—Three weeks later, Lilith, Seth, Kate and Hector met Peter at the Renu Center. Although she had seen others before and after the treatment, she found Peter's transformation especially dramatic. Now Lilith knew how her family and friends must have felt seeing her and Seth rejuvenated

Brown hair a half-inch long covered Peter's previously bald head, and his skin glowed with health, making him look at least thirty years younger. He walked toward them with an assured, brisk pace.

Lilith wasn't prepared for his embrace.

"You were right!" He lifted her off her feet. "My Stage Four cancer is really gone."

She laughed and smoothed her shirt when he sat her down. "I'm so happy for you!"

"If it hadn't been for you and your experience with pancreatic cancer, I wouldn't have tried the treatment. You and Renu have given me back my life. I can't thank you—all of you—enough!" He grinned at Kate, Hector, and Seth.

Lilith took both his hands in hers. "Now it's your turn to help us save other people's lives."

He squeezed her hands, then turned toward Kate and Hector. "This is going to make us a fortune!"

Kate cut her eyes at Lilith, who was taken aback that money was top on his mind. Why did it surprise her? He was the embodiment of a self-made man, and everything about his business said "money."

Unfazed, Hector said, "Our staff has been calculating what it will cost to convert your clinics and train the needed personnel. Administering the serum is pretty straightforward for good medical technicians. But the main issue is employees need to learn how to support people as they go through the rapid changes."

"But you know all about that," Seth said.

"Right." Peter nodded. "The patients have psychological, as well as physical needs. But my staff can easily handle that." He looked at Hector. "I'll have my attorneys call you this afternoon."

———

EIGHT DAYS LATER, the Pioneers and the Renu Board met to sign the finished contract. Kate smiled at Lilith and Seth. "If things go as planned, the first hundred clinics will open in two months. Then three hundred more will open each month as training and remodeling are completed."

"How many patients will each clinic be able to treat?" Seth asked.

"Each clinic location should perform at the same level as here, which will now officially be called the Renu Research Center. So, about a dozen a week," Kate said.

"Then we should need to convert only about half the clinics," Peter said.

"About thirty-five hundred clinics?" Seth asked.

"Yeah," Peter said. "We estimate about 2.5 million people die each year in the U.S. of diseases Renu can treat. That's a huge market!"

"Exactly!" Her voice echoed Peter's excitement. "With economies of scale, we can lower the price significantly as more clinics are opened, while still generating the type of returns our investors expect. Next year, by the time all the clinics are open, we should be able to charge about a third of what we do now."

"And we won't have to limit it to just our subscribers, although they will still get first preference, right?" Lilith said.

"Of course," Kate replied.

"I think it's going to work well for everyone," Seth added.

"Next year, we can expand into Europe. Then Asia." Peter's voice raised with excitement.

"Not to be a wet blanket, but let's not forget the 'side effect,'" Ralen said as he signed the forms. "It's going to become a much greater issue when we're able to treat a significant portion of those with terminal illnesses."

Kameitha typed a query on her phone. "The latest estimates show between five and ten percent of the world population is gay or bisexual. Say you go with the high figure—that's about 7.4 million."

"If the treatments add another 2.5 million per year, it's going to create a huge cultural change in a short time," Ralen said. "In other words, in three years, the gay and bisexual population could double."

"Not to mention the number of deaths declining," Kameitha added.

"It's a lot to consider," Kate said.

"But the alternative is death and suffering," Lilith said. "And discord between those who get the treatment and those who don't."

Kameitha shrugged. "Looks like it would be a rough ride either way, so I'd rather see us help as many people as we can."

"I agree," Ralen said. "And if most resources that are now spent on the terminally ill are freed up, it will allow other pressing societal issues to receive attention."

"And there will be a lot of healthy people like us who will want to make the most of their longer lives by solving some of those problems," Lilith said.

"We just need to take as many precautions as possible to lessen the backlash," Kate said.

As the other Pioneers signed the documents, Kameitha's tablet dinged. She gasped. Lilith followed her out of the room. Tension radiated from Kameitha like an invisible barrier and tears welled in her eyes.

"What's wrong?" Lilith asked.

Kameitha shook her head. "Not here."

As the door slid shut behind them, Kameitha slumped against the outside wall and handed Lilith her tablet. "I'm so sorry." She covered her face with her hands.

Lilith gave Kameitha's shoulder a gentle squeeze. "Whatever it is, we'll get through it." She tapped the screen to activate it and followed the link Jeremy had sent Kameitha. Although she felt prepared for whatever she might find, Lilith sucked in her breath when she saw the photos showcased on the social media site. A headline blazed in bold red italic letters: "Renu sex serum." She skimmed a story beneath a photo of her and Kameitha kissing and holding hands. Rev. Danny Day referred to Renu's serum as a "devil's brew that taints biological purity."

"But how...?" Lilith's voice trailed off.

Kameitha lowered her hands and shook her head. "Maybe Jeremy's had a drone following us. It looks like it could have been taken when we went to see how the house in Eden was progressing."

"You're right," Lilith said. "It does look like the mountains in the background."

Kameitha reached for Lilith's hand. "Does Gemini know we're together?"

Lilith took a deep breath and shook her head. "Not exactly. She knows we're living together, and I've been wanting to tell her about our relationship, but the time never seemed right."

"At least she hasn't been protesting against the Center like Jeremy has," Kameitha said.

Lilith squeezed her hand, hoping Kameitha would feel her support.

"I can't find a way to make him see that we're trying to help people. You'd think it would matter to him that Renu saved my life!" Kameitha's voice caught on the last words.

"It matters to me." Lilith pulled Kameitha close and held her until she calmed. "C'mon. We should show this to the others. It's like you said earlier—we knew it would be an issue sooner or later."

"I guess Jeremy's making sure it's sooner." Kameitha looked up at her with glistening eyes.

"All you can do is love him and hope he eventually understands." Lilith gave her a one-armed hug and took a step toward the door. "Let's get this over with."

Still favoring her ankle, Kameitha limped back into the conference room, and Lilith followed. With the signing completed, some of the Pioneers stood, ready to leave. Others were closing laptops and checking phone messages.

Kameitha cleared her throat. "I have something to show you before you go." She connected her tablet to the projector. The holo-image of Lilith and her kissing blazed to life at the front of the room. "Zion's Sword Church posted it, along with quotes from our 'good friend,' Rev. Danny Day."

Hector sighed. "Well, it is what it is. But the timing sucks."

Peter nodded. "I have to admit, when I signed the release form before taking the treatment, it was hard to imagine how profound the changes in my sexuality would be."

Lilith shrugged and smiled at Kameitha, Seth and Ralen. "It's made our lives much richer."

"For some of us, empathy doesn't come easily," Peter said. "Before I had the treatment, I couldn't really understand what it was like to be anything but a heterosexual male. I saw everything through that perspective. It's hard to change ingrained beliefs."

"We need to prepare for a backlash," Kate said. "While people are generally more accepting about alternative lifestyles than they used to be, a lot of intolerant people will feel threatened."

"And public perception is already skewed about how many people have same-sex attractions," Hector said. "Most estimate the number at about double the actual ten-percent rate. Those who are phobic will find a true increase especially threatening."

"On the other hand, more than half the population believes homosexuality should be considered an acceptable lifestyle," Kate said.

"But will they feel the same when gay or lesbian tendencies are medically enhanced late in life and affect someone they love—a husband, sister, or mother?" Kameitha said.

"Or themselves," Lilith said.

"That's the challenge, all right." Seth shrugged and fidgeted with the strap on his backpack as he looked toward the door.

"That's what Rev. Day is counting on—alternative lifestyles are great in the abstract, but maybe not when someone you know changes practically overnight," Ralen said.

Lilith bit her lip, then texted Gemini, asking to meet as soon as possible. She didn't know the best way to tell her, but she wanted to talk with Gemini before she saw the post online.

"But this isn't really about being gay," Kameitha said. "Even though they want to make it look that way by photographing Lilith and me kissing and holding hands, I'm also in a partnership with Seth and Ralen. It's not just about sex."

"The same is true for us." Hector motioned toward his partners. "It's called polyamory—having more than one loving relationship

175

at the same time, with the full knowledge and consent of all involved."

"Exactly," Yi said. "When I started trying to understand what was going on with me, I learned it is a lot more common than I ever thought."

"Really?" Seth asked.

"Several studies have shown as many as a third of relationships allow for non-monogamous activities," Yi said.

"A third?" Lilith asked in a skeptical tone. Had she known that many people who'd kept their intimate relationships hidden from her?

"It's just not obvious because there's no contract like a marriage license," Yi said, as if echoing her thoughts. "Often it's kept private between the parties involved."

"I'll get started on talking points," Kate said. "In the meantime, we should expect more reporters hanging around than usual. Just don't go out alone, and for now, don't comment."

Lilith's phone chimed. Gemini said she would be home in an hour. Lilith sighed with relief and tapped a note back saying she was on her way.

Chapter 32

MIDWAY, UTAH—Lilith stood on Gemini's porch, breathing deeply. Her nerves danced, though she told herself everything would be okay.

She pushed the doorbell and heard Gemini call out, "Come in! The door's open."

Lilith entered and Gemini motioned her to the kitchen. "I was just fixing a cup of tea. Like some?"

"Sure." Lilith put her purse on the countertop and took a seat on one of the red leather bar stools.

"What's up? You sounded stressed." Gemini set a steaming cup of tea on a coaster in front of her.

"Well, yes, a bit." Lilith scooted her stool closer to the counter. "I need to talk with you about something. We kind of touched on this when I told you about the house we're building in Eden."

"Okay," Gemini said warily as she stirred a spoonful of sugar into her cup. "That was a bit of a shock, but I've gotten used to the idea. How are things going?"

"The utilities and foundation are in place." Lilith toyed with her necklace, then tapped her fingers on the countertop. "It will start to look like a house soon. I'd love to show you around."

"I can't wait." Gemini grinned at Lilith's scrunched eyebrows. "No, really! And I think the kids are intrigued, too. It's hard to imagine anything nicer than your home in Park City."

"It's really a lifestyle thing." Lilith cringed inwardly at the defensive tone in her voice.

"I get it." Gemini bobbed her head. "You want to be around the people who've been through what you have."

Lilith swallowed hard, gathering her courage. "It's more than that. Since the treatment, I've grown very close to Kameitha. We're seeing each other... romantically."

Gemini glared at Lilith. "You're having an affair?"

"No, it's not like that. Seth knows about Kameitha and me."

"So, what does he think?"

"Well, he and our friend Ralen have grown close, as well," Lilith said. "Increased libido and same-sex attraction are side effects of the treatment. In fact, the four of us—Kameitha, Seth, Ralen and I—are in a committed relationship."

"A relationship?" Gemini's forehead furrowed as she looked into Lilith's eyes. "You've got to be kidding me. Like sex?"

Lilith nodded. "I know it's happened really quickly, but we love each other. And we're all happier living together."

"Really, Mom? TMI." Gemini's cup clanked loudly as she sat it on the stone countertop. "I don't even want to imagine it."

"Well, that's just it. You don't have to, because Kameitha's son posted pictures of us kissing." Lilith pressed the display button on her tablet and a holo popped up.

"Wow!" Gemini waved her hand at her face like she was faint. "I didn't see that one coming."

"I wanted to tell you about our relationship earlier, but the timing never seemed right. Not that it's better now—I just didn't want you to hear about this from someone else first."

"Nice of you consider that," Gemini said sarcastically. "Actually, I'm surprised the kids didn't beat you to it. They're usually on top of anything that hits social media." She paused and sighed, as if resigned to the situation.

Lilith felt the heat as Gemini's mood shifted. Her gaze, full of judgment, raked over Lilith. Defensively, Lilith said, "It's not just about sex."

Gemini shook her head, then stood and paced. "Okay. So first you disappear into the Research Center and I think you're giving up your last chance to live." Her voice continued to rise. "Then you show up not only looking younger than me, but totally cured of cancer. Now you're telling me you're suddenly lesbian? At age ninety-two!"

Lilith bit her lip. "That's one way of looking at." When Gemini remained silent, Lilith added, "Actually, it's called polyamory—and I'm bisexual, not lesbian."

Gemini put her hand to her forehead. "What's it going to be next week?"

"What do you mean?"

Gemini waved her hands as she continued to pace. "Seems like when I come close to getting a handle on things, something else changes."

"Like I said, I would've told you earlier, but I didn't want to upset you more than you already were," Lilith said.

"You sound like one of the kids, making excuses." Gemini stopped pacing and stared at Lilith. "It's not the kind of secret you can keep."

"And I didn't want to, Gemini, especially not from you and the family." Lilith reached for Gemini's hand. "Kameitha and Ralen are wonderful people, as I'm sure you will agree when you get to know them."

Gemini pulled away. "Guess that explains the rush to sell their houses and move into your place."

"Getting their homes sold quickly was partly based on financial reasons. But yes, we also wanted to spend more time together," Lilith said quietly.

"So, is that all?" Gemini reached to shut down the holo projection on Lilith's phone.

Lilith's jaw tightened as she tried to control her swirling emotions. She took a deep breath to release the tension. "No, I also have good news. We can get Lacy's friend Sadie into Renu for treatment much quicker than we thought."

Gemini closed her eyes and looked away. "No. You can't." She shook her head. "Sadie died last week."

A lump rose in Lilith's throat, and the excitement she'd felt about the expedited treatment faded.

"She was only forty." Gemini's voice wavered.

"I'm so sorry," Lilith said in a soft, halting voice.

"Me, too," Gemini said. "Lacy's taking it hard. I liked it better when she was angry."

"I wish we could've done something sooner."

"Me, too," Gemini said.

"We just signed contracts today to partner with Xtreme Care Clinics," Lilith said. "Derek's vision of a clinic on every corner like Starbucks may be coming true sooner than we imagined. Instead of treating a few hundred each year, now we'll be able to save thousands."

"I'm sure that's great," Gemini said, "but I'm not going to lie to you. You're my Mom, and I'll always love you, but this is all getting to be a bit much."

"It's a challenge for all of us—something no one has ever dealt with before throughout human history." Lilith swallowed hard, trying to ignore the fear rising within. "Given that, I don't guess it should come as a surprise that it isn't easy."

"But I don't even know how to relate to you anymore."

Lilith's heart felt like it was made of lead. "Please, don't let this come between us."

"Right now, Mom, I need a little time to put things in perspective." Gemini stood and took a few steps toward the door. "You've always preached to me that adults think about how their actions affect others. I don't believe that's been a big factor in your life lately."

Hurt and confused, Lilith followed her. Was Gemini throwing her out? She thought of the many families she'd seen torn apart over the years, often from simple misunderstandings. Never would she have believed her relationship with Gemini could be threatened. Until now.

Lilith tried to sound calm, but her voice betrayed her. "It's true, I try to live my life to the fullest, but that includes being the best mother to you that I can be. I always want what's best for you and the kids. I'm sorry if it doesn't look that way to you right now."

"We'll talk later, Mom," Gemini said coldly. The door slid shut, leaving Lilith outside. Alone.

Chapter 33

PARK CITY, UTAH—Kameitha met Lilith with a worried smile when she returned home. "How did it go?"

Lilith shook her head. "She's overwhelmed. I think this—" she gestured from herself to Kameitha, "us—was the last straw. One thing too many for her to handle."

Kameitha patted the cushion next to her on the couch and looked into Lilith's eyes. "It will be all right. Gemini's a smart woman and a loving daughter. It's just a lot to take in." Kameitha kissed her forehead, then gave Lilith a hug.

"I keep telling myself everything will be fine." Lilith felt the tears welling up inside. "But it feels like I'm losing her."

"That's not going to happen." Kameitha slammed her fist on the couch. "I hate that my son is the cause of all this. I'm so sorry!"

Lilith shrugged. "If it wasn't him, it would've been someone else. Any way you look at it, I have to take responsibility for how others' lives are changed because I chose to undergo the treatment."

"Their lives would've been affected in much worse ways by your death," Kameitha said. "Don't forget that."

"Exactly!" Lilith said. "It was all about staying alive. We had no idea the treatment would cause changes in sexuality and only a hint about the possible changes in appearance. Even after all the years of testing, a serum that would reverse any terminal illness, much less all of them, was beyond our ability to comprehend. And now it's a reality."

"Yeah, somehow that's gotten all twisted around, hasn't it?" Kameitha said. "The protesters. Even our friends. No one seems to really understand."

"I know life isn't fair, but this sucks," Lilith said.

Kameitha chuckled. "It does! But I can understand how someone like Gemini—and, to some extent, my son—find it difficult to understand or accept. Sometimes I feel overwhelmed by all the changes, don't you?"

"Sure. And logically, I can see their point," Lilith said. "But emotionally, it's a different matter. I've always been there for Gemini and the grandkids, and their kids. I haven't always agreed with what they did, but I wanted them to be happy. I expect the same in return, not being judged for doing what I needed to do to survive. Or to thrive. Is it too much to ask my family to give me the same consideration I gave them, for once?"

"Of course it isn't. You deserve that," Kameitha said. "But I can't think of anything you can do now to make things better with them, can you?"

Lilith stood and walked to the patio doors overlooking the mountains. "No, and I guess that's what's most frustrating—not being able to control things or people. It's just a wait-and-see game. I hate that!"

Kameitha walked over and took both of Lilith's hands in hers. "The good thing is we have each other. You're not alone. I'm here for you."

"I am, too," Seth said.

Lilith and Kameitha jumped. "Oh, Seth, I didn't hear you come in," Lilith said.

"I just got here," he said from across the room. "Sounds like your meeting with Gemini didn't go too well."

Lilith sighed. "The quick version is that she needs time to come to grips with our new lifestyle."

"Don't let it get you down," Seth said. "We have time, Lil. We knew if the serum worked, Renu would change the world. And that's exactly what it's doing."

"Somehow I didn't picture how that would work within our family." Lilith sighed again.

Seth grinned. "If you had, I'd think you were a witch."

Kameitha laughed.

Lilith rolled her eyes. "You're so full of it!"

At the sound of the front door opening, they turned to see Ralen enter. "What's going on?" he asked.

"I'll bring you up to speed later," Seth said. "Let's head over to the club." He put his hand in the small of Lilith's back and leaned over to kiss the back of her neck as he guided her toward the door. He picked up his laptop on the way out.

"So, ladies, we've been working on something this morning that might make you feel a little better," Ralen said.

Usually they would've walked the few blocks to the clubhouse at Promontory, but with Kameitha's injured ankle, they drove. After they placed their orders, Seth positioned his laptop so everyone could see the screen.

"Do you remember the figure the groups viewed as the tipping point for Renu, as far as gaining acceptance?" Seth asked.

"Sure," Lilith said. "Around seven thousand people."

"When we were talking about fewer than fifty people being treated each month, it would've taken years to reach that number," Ralen said.

"But now, with the Xtreme Care Clinics, things look much different," Seth said.

"Want to guess how soon we may reach it?" Ralen asked.

Kameitha and Lilith exchanged a look, and both shrugged.

"In a year?" Lilith guessed.

"You're not going to believe this," Ralen said. "We're looking at less than three months after the clinics are converted, if things go as planned."

"Really?" Kameitha said. "Seven thousand will have been treated by May?"

"That's assuming the clinics are all able to treat a dozen per week," Seth said.

"That still seems pretty ambitious," Lilith said.

"And what about the money—I know Kate estimated the cost could be cut by two-thirds when all the clinics are open, but that's going to take at least a year," Kameitha said. "Since the treatment's experimental, insurance won't touch it."

"They worked out a financing plan today," Ralen announced triumphantly.

"How does that work?" Lilith stared at him curiously.

"For one thing, they're dropping the cost to $600,000," Seth said. "One option is to make a $50,000 initial payment, followed by a thirty-year payment plan at two percent interest. That brings the monthly cost to two thousand dollars."

"That's a lot better, but it's still pricey!" Kameitha pulled out her phone again and tapped in another search. "The average income for retired folks is less than forty thousand dollars. They aren't going to have that kind of money."

"The Board's still trying to find ways to make it more accessible to everyone," Seth said. "But Peter got them to expand the foundation's coverage. So, in addition to the free treatments, another ten percent will be offered an income-based fee scale."

"And the price of the treatments will continue to decrease after the initial expenses are recovered," Ralen said. "They're working on a five-year plan that should see the longevity treatments becoming an integral part of the healthcare system."

"Working with the FDA?" Lilith said skeptically.

"Someone has to do it," Ralen joked

"I don't know if it's going to be that easy," Kameitha said. "Already just in our foursome, we've had family problems—my son, especially, but also Gemini. From what I hear, that's the rule, rather than the exception."

"I hear what you're saying, but Kate says they're getting more calls from people demanding the treatment than they can answer," Ralen said. "She can't hire people fast enough to keep up with inquiries."

"It's like a storm brewing," Lilith said. "All these different currents are converging—those who want the treatment, and those who can't accept it. When they meet, it could be explosive."

Chapter 34

SALT LAKE CITY, UTAH—Jeremy Banks watched from the parking lot as Rev. Day escorted two men from his office. He'd seen one of them before—a stocky man in a white suit with a striped bowtie. An actor maybe? A politician? The other man—a thirty-something blond with a weasel's face—was definitely a stranger to Jeremy.

They paused and Rev. Day clasped the men's hands between his. Smiling broadly, he leaned over and whispered something to them that Jeremy couldn't hear. They laughed.

As they walked away, Rev. Day spun around to face Jeremy. "Don't just stand there. We have work to do!"

Jeremy jumped, startled, when the pastor's big hand patted him on the back as they walked through the doorway.

"That drone footage…" Rev. Day shook his head. "You really have proven your dedication, my boy. Now I need you to make one last effort to save your mama's soul. It's the faithful son's duty."

"But you saw what she… and that woman… did!" Jeremy protested.

Rev. Day rested his pointer finger on Jeremy's chest. "And if—no, *when* you don't succeed, we will contain this evil and keep it from spreading. Think of it like cauterizing a festering wound."

35

February 2030

PARK CITY, UTAH—Lilith sat at her desk, wondering where the time had gone. Tomorrow the first dozen patients would arrive at the Xtreme Care Clinic in Eden where Kameitha's ankle had been treated, and where she had noticed the red X on the sign. It was one of the first hundred public Renu clinics scheduled to open this month.

Peter and Kate had decided to launch them without fanfare. Only the Tree of Life symbol replacing the red X on the sign and Renu's name on the door announced the changes.

Lilith thought it was a wise approach. She still had qualms about Rev. Danny Day and his followers. They had been eerily quiet the past two months—no more leaked photos or scathing comments from Rev. Day—which made her wonder what was brewing. Even Jeremy had kept a low profile since his post of Kameitha and her kissing.

Things had gone so well that Lilith felt hopeful. If Renu could get the clinics launched as planned, they might reach the tipping point quickly. And that would help on many fronts.

The Renu Board had done all it could to prepare for problems, including a fat allocation to fund security at the new clinics. Patient screening included a background check to ensure they weren't affiliated with Rev. Day's church. For now, anyway, they couldn't take the risk of having protesters on the inside disrupting the treatments. Lilith felt sure the time would come when many of his followers would legitimately seek treatment, but Renu needed to get the clinics on firmer footing before they could accept that risk. The protesters still picketing the Research Center were proof enough the evangelist and his followers hadn't forgotten about them.

Kameitha tapped on the frame of Lilith's open door. "Hey." She poked her head into the room.

"Oh, hi," Lilith said.

"Got a minute?"

"Sure. What's up?" Lilith turned from the computer screen.

Kameitha moved papers off the turquoise-and-green armchair by Lilith's desk and sat. "I ran into Nan outside. Looks like she's as excited as Seth about the progress their groups are making on the new serum."

Lilith nodded. "Seth said Dr. J is already talking about doing human trials. Can you believe it? It took more than fifteen years to develop the treatment we used, and only a couple of months to get the new serum to this stage."

"That's amazing progress!" Kameitha agreed.

"Seth thinks it's because the medical team knows so much more because of their work on the treatment we took," Lilith explained.

"That had to help."

"If they could get the new serum ready by next year when all the clinics are up and running, what a difference that would make!"

Puzzled when Kameitha didn't respond, Lilith followed her gaze out the window.

"Something on your mind?" Lilith asked.

Kameitha shivered and refocused on Lilith. "It's silly, I guess, but I'm just waiting for the other shoe to drop."

"You mean Jeremy?"

She shrugged. "Yeah. But more than that. Have you heard anything from Gemini or the grandkids lately?"

"No." A familiar lump rose in Lilith's throat, one she'd had the past two months when she'd thought about her daughter. "I've left several messages for her, but she hasn't responded."

Kameitha pressed her lips together. "From what I'm hearing, the rest of the Pioneers are having similar problems. The change we experienced is so sweeping, it's really hard for our families and friends to accept."

Lilith sighed. "I know. But I don't know what to do about it, except to keep reaching out to the ones we love."

"That's just it." Kameitha frowned. "We can't even get the ones closest to us to understand, and now we're being asked to reach out to a wider audience."

"Oh?"

"I got a call today from an old friend who's an editor for 'Science America.' They want to make Renu the cover story, but only if they get an exclusive."

Lilith paused, considering the offer. Mainstream media often picked up the top stories from the popular science journals. "That would be huge, but I'm not sure we're ready for it yet. Have you talked with Kate?"

"No, I wanted to see what you thought first." Kameitha shifted in her seat and gave Lilith a hopeful smile. "With their lead times, the story wouldn't run for a couple of months. By then, hundreds of clinics will be open."

"True." Lilith nodded. "And more than a thousand people will have completed the treatment. We can't put off major media coverage forever. At least 'Science America' would be more interested in facts than sensationalism."

"That's what I was thinking," Kameitha agreed.

"Let's see what Kate says," Lilith suggested. "Her marketing plan included the top science magazines, but I don't know her timeline."

"This could be our best shot—to lay the groundwork as the new clinics open," Kameitha said.

"Who knows—maybe it could even help Gemini and the others understand this better," Lilith said.

"Wouldn't that be nice!" Kameitha said. "But I'm not holding my breath as far as Jeremy's concerned."

Lilith considered Kameitha's remark. "I guess it could also make things worse—stirring the pot, and all that."

"You just never know." Kameitha gave her a concerned look, then jabbed Lilith's shoulder lightly with her fist. "But making decisions like this is why Kate gets the big bucks."

———

WHEN THEY ARRIVED at the Research Center, a Wolf TV van sat in the circular drive.

"Huh," Kameitha mused as she pulled into the parking lot. "I wonder if Kate called them here."

Lilith unbuckled her seat belt. "Or maybe they heard about the clinics opening?"

The cameraman started setting up by the fountain as they followed the reporter into the lobby. Lilith recognized the young female reporter as the same one who'd previously covered the protesters.

Kate greeted the young woman by the security desk, then motioned toward the door and said, "I'll join you outside in just a moment." She faced Lilith and Kameitha with her brows scrunched in a puzzled expression. "Do we have an appointment?"

"No," Lilith said. The door slid shut behind the reporter. "We don't mean to disrupt your day, but we'll only need a few minutes after your interview."

Kate nodded. "Of course. You can wait in my office. I won't be long."

Kameitha and Lilith sat in the red leather chairs facing Kate's desk. It took Lilith a few minutes to recognize the pattern of the ornate ironwork beneath the oval glass desktop. Mirror images of the Renu logo, the Tree of Life, joined—trunk to leaves and leaves to trunk—to form a continuous figure.

Lilith pointed at the desk. "That's new."

"I was thinking the same thing," Kameitha said. "It's beautiful."

"It's interesting how the trunks' double helixes weave into the leaves," Lilith said.

"Very symbolic, don't you think?" Kameitha said. "It's such a connected process. As we change, we reach out to others, who also change."

Lilith nodded as the door slid open.

Kate took a seat at her desk. "This is a nice surprise. I think. Everything okay?"

"Can't we just drop in for no reason?" Lilith said lightly.

"Of course," Kate said, her voice suspicious.

Lilith grinned. "All right, so we do want something. We need your guidance."

Kate wagged a finger. "I knew it wasn't just a social call."

Lilith shrugged and tilted her head toward Kameitha. "It's all her doing."

"A friend at 'Science America' saw Dr. J's journal article and wants an interview about Renu," Kameitha said. "She says we can have the cover if it's exclusive."

"You did exactly the right thing by coming to me. And the timing couldn't be better!" she said.

"My friend will be glad to hear it," Kameitha said. "I'll forward her contact information to you. Of course, I can't guarantee she'll have softball questions. She's very serious about her job."

"No problem with that," Kate said. "'Science America' is the top science magazine. That's the best publicity you can get. Almost two hundred people have now completed the treatment, so there are a lot of people who were dying and are now healthy."

"That many?" Kameitha said.

"What about the side effect?" Lilith asked.

"Yes, it's still there, too." Kate sighed. "It doesn't make things easy."

"You never reacted to Rev. Day's claims that Renu's serum is the devil's brew," Kameitha said. "I'm sure his issue of 'biological purity' will come up again. My son and Day's other rabid followers will see to that."

"That's true. But you don't repeat a negative like that—it just reinforces it in people's minds." Kate rose and walked across the room. She clicked a remote and a window disappeared. She motioned toward the workstation concealed behind the holoscreen's illusion. "Join me."

Chapter 36

RENU RESEARCH CENTER, OGDEN RIVER SCENIC BYWAY—"You're full of surprises, Kate," Lilith said.

Kate chuckled. "I try to be."

"Why do you keep your workstation hidden?" Kameitha asked as they followed Kate across the room.

"To make the office more impressive, of course." Kate took one look at them and laughed. "Just kidding! It's mainly for added security. Hector insists. It's a technique developed in the Cyber Wars that corporations now use to guard trade secrets from in-house spies. Randomized holoscreens incorporate complex passcodes. Tomorrow the workstation—and data—may be hidden on the other side of the room by the image of a chair or a potted plant."

Kate touched an icon on the monitor's clear screen, which levitated in front of her. It projected the image of a bar chart, which now hovered beside them.

"This shows the projected growth in the number of people treated as new offices open." The height of the multicolored bars jumped from nothing to higher than their heads. "The first hundred centers that open tomorrow are fully booked through the end of the year by our existing list of Renu subscribers and referrals, without any publicity. All are terminal cases. I expect media in every city where those are located to pick up today's interview via the wire service. I also released the locations of the next three hundred clinics to Wolf. I'm sure those cities will run the story, too."

"Then I guess it's too late for my friend to get an exclusive," Kameitha said.

"Not at all," Kate said. "The scientific data I provide her will be exclusive. And it will offer hints about the new protocol, just enough to tantalize those who may be resentful of a cure that's only available to those terminally ill."

"Or those who feel threatened by expanded sexuality," Lilith added.

"The idea is to broaden the playing field," Kate said.

Kameitha nodded. "So, you're trying to give more people a stake in the game."

"Yes," Kate said. "Not if, but when Rev. Day comes out strongly against us, we'll need their support. Hector said the good reverend has a lot of powerbrokers in his pocket, including those with political connections."

"Why am I not surprised?" Lilith had seen many overly zealous evangelists in her long life. Some had come close to eliminating the separation between church and state, which was fundamental to the nation's political structure. Filled with dread, she shook her head, thinking back to what Rev. Day had already said about Renu. "Things could get ugly fast."

"As your groups continue to provide us information from remote viewing sessions, we'll refine our publicity and expansion plans," Kate said. "But for now, developing the new protocol and getting as many terminally ill people cured as possible look like the best approaches."

"Plus, they are the right things to do," Kameitha said.

Lilith smiled in agreement, but she felt uneasy. Although the Pioneers had talked about the way the world would change, it had never hit home like when she'd seen Kate's charts. The progression from blue to red as the bars rose toward the tipping point in a matter of months made it clear just how fast the changes would come, picking up speed as each new clinic opened. Lilith was still pondering the unprecedented pace and scope of the changes when they reached the car.

"Ready to head home?" Kameitha asked as she opened the driver's side door.

"Sure." Lilith sat in the passenger's seat, staring straight ahead.

"You seem preoccupied. Is something wrong?"

"Not really," Lilith said. "Those charts got me thinking about history."

Kameitha grinned as she started the car. "Now you're getting serious on me."

"A little." Lilith shrugged. "Kate's holoscreen security reminded me of how much things changed when computers first became popular. Remember the days before computers?"

Kameitha nodded.

"The digital revolution changed the way we lived—in some ways, we became more isolated, interacting online rather than in person, and yet we were more connected globally than ever before."

"Until the Cyber Wars," Kameitha said. She turned onto the interstate, heading toward Park City.

"True, we lost a lot of ground then, but things never returned to the way they were before," Lilith said. "The digital revolution changed society at a fundamental level, just as the industrial revolution did a few decades earlier. Industrialization and urbanization even changed how most people defined 'family.'"

"You mean how nuclear families replaced extended families living together?" Kameitha said.

"Exactly."

"So, what are we starting—a medical revolution?" Kameitha asked.

Lilith thought a moment. "I don't know what it should be called. It could be seen as a leap forward, similar to when vaccines and antibiotics were introduced, but I know it's going to have a more profound influence on the way we all live.

"And in a much shorter time than the digital revolution, particularly with the expanded sexuality," Kameitha added.

"That will be the most apparent change because it will be immediate," Lilith agreed. "Just think—within a year, there will be thousands like us, wanting a different lifestyle. The nuclear family won't be as desirable anymore."

"Hmmm, I can't help but think about the Sixties. Maybe this is a 'new and improved' sexual revolution?" Kameitha winked at Lilith.

"Well, I'm sure not complaining about that." She reached over and squeezed Kameitha's knee. "But the change is so fundamental it affects everything—even the kind of house we want."

"I think you're right," Kameitha said. "There'll be huge demand for houses suitable for multiple couples and families—the new extended family."

Lilith nodded. "And before long, governments and businesses will need to rethink things like retirement benefits."

"Even if people could afford to sit around and do nothing, don't you think most will want to stay active?" Kameitha said.

"If they are healthy," Lilith said.

"Well, that's what our treatment is all about—restoring health," Kameitha said. "Which brings up something I've been thinking about. Now that we probably have decades longer to live, what are we going to do?"

"Good question," Lilith said. "Of course, Renu will keep us busy for quite a while. And dealing with the naysayers."

"I'm afraid some people will never accept it," Kameitha said.

When Lilith pulled into their circle driveway, Jeremy stood leaning against his car in front of the house.

Chapter 37

PARK CITY, UTAH—Kameitha sucked in her breath. "What's *he* doing here?" Rather than park in the garage, she stopped in the driveway behind Jeremy's battered blue Chevy. She turned off the car and gave Lilith a pleading look.

"It will be okay." Lilith said, reassuringly. If only she believed it. She placed a steadying hand on Kameitha's shoulder.

Kameitha frowned. "We'll see." She opened the car door and stepped out, her gait stiff from tension.

Lilith followed, her pulse racing. She kept her eyes trained on Jeremy, wary of any threatening movement he might make. She didn't trust him.

When Kameitha was within arm's length of Jeremy, she said in a steady voice, "This is a surprise."

Jeremy straightened, looming a head taller than his mother. He scowled down at her.

"The Reverend sent me," he said harshly. "*He* honors the sanctity of family, as we're instructed in the Bible. Even though you have polluted your body, Rev. Day says it's my duty as your son to offer you redemption. Leave this place and this—Jezebel." He motioned toward Lilith. "Repent of your sins against nature."

Kameitha shook her head. She spoke softly, but with resolve. "You know I love you, Jeremy, but I don't need you or your preacher to absolve me of anything." She stepped toward him until they stood toe-to-toe. Her mouth pressed into a thin line. "And furthermore." She pounded her finger against his chest. "If you can't treat me and the people I love with respect, then just stay away. You hear me? You don't have to approve of my lifestyle, but you *do* have to act civilly in my presence."

Jeremy's lip curled, and he snarled, "I told him you weren't worth the effort." He pushed Kameitha back and jerked open his car door. "Soon you'll wish you'd taken this offer."

He slammed the door shut, then revved the engine and sped away.

Lilith slid her arm around Kameitha's waist and pulled her close. His car disappeared around the corner. The vacant look in her eyes tore at Lilith's heart. "I'm so sorry."

"I wonder if I'll ever see him again," Kameitha said.

Lilith brushed a tear from Kameitha's cheek and guided her into the house. Lilith sat on the sofa next to her, wondering how to respond when she had the same question about Gemini.

"I wish I knew what to tell you, my love." Lilith stroked her hair.

Kameitha stifled a sob.

"There's something I want you to understand." Lilith gently lifted Kameitha's chin so their eyes met. "As wonderful as you are to stand up for me, and for us, his words hurt me *only* because they hurt you."

Kameitha's black eyes flashed. "No, Lilith. He wasn't raised like that. I don't know how he and I came to this point, but some behavior is simply not okay."

"I understand," Lilith said. "But please, don't ever feel like you have to defend me."

Kameitha began to shake in her arms. "It's just not fair! When death spares you, it's supposed to be a reason to celebrate."

"I know." Catching sight of Seth and Ralen at the front door, Lilith motioned for them to enter. "We all expected our families to be our biggest supporters. That just didn't happen, but I'm here for you."

Seth knelt in front of Kameitha. "We're *all* here for you. Don't ever doubt it." He looked up at Lilith and mouthed "Jeremy?"

She nodded.

"I know it doesn't look like it now, but things will get better," he said. "It's just going to take time for him—and everyone else—to see the bigger picture. Don't give up on him."

Kameitha shook her head. "When Jeremy gets something in his head, that's that."

"But he hasn't always been this way, so that means he can change again," Seth reasoned.

Ralen sat beside Lilith, draping an arm around the two women as he reached for Seth's hand. "Remember, Kami, it's like we said from the get-go—we're all in this together. We've got your back."

Warmth lit Kameitha's face, and the corners of her mouth turned up. "I know. That's the only thing that keeps me going."

Lilith looked from one partner to the next, relishing Ralen's strong hand caressing her back and the sweet smell of Kameitha's hair brushing her face. Her eyes met Seth's, and the love they'd shared for so many years seemed to intensify.

Seth smiled at Lilith and reached for her hand as he stood. "The four of us are meant to be together," he said.

Ralen gently pulled Kameitha into his arms, holding her close as they walked down the hall. Seth and Lilith followed them to the bedroom. Seth lowered Lilith onto the king-sized bed beneath him. Beside her, Ralen and Kameitha embraced.

Then Seth drew all Lilith's attention as he lowered his body onto hers. He kissed her long and deep. It took Lilith's breath away. He drew back and pulled her blouse over her head. She pressed her fingers into his back, closing the distance. As they moved together, he met her eyes with an expression filled with longing.

Starting at her fingertips, Seth traced a line of kisses along the inside of her arms, his lips gentle against her tender skin. She closed her eyes in ecstasy as gentle flicks of his tongue made circles along the curve of her waist. Then the crease of her thigh. The sensation was as intense as a tickle, but suggestive of more tantalizing things to come.

But it was Ralen who delivered. He didn't give Lilith time to miss Seth's attentions, which were now lavished on Kameitha. Ralen propped on his elbows so his body hovered inches above Lilith's. The proximity heightened her desire—tantalizing close, but not touching. Ralen lowered his lips to hers for a soft, lingering kiss. She arched her hips to meet his, but again he pulled beyond her reach, teasing her.

He rolled onto his side as Seth did the same, leaving Lilith and Kameitha nestled between them. Lilith tugged Kameitha's blouse over her head. They drew close, their bodies touching from head to toe as they kissed. Lilith slid her hand down Kameitha's smooth, flat stomach, as Kameitha stroked her.

As their frenzy grew, Seth and Ralen worked together to free them both of their remaining clothes while shedding their own.

Seth lay back down behind Kameitha and reached to caress Lilith. She gasped with pleasure as Ralen thrust deep within her. He rested one hand on Seth's hips as Seth joined with Kameitha. The four moved together as one in a tangle of limbs and kisses and sighs.

Lilith's body vibrated with pleasure as they teased her senses, drawing her toward climax. When Kameitha cried out, the sound of her lover's pleasure brought Lilith to peak, too. Ralen and Seth closely followed. With their passion spent, they relaxed into each others' arms.

As Kameitha drifted off to sleep minutes later, Lilith met Seth's eyes. "Thank you," she whispered, then yawned and nuzzled deeper into Ralen's embrace. She was truly loved. No matter what the world threw at them, they had each other.

Chapter 38

SALT LAKE CITY, UTAH—Jeremy Banks withered as the men's judging eyes raked over him and their unspoken taunts echoed in his ears.

"You're no true believer," Rev. Danny Day said.

"You're too weak," the weasel-faced man said.

The two men smirked and walked away together, carrying the explosive devices the weasel had brought. Leaving him behind.

Jeremy would show them, even if it meant his mother must die. It was her fault, after all. He'd warned her, repeatedly, yet she'd turned her back on God's plan. The words of Ecclesiastes 3 echoed in his mind:

To everything there is a season, and a time to every purpose under the heaven:

A time to be born, and a time to die; a time to plant, and a time to pluck up that which is planted;

A time to kill, and a time to heal; a time to break down, and a time to build up...

Chapter 39

PARK CITY, UTAH—At first, Lilith wasn't sure what had caused her to wake. Then the noise came again. She propped herself up on her elbows to see the clock on the nightstand. Who would be calling at 3 a.m.? She reached over Ralen, who groaned once, then continued to snore. She snapped awake at the sight of a blank caller ID; she hadn't seen that in decades. She dampened the vid screen and picked up the phone.

Lilith punched the "on" button as she scooted toward the foot of the bed. "Hello?" she whispered.

Silence.

The quiet conveyed a sinister feel that raised a cold chill along her spine. Lilith grabbed a blanket draped over a chair by the door and wrapped it around her as she walked down the hall toward the kitchen. "Who is this?" she demanded,

Heavy breathing replied.

"This isn't funny." Lilith started to hang up when a deep, muffled voice said, "Stop the treatments or you all will die. You've been warned."

The phone went dead before Lilith could reply. She flushed with anger but couldn't shake the feeling of foreboding. This wasn't a prank. Whoever had been on the other end of the phone meant them harm.

She pushed the code to redial the last caller. Instead of a phone number, the numeral one repeated across the screen. "What the?" she muttered. Maybe Seth could figure out how to track the call. Otherwise, they'd have to get help from the authorities. Whatever it took, she was going to get to the bottom of this.

She had begun to calm down when Kameitha joined her at the breakfast bar a few minutes later. "Did I hear the phone?" Kameitha asked groggily.

Lilith nodded.

"Is everyone all right?" Kameitha said anxiously.

"Yes, it wasn't any of the kids or our friends," Lilith said. "Nothing like that."

"Oh, good." Kameitha sighed. "Then what... someone partying and got the wrong number?"

"I wish that's all it was." Lilith rose and poured cordial glasses of Amaretto for herself and Kameitha. Lilith took a sip of the sweet liqueur. "It was a threat."

"From whom?" Eyes wide, Kameitha downed the Amaretto in two gulps. "Jeremy?"

"No, I'm almost certain it was someone else." Lilith took another sip. "It felt... more sinister." She told her what the caller said.

Kameitha pulled her robe closer, hugging herself. "Why can't people just leave us alone?"

Lilith huffed. "Since when has that happened?" She took their empty glasses to the sink. "But this was more than just being judgmental. And its timing—on the eve of the clinics' opening—concerns me."

"Sounds a lot more personal to me," Kameitha said in a worried voice. "Maybe we should wake the guys?"

Lilith shrugged and looked at the wall clock. "There's not much anyone can do right now. I'll text Kate, then call around 5 a.m. I don't think any of the workers will arrive at the clinics before then."

"Do you think an additional security sweep will be sufficient?" Kameitha asked.

"It would be a good start." Lilith sent Kate's text. "C'mon, there's nothing more we can do for now. Let's try to get back to sleep. It's going to be big day."

Kameitha tousled Lilith's hair. "You go ahead. I'm too wired."

Lilith pulled her close and kissed her cheek. "Are you sure? We could cuddle."

Kameitha gave her a half-hearted smile and looked away. "It's tempting, but I think I'll read a while."

Rather than rejoin the men, Lilith went to her room. She wanted to play her favorite sleep track, a hologram of the seashore that surrounded the bed, accompanied by the sound of waves. If anything could lull her to sleep, that would be it.

She pulled the pillows around her and nestled in, listening to the roar of the surf and thinking back to earlier that evening. It wasn't the first time they'd all shared a bed, but it was by far the most intense. She replayed the sensation of Seth's kisses, Ralen's sensuous touch, and Kameitha's tender loving.

To have encountered them separately as lovers would've been amazing, but all at once overwhelmed her senses. Synergy—that was the word—so much more than a sum of the parts. It was altogether new, and it filled her heart with bliss. They were no longer couples but a unit. Lovers. Family.

————

THE NEXT THING SHE KNEW, Lilith awoke to the alarm she had set to call Kate before the clinics opened. She dressed and headed to the living room, expecting to see Kameitha curled up on the couch. Not finding her there, Lilith grinned, thinking how she'd tease Kameitha later about being such a loner. Maybe she'd been able to get some rest after all.

Lilith started the coffee while her phone voiced her messages from the night before. A reply text from Kate showed she had already ordered additional security measures, including complete sweeps for bombs before the clinics opened.

She called Kate. "I see you're taking the threat seriously, too." The vid screen showed Kate still in her PJs but looking alert.

"Of course. There's too much at stake to get careless."

"We're going ahead with the openings?"

"Unless we discover a reason not to," Kate said. "I notified the police, of course. They'll want to speak with you, I'm sure."

"Thanks," Lilith said. "Although I can't tell them much. Perhaps they can track down the caller's number. I couldn't get anything."

"That's odd," Kate said. "I wonder how they circumvented that."

"They must have technical expertise."

Kate paused. "Like Jeremy?"

"Jeremy? He dropped out of college after only one semester."

"Didn't you know? He was quite the savant," Kate said. "Kameitha said he was born knowing how take apart and fix anything to do with computers or electronics."

"Well, that's not good news," Lilith said. "But I still think it was someone else. It just didn't *feel* like Jeremy, if you know what I mean."

Hearing footsteps behind her, Lilith turned to see Seth and Ralen walking down the hall together. They wore matching blue-striped pajama bottoms, but no tops. Lilith admiringly appraised their firm abdomens and chests. In the months since the treatment, they had grown even more fit and youthful looking. Lilith hoped they thought the same of her.

"The guys are up," she told Kate. "We'll talk more later."

"Be safe," Kate cautioned, then hung up.

"You're up early," Ralen said, taking a seat at the breakfast bar.

Lilith shook her head. "It's a good thing the house wasn't on fire. You two sleep like rocks."

"What?" Seth asked, filling cups of coffee for them both.

"We had a call at three," Lilith said. "A threatening call."

Seth put his cup on the counter and gave her a puzzled look. "A threat? I don't like the sound of that."

She brought them up to speed, including the measures Kate had taken.

"I'll take a look, but if the number didn't show up when you pressed the tracker button, I don't know what else to do," Seth said.

"From what I hear, the phone company can check callers, but they will only notify the authorities of anything suspicious," Ralen said. "I'll give them a call."

By the time Seth and Lilith finished making breakfast, it was time for the workers to start arriving at the clinics. While Seth set the table and Ralen went to wake Kameitha, Lilith turned on her computer's GPS street view outside the Eden clinic. A dusting of snow covered the almost-empty parking lot. The sidewalk remained clear except for an occasional passer-by heading to the adjacent tea shop, and a security guard on his regular rounds.

"So far, so good," she said. "No protesters."

Ralen returned. Frowning, he exchanged a worried look with

Seth before asking Lilith, "Do you have any idea where Kameitha is?"

For the second time that morning, tingles shot up Lilith's spine. "She's not in her room?"

Ralen shook his head. "I checked the garage. Her car's gone."

"But where would she go?" Lilith grabbed her phone and punched in Kameitha's number. After six rings, it went to voice mail. "Kameitha—call me!" She hung up, texted her, then watched for a minute or two. "She's not responding."

"It's not like her to just disappear like this," Ralen said.

"If she thought Jeremy made the threat, she might try to keep him from doing something stupid." Seth sighed.

"That would be like her—to think of someone other than herself," Ralen said.

"I don't trust Jeremy," Lilith said. "She shouldn't be around him, especially not alone. If he was the caller, he's even more dangerous than I thought."

"Do you know where Jeremy lives?" Ralen asked.

Lilith shook her head. "Last I heard, he'd been kicked out of his apartment and was sleeping on a friend's couch."

Ralen frowned. "Same here. I just hoped you'd had a different experience."

Seth looked up from his computer. "I'm not finding anything on a directory search for him except Kameitha's old address."

She left another message on Kameitha's phone. "I hope you're not trying to contact Jeremy. That would not be good. Call me!" Lilith hung up and turned toward Seth. "I just don't get it. I was so proud of how she stood up to him."

"But that was before last night's threat," Seth said. "Now it's personal—directed at us. At you."

Lilith lowered her head as the weight of Seth's words settled. He was right. It wasn't just about politics or religion anymore. Last night's threat was personal. It didn't rule out attacks on the clinics, but it was aimed at their household. Or was it? Had any of the other Pioneers received threats?

She glanced at the clock. Only 6:30 a.m. Lilith decided to check with Hector and Monique anyway. If they'd gotten a threat, they'd be up. If they hadn't, they should know about it before the clinics opened at seven.

As Lilith waited for Hector and Monique to answer her call, she wondered how many of the Pioneers were already on their way to the clinics they'd chosen to mentor. Each of them would act as a consultant to nine clinics, giving the staff and patients the benefit of their experience.

Hector's group had foreseen ways to implement the concept during their controlled remote viewing sessions. Then they learned the franchise already had a training program in place that could easily be adapted.

"Good morning!" Monique answered cheerily. "You must be excited to call so early."

"Ah, good," Lilith said. "You were already up?"

"Of course." The vid screen captured the smiling faces of Xavier, Lorenz and Nan gathered around a table, drinking coffee and tea. "We have planes to catch and places to be."

"Sounds good," Lilith said. "We'll give Hector another minute to join us."

Monique sipped from a cup and nodded. The screen shrunk to make room for Hector's image. His hair was tousled, and he wore red plaid flannel pajamas. "Yeah," he grunted. "Oh, it's you. And Monique, too?"

Lilith grinned and pressed the button to make their images project as holograms. "Yeah, double trouble. Sorry about that, Hector, but I need to tell both of you about a threat we received last night."

His expression changed from one of irritation to concern. Monique grimaced.

"What happened?" Hector asked.

She told them, then said, "I take it that neither of you received a call?"

Monique shook her head, and Hector said, "No."

Then she told them of Kameitha's disappearance. "I don't suppose she contacted you?"

They both shook their heads. "I'm so sorry," Monique said. "Could there be another explanation for why she's gone? Maybe it's not a bad thing. She has clinics to visit, too, right?"

"If it was something like that, she wouldn't have left without telling one of us," Lilith said. "And she would've answered my calls."

"You're right, of course."

"We'll see if we can find any leads," Hector said. "In the

meantime, I'll work with Kate to ensure no one takes any chances at the clinics."

As Lilith ended the call, Ralen and Seth sat on either side of her on the couch. "We'll find her," Seth said, taking her hand.

"And she'll be fine," Ralen reassured her, putting his arm around her shoulders. "But it looks like the threat was specific to us. We need to be sure we're taking every precaution around here. That will be my task today."

"Our task," Seth corrected him. He followed Ralen to a bedroom they'd converted into an office.

Lilith watched them go, at a loss for what she could do. Drawn to Kameitha's bedroom, she sat on the edge of the bed and smoothed the blue duvet. Silence surrounded her. Just knowing Kameitha was gone made the room seem darker. Lonelier.

She checked the closet. Kameitha's carry-on bag was missing from the top shelf. Lilith leaned against the doorframe and softly said, "Don't do anything crazy."

Chapter 40

PARK CITY, UTAH—Lilith fumed. The police had come and gone by mid-morning, assuring them that identifying the caller wouldn't be a problem. While that was encouraging, they'd refused to classify Kameitha as "missing" or track down her car for at least twenty-four hours. How could Lilith prove something was amiss when there was no sign of a struggle?

She checked her phone again, as if wanting it to ring would make it happen. It certainly wasn't working so far. She'd left so many messages that no room was left in Kameitha's voice mailbox. Why didn't she call?

Lilith paced across the living room, her mind racing. How could she find Jeremy? Or would Kameitha have gone somewhere else? What could she hope to accomplish alone... without her? It hurt that she had left without a word. They should be facing this threat together.

Ralen walked over and put his hand on Lilith's arm. "Let's go to her house and talk with the neighbors."

Lilith saw the concern in his gray eyes. "You think she might've gone back there?" Lilith was doubtful, but the suggestion offered a glimmer of hope.

"I don't know. But I seem to recall Jeremy hung out with one of the neighborhood women. It's the only thing I can think of... it's not like Jeremy's held jobs for long enough to matter. And he wasn't exactly a scholar."

Lilith nodded. "Let's go."

"I'll stay here, in case she comes back," Seth said. "Keep me posted."

After they visited the neighbors on either side of the home where Kameitha had lived, Lilith sat in Ralen's car feeling as dejected as he looked.

"I really thought Anna would know where Jeremy might go," Ralen said, putting the car in gear. "I guess it's been too long, or maybe she just didn't want to say."

"What are we going to do now?" Lilith said. Her stomach felt like an empty pit.

Ralen backed out of the driveway onto the street. "I'm out of ideas. We'll just have to wait and see if she calls us."

Lilith bit her lip and nodded. "I guess you're right." Kameitha would be okay. She had to be.

Seth looked up eagerly when they returned home, but his smile quickly dissolved after seeing their faces. "Nothing?"

Ralen shook his head. "No one seemed to have a clue."

Lilith sat on the couch and flipped open her laptop. For the fourth time that day, she checked to see if any protesters had shown up at the Eden clinic. All was quiet. She closed it and stood.

"I can't just sit here," she said. "I'm going to the clinic."

Seth walked to the door with her. He helped with her coat, then let his hands linger at her waist. "You." He put his finger on the tip of her nose. "Don't do anything crazy."

She brushed his hand away. "You." She poked his chest. "Don't be annoying." She grinned at him and opened the door. She knew there wasn't much for her to do at the clinic, but something was better than nothing. And right now, she couldn't handle the idea of staying at the house waiting for Kameitha to show up.

Her thoughts were on a continuous loop during the hourlong drive. Was Jeremy really the kind of person who would hurt them or his mother? While it was true his girlfriends didn't stay around long, she'd never noticed any suspicious bruises. She'd always figured it was his holier-than-thou attitude that drove them off, but could she be wrong?

As she neared the Renu Research Center, the protesters caught Lilith's attention. She'd gotten so used to seeing them, she hardly noticed them anymore. She slowed the car and quickly scanned the crowd but didn't see Jeremy.

She drove on, reaching the new clinic in Eden about thirty minutes later. Although another facility in the area had seemed excessive, they had initially agreed to it for sentimental reasons. This was where they'd made the connection to the "X" in the remote viewing sessions.

Now, though, it allowed them to convert the Research Center to test the new serum, with trials beginning there next week. All patients for the original longevity treatment would go to the new clinics.

As she pulled into the Eden clinic's parking lot, Lilith noted the subtle changes—new signage and the Renu tree of life painted on the front window. A receptionist greeted her as she entered, "Ms. Davidson, I wasn't expecting you this early."

"I couldn't sleep so I decided to come on in," she said. Chairs sat empty along the sides of the room, which formed a U-shape with a fountain in the middle beneath the large bay window facing the street. Lilith took a seat, marveling at how the trickling water was the only sound until footsteps approached.

"This is a nice surprise." The director wore aqua scrubs bearing the Renu logo. She brushed back black, wavy, shoulder-length hair, and held out her hand.

"I just wanted to make sure everything is going smoothly." Lilith shook her hand. She recognized the director from last month's training session. Like the other Pioneers, she had spent a day with each of the directors assigned to the nine clinics she would mentor.

The director nodded. "Couldn't be better." She tapped her knuckles on the receptionist's desk. "Knock on wood."

"Did everyone show up?"

"Yes," she said. "We have a full house, and they've already begun treatment."

"I've checked the GPS a few times." Lilith motioned to her phone. "I haven't seen any troublemakers."

"No, it's been quiet," the director agreed.

The receptionist looked up. "Well, we did have that one little incident."

"What do you mean?" Lilith asked.

"The power went out." The director waved her hand

dismissively. "It was just for a few minutes. Nothing to worry about." She frowned at the receptionist, who avoided her gaze.

A prickle of alarm raised the tiny hairs at the nape of Lilith's neck. "Did the backup generator come on?"

"I was just going to check on it when the power came back on," the director said. "I figured the power wasn't off long enough to trigger it."

Lilith nodded, but wondered if that was the case. She'd have to ask Seth.

"And the patients liked their suites?" The rooms had been the topic of a lot of discussion. Peter wanted just basic amenities. Lilith and the other Pioneers had taken a firm stance, insisting that a few luxuries—like gourmet food and top-quality linens—helped offset the trauma of the change in some small, but important, way.

"Yes, the suites are great," the director said. "Quit worrying. Everything is fine."

While Lilith said her goodbyes, her thoughts turned to the days she'd spent at Renu. At the time, she had no idea if she and Seth would live through the ordeal. So much had happened since then— her whole life had changed. And now people at a hundred clinics across the nation were starting their journey to renewed health and vigor. The magnitude of it overwhelmed her—they'd *actually* done it. She hoped these people found as much joy in their new lives as she had. Until now.

She got in her car and stared at her phone. Still no message from Kameitha. On impulse, Lilith stopped at the Research Center. Kate met her at the front desk.

"You look awful," Kate told Lilith as they walked to her office. "Have you had another call?"

"No," she said, her throat closing and tears welling as she formed the words, "Kameitha's missing."

Kate sat silently, as if it took a moment to process what she'd said. "What do you mean, 'missing'?"

"I mean she left." Tears streamed down Lilith's face. "When I woke this morning, she had taken an overnight bag and gone, without even leaving a note. And she won't answer my calls."

"I'm so sorry." Kate tapped a pen on the glass desktop. "Was everything okay between you? Maybe all the changes just got to her. A lot has happened."

Lilith shook her head. "Even after Jeremy showed up in our

driveway the other day, she seemed totally committed to me—to us. But the call shook her... as it did all of us."

"Kameitha has what I would call a strong warrior personality," Kate said. "She seems meek until you threaten her key values. Then she becomes fierce."

"I've seen that, even when she was dealing with Jeremy," Lilith said. "But I don't see what it has to do with her disappearance."

"I could be way off base, but what if she wants to do something to protect Jeremy that she doesn't think you'd agree with?" Kate said. "She may have thought it was easier to disappear than to confront you."

Lilith considered Kate's words as she drove back to Park City. Her first question about their relationship had really hit home. Could Kameitha have realized she wasn't in love with her after all? That would explain her disappearance. But Kate was also right about Kameitha's fierce protectiveness. Maybe she'd learned Jeremy wanted to reconcile? Lilith huffed. When pigs fly.

She tried to focus on next steps. When Lilith arrived home, she was glad to find Seth and Ralen already had a plan underway.

Chapter 41

PARK CITY, UTAH—About half the Pioneers filled the living room, gathered in two small groups. Stacks of blank paper and pens on the table in front of them clued Lilith to their task. They busily filled in pages with data written in outline form across and down the page, interspersed with sketches.

Seth pulled her aside and told her quietly, "After you left, we suddenly realized we were overlooking the obvious—remote viewing could give us some of the answers about Kameitha and the caller," he said. "We rounded up those who hadn't left on their mentoring visits."

Lilith laughed softly and shook her head. "You'd think, after all these years, that would be the first thing to come to mind when something crazy like this happens."

"I know," he agreed. "Emotion can sure high-jack our reasoning power, can't it? Each table has a different task—blind to them, of course, to avoid mere speculation about the issue."

"Good." Lilith kept her voice low. "Do they know Kameitha's missing?"

"No, we can keep that part blind. I think they assume it's about the threatening caller. We couldn't avoid a little front-loading."

"I'll be interested to see what they come up with," she said.

One by one, the viewers scribbled the time, then "Break" or

"End of Session," at the bottom of their paper. Some went to the kitchen, others to the bathroom, and one went outside.

Ralen and Nan motioned for Lilith and Seth to come over. They sat in the viewers' empty chairs. Ralen pointed at Nan's transcript. "I thought you'd be interested in this. Her task was to explore the sensory impact for the target an hour before the event, and two hours afterward." Sensory impact, or SI, was the term for how someone at the event would perceive things, versus how the viewer or another outsider would.

The first list of impressions included such things as: "I'm confused." "I'm outraged and disappointed." "I feel torn between those I love."

Hours after the event, SI descriptors shifted to: "This can't be happening." "How can I protect them?" "I must do whatever it takes."

"I was alarmed by the strength of the feelings I perceived," said Nan, "so I went even further out, to five hours after the event. Then I got impressions like: 'They'll never understand.' 'I don't know if I'm strong enough to do what I must.' 'I'll never forgive him for making me choose.'"

Lilith tried to make sense out of the cryptic messages, which tracked Kameitha's feelings prior to and after the threatening call. She knew Nan was their most gifted viewer for that type of work, so she didn't question its accuracy. Just its meaning.

But Nan wasn't finished. "The signal line just snapped off after that. It was the strangest thing ever, like the target realized she was being monitored and blocked it."

Lilith nodded, catching that Nan knew the target was female. Although she couldn't tell her without affecting Nan's future sessions on the topic, Lilith knew Kameitha was skilled at blocking attempts at what some called remote influencing.

"Did you get any sense of danger or coercion?" Seth asked.

Nan shook her head. "Plenty of tension, to be sure, and lots of anger and drama. But not physical danger."

"Of course, that can always change," Ralen said. He caught Lilith's frown. "Yeah, I know. I can find a dark cloud for any silver lining."

Seth smirked. "You said it." He turned back to Nan. "Before you viewed the SI, did you get a feel for the target's location?"

"Nothing definitive, although I kept thinking of cherry pie for some reason," she said. "Maybe I'm just hungry."

Lilith grinned. "Who can account for the subconscious? And cherry pie sounds pretty good. Go take your break, and thanks."

"Sure," Nan said. "I hope we'll get feedback that shows the target overcame her predicament."

"Me, too," Lilith said, "though that feedback may have to wait a while. I'm afraid things are still unresolved."

"I understand." Nan stood and headed toward the kitchen for a break.

One by one, the viewers returned to the tables and continued their sessions. Now they were told to get information about the threatening call. By dinnertime, they had all turned in their results and left.

"Look at these descriptors of the caller." Lilith shuffled through the papers and handed them one by one to Seth and Ralen after she read from each. "Powerful, influential, angry, political, corrupt, egomaniac, zealot… and this one." Lilith shivered. "Sociopath."

"Just the kind of person who would carry out that threat," Seth said.

"But this physical description doesn't match with Jeremy or the Reverend, except that he's male," Ralen said. "Short, fair-haired, mid-forties, blue-eyed, blond."

"That doesn't mean one of them didn't put him up to it," Seth said.

"That's true," Ralen said.

"This isn't making me feel any better," Lilith said, wrapping her arms in front of her, hands to elbows. "It confirms my fears that we're up against someone who's serious about stopping Renu. And who hates us."

"Well, we've done our best to get as many clinics open as quickly as possible," Seth said. "Maybe that will be good enough."

"And we know Kameitha's not in any immediate danger," Ralen said.

"That's all good, but I still want to know where she is," Lilith said. "I really need to talk with her."

Chapter 42

RENU RESEARCH CENTER, OGDEN RIVER SCENIC BYWAY—Two days later, the limo pulled in front of their home to take them to the Research Center. The other Pioneers had returned from their clinic visits to be at the Research Center for the weekly check-up. Lilith had remained in Park City with Ralen and Seth, doing their mentoring by vid phone while awaiting word from the police. At least she had finally convinced the police to declare Kameitha a missing person.

Nothing at Renu had changed, but, for Lilith, everything was different without Kameitha. She couldn't even ignore the protesters like she normally did. Now Lilith examined each of their faces to see if they were hiding something. Did they know where Kameitha was? She studied their slogans and taunts, searching for double meanings.

Lilith pointed to one of the protesters brandishing a "Save your life, Lose your soul" placard. "If they think you save your soul by dying rather than taking the treatment, do you think they'd consider killing Kameitha to save her soul?"

Seth and Ralen exchanged a glance. "Lil, we don't have any reason to think they have Kameitha."

Lilith pressed her lips together and looked away. She knew she was over-reacting. Yet, as the hours dragged by, Lilith became more convinced that Kameitha would've contacted her if something hadn't happened. Despite what they'd learned from the remote viewing sessions, she was sure someone must be preventing Kameitha from coming back or calling.

As they entered the building, Kate asked, "Have you heard anything?"

Lilith shook her head. "How about you?" Kate had assigned Renu's security service to investigate the caller and Kameitha's disappearance.

"Nothing new on the caller," Kate said. "I'm sure she'll be in touch soon." Her eyes crinkled with kindness.

"I hope so," Lilith said, but after another sleepless night, she was less than optimistic. She went through the motions—a habit after months of routine exams. The tech took her vitals and drew blood, then Lilith walked through the scanner. By the time the doctor came in to give her a physical exam, results showed on a holographic monitor.

"Your blood pressure is a bit elevated today, but nothing alarming," the doctor told her after the exam. "You're good for another week."

She joined the others in the limo. The trip to the construction site had become a part of the Pioneers' routine. After their checkup last week, they'd crept along as part of a procession of concrete trucks. Today they joined flatbed trucks loaded with boards, floor joists, wall studs, and roof trusses.

As they drove up the long, curving driveway, Lilith thought back to the day Kameitha fell and they'd rushed her to the urgent care clinic. They'd had so much hope that day. But shortly afterward, Jeremy's story broke, and now Kameitha was gone. She couldn't get her head around everything that happened, or the helplessness she felt.

When the limo stopped at the top of the ridge, Everett waited for them.

"What's going on this week?" Seth asked the foreman as they toured the site.

"Looks like the weather's going to continue to be unusually mild," Everett said. "We should be able to finish the framing soon."

Two of the wings were roofed, and workers had started on the third. Despite her malaise, Lilith marveled at the size of their new home. It spanned the top of the ridge, with breathtaking views of the surrounding mountains.

They stood in the octagonal hub where the wings joined. Kitchen plumbing had been roughed-in at the center of the hub, leaving room on the perimeter for the living areas.

"We've begun the finishing touches in the first wing." Everett pointed to the lower level, which already had windows in place. "It has the large theater, which seats twenty. The smaller one is in the wing we're building now. Once we get it roofed, things will go even quicker."

By the time the limo dropped off the others on their way home, half the day was gone. Lilith fidgeted, anxious to see if Kameitha was at home. As they pulled into their driveway, Lilith's hope rose at the sight of a car in front of the house. When she recognized it, a new set of emotions arose—anticipation mixed with caution and longing.

As they pulled up, Gemini stepped out of her car.

"This is a pleasant surprise," Lilith said. "Have you been waiting long?"

"I just got here." She gave Lilith a hug. "Seth told me about Kameitha, and I figured you might need moral support."

They walked into the house arm in arm. "I'm glad you're here." Lilith pulled her tight. "I've missed you so much, Gemini. I simply didn't know what to do or say to make things better."

Gemini sighed. "I'm sorry, Mom. I've spent the last couple of months telling myself I was right to put distance between us. But I never felt good about it. At the end of the day, you're still my mother, no matter what. You wouldn't abandon me, and I won't do that to you, either."

"I appreciate that, more than you know," Lilith said.

"Seth tried to reason with me a couple of times but hearing what you're going through with Kameitha made me realize how selfish I've been," Gemini said. "You taught me better than that."

They sat together on the couch, and Gemini turned so she faced Lilith. Hot tears streaked down Lilith's cheeks as she let herself collapse into her daughter's arms. "Thank you," she whispered.

As Lilith dried her eyes and regained her composure, Seth walked over with two steaming cups. "Thought you could use some tea." He placed the cups on the sofa table and paused a moment to massage Lilith's neck.

She beamed up at him gratefully as she took a sip. After all these years, he still surprised her by knowing what she needed before she did. He'd even tried to get Gemini to contact her. Her heart warmed with the knowledge that she could always depend on him to be there for her.

Seth smiled back at her, then gave Gemini's shoulder a gentle squeeze in passing. "Good to see you, kid. It's been too long."

"Hey, Seth." Gemini smiled at him. "What can I do to help?"

"Just being here is plenty." He walked over and stood by Ralen, who had just entered the living room from the kitchen.

She nodded. "I wish I could do more."

"We all feel that way," Ralen added.

"You haven't heard anything at all from her?" Gemini asked.

"No," Seth said.

"Or from the caller?" Gemini said.

"We just got the one threat," Ralen said.

"But that was enough," Lilith added.

A knock at the front door drew their attention.

"That must be the detective," Seth said, as Ralen went to answer it.

"Detective?" Lilith asked.

"He called earlier and said he wanted to come by," Seth said.

Lilith sat straighter, her heart pounding. Had he found Kameitha? Was she okay?

Gemini reached over and took her hand as a stocky man who appeared to be in his sixties entered with Ralen.

"This is Detective Stan Roberts," Ralen said. He motioned the plainclothes officer toward a chair opposite the couch where Lilith and Gemini sat.

After introductions, Detective Roberts opened his tablet. "I know you've been anxious to hear something, and I wish I had more to tell you. But we did track down the source of the threatening call you received."

Lilith hadn't realized how hopeful she'd been until he said that. He wasn't here to tell her they'd found Kameitha. It was about the caller.

"The call was made from a disposable phone, so the telecom company couldn't identify the caller," the detective said. "I'm sorry we don't have anything more definitive."

"What about Kameitha's car—have you located it?" Lilith asked.

"Sorry, m'am," he said. "Nothing there, either. But we have

been monitoring Rev. Day's headquarters. Because of the protesters at the Renu Research Center, the judge approved our request to initiate surveillance. Our system has facial recognition software that will alert us if she or her son enters the building. And our traffic cams will signal if Ms. Banks' car is spotted."

"Is the traffic monitored only within the city?" Ralen asked.

"We get data from surrounding cities, as well," the detective said. "Although we've been working toward an integrated national system for decades, it's not there yet. Still, if she's driving her car anywhere in the area, we'll know about it."

"What about her son, Jeremy—have you located him?" Gemini asked.

"Not yet, but we have a few leads." The detective picked up his hat and rose to leave. "Be sure to let me know if you get any further threats, or if you hear from your friend."

"Thanks for coming by," Seth said.

Ralen escorted him to the door, then returned to the living room.

"Well, at least they're doing something," Seth said.

"I'm trying to imagine how they're getting around if they're not using Kameitha's car," Lilith said.

"I could've told you her car wasn't at Rev. Day's center," Gemini said.

Alarmed, Lilith said, "How would you know that?"

"I've checked several times in the past few days since Seth called and told me what happened," she said.

"That's too dangerous," Lilith said. "Don't go near that place!"

"They don't know me," Gemini said calmly. "The only ones who could connect me with you would be Jeremy or Kameitha, and they never showed up while I was parked across the street watching."

"Still, they're not rational people," Lilith said. "You don't need to be around them. Leave it to the police."

"Like you do," Gemini scoffed good-naturedly. "I know you've been driving by there, Mom. I saw you twice just in the short time I was there."

Lilith cut her eyes toward Seth and Ralen, expecting a reaction. She didn't have long to wait.

"You've been doing *what?*" Seth's voice was sharp and loud. He slammed his palm against the couch. "Lilith, are you crazy?"

"What were you going to do if you saw her?" Ralen asked.

"You heard the description of who we're dealing with here, Lilith. A *sociopath*! You need to use common sense," Seth scolded her.

"I didn't stop," Lilith said defensively.

"But you would've," Seth said. "You know you would've... *I know* you would've."

"Well, okay, I probably would have. But it didn't happen. I didn't see her." Her tone weakened on the last words as the sorrow seeped back into her voice.

"I know, I know," Seth said, backing down. "Just don't make this any worse than it already is. *Please* stay away from there! We can't be worrying about you, too."

Lilith sighed. "Okay. Now that I know the detective is monitoring the place, I can see it's not helping anything. But I can't just sit here doing nothing."

"That's true, Lilith," Seth said. "Sitting here isn't going to help Kameitha, no matter where she is. You have obligations; we all do."

"What? You want me to just go on like nothing's happened?" Lilith heard her voice's shrill tone and cringed inwardly, but she wasn't going to walk away from Kameitha like she'd never been a part of their lives.

"I'm not saying that," Seth said. "It's just that obsessing over her disappearance isn't helping you find her. It's just hurting you, and those who love you."

After an uncomfortable silence, Gemini stood and slipped on her coat. "Why don't you come over later, Mom? We need to catch up, and the grandkids want to see you."

Lilith smiled at the thought that they had missed her. Maybe there was still hope for the family to weather these changes without disintegrating. She hoped so. "I'll do that."

"Let's make it dinner." Gemini turned to Ralen and Seth. "You're welcome to come, too, but only if you don't pressure her any more about Kameitha."

Chapter 43

MIDWAY, UTAH—Lilith's stomach knotted with anxiety as Seth pulled into the last parking spot in front of Gemini's four-car garage. She hadn't spoken with Lacy since her friend Sadie died, and she was dreading it.

Sensing her mood, Seth and Ralen each took a hand as they went up the sidewalk. "Come along," Seth said soothingly.

"Everything will work out," Ralen reassured her.

Their actions were so over the top, they made Lilith laugh. "Thanks, guys. You're the best." She squeezed their hands.

Then Rachel answered the door with a scowl, dampening the mood. It took Lilith only an instant to guess they weren't the cause of her displeasure, noting the phone in the teen's hand and her earbuds.

"Get Gran and Pops a drink," Gemini called out from the back of the house.

"It's Faye's turn," Rachel yelled and stomped out the back door, heading toward the bunk house.

Seth chuckled as they headed toward the kitchen. "Well, some things never change. What can I get you?" he asked Ralen.

Faye wandered over while Seth was shaking their martinis. She placed an olive in each frosted glass.

"Thanks, Faye," Seth said.

"Sure, Pops." She stared at Ralen.

"Sorry. I guess introductions are in order." Seth lowered the shaker and motioned toward Ralen. "This is our friend, Ralen." He gestured toward the teen. "Ralen, this is our eldest great-granddaughter, Faye. That was Rachel who greeted us at the door."

"My pleasure." Ralen dipped his head to Faye.

She grinned at him. "So, you're living with Gran and Pops now?"

Ralen nodded, his dimples showing when he smiled at her. "For the past few months."

Derek wiped his hands on a dishtowel as he rounded the corner, with Lacy following. "I'm Derek—Faye's dad—and this is my sister Lacy." He extended his hand.

"Good to meet you both," Ralen said. "I was just going to tell Faye how excited we are that our new home will be ready soon."

"Yes, how's that going?" Gemini asked as she joined them.

"Quite well," Seth said. "It's been such a mild winter that work is well ahead of schedule."

"And your grandfather has outdone himself on bringing innovative technology to every facet of the project," Ralen told Derek.

"I'm looking forward to seeing it," Derek said, looking quizzically at Seth.

"It's nothing much," Seth said modestly.

"No, just a few *little* things, like bladeless wind turbines and solar roadways," Ralen explained.

"Very cool," Derek said as they took their drinks and moved into the great room.

Gemini motioned toward facing sectionals that made a U-shape in front of the fireplace. "Have a seat. Dinner will be ready in about five minutes." The glass doors to the deck let in the fiery glow of sunset, giving the room a warm, homey feel.

"If the weather holds, we could move in as early as next month," Seth said.

Lilith waited until Lacy sat, then took the seat next to her. "How are you, dear?"

"I'm fine, Gran." She fidgeted with her hair. "So, what do you think about the new house?"

"It will be wonderful, I'm sure." Lilith gathered her courage,

228

deciding not to skirt the issue. "But I want you to know how sorry I am about Sadie."

Lacy nodded. "Me, too. She was a great person."

Lilith reached over and brushed Lacy's hair back from her face. "She was lucky to have a friend like you."

"It didn't matter," Lacy said, her voice tense. "I couldn't help her."

"And I'm sorry I couldn't help her either," Lilith said. "Time worked against us."

"I don't want to hear it, Gran," Lacy said angrily.

"I know it's hard to accept," Lilith said. "It's just not fair that someone so young and full of life would die."

"Her children are the same age as mine, and now they don't have a mother."

"I'm so sorry," Lilith repeated. "I know how much it hurts. I've lost friends, too, so many of them. And it never gets any easier."

"But *she* didn't have to die." Lacy glared at Lilith. "After all, *you* didn't have to die."

Lilith took a deep breath, trying to keep her emotions in check. It had been an ongoing struggle over the past months. Perhaps everyone who lived while others died had to find a way to live with the injustice, but it seemed worse because she—and all the Pioneers—had already lived full lives.

Derek walked over and knelt at his sister's side. "Lacy, give Gran a break," he said gently. "She told Mom as soon as they could take someone for treatment, but it was already too late. You need to take that up with God or fate or whatever."

Lilith took a deep breath, grateful for Derek's words. Even at her age, she still grappled with the fickleness of life and death.

Seth moved closer to Lilith, wrapping an arm around her shoulders. "Now that the clinics are opening, we're going to be able to save a lot more people."

"A friend told me about the Eden clinic the other day," Derek said. "Just like I predicted, it won't be long until there's one on every corner!"

Lacy wiped away a tear, then rose and walked away. Lilith watched her go, sad that she couldn't make things easier. Lacy disappeared into the kitchen as Gemini left it to rejoin their group.

Seth nodded. "As it turns out, I think you were inspired. Have any other predictions popped into your head?" he joked.

"Nothing good, I'm afraid," Derek said with a sigh.

"What do you mean?" Lilith asked.

"It's just with the news coverage you've had, then the threat, and now your friend's disappearance, I'm not feeling too optimistic," Derek said.

Gemini groaned dramatically and sat beside Lilith. "Ignore him. He's just being a pessimist."

Lilith grinned. "Maybe so, but lately it's been hard to look on the bright side."

"Just the fact you're alive and doing well is a lot," Gemini reminded her.

"You're right, of course," Lilith nodded. "I should be more grateful."

Gemini checked the time just as a beeper sounded in the kitchen. She rose and moments later, the smell of baked bread and savory stew filled the room. Sam and Evan appeared as if conjured by the food.

Lacy carried a covered basket of bread to the table. "Get your sister," she told Sam.

"Aw, Mom," he said.

"Do it." She pointed a finger at him, and he left the room.

"And you help your grandmother," Derek told Evan, who sighed, but soon returned with another bread basket.

Rachel brought in chilled bottles of sparkling water and filled the glasses, while Gemini placed two oversized crockpots on a sideboard. "Hand me your bowls and I'll fill them for you," she suggested. "We have vegetable soup and chili."

As they gave their preference for white or red wine, Derek poured their drinks at the bar. When Faye arrived, he put her to work taking the glasses to the table.

They had all just taken their seats when the doorbell rang. "Who could that be?" Lacy said.

"I'll get it." A moment later, Derek returned, his face a shade paler. "Pops, there's an officer of the court here to see you. And Gran and Ralen. He has summons."

Lilith's heart fluttered. When Derek had said an officer of the court, her first thought was something terrible had happened to Kameitha. But it wasn't a police officer. A summons would be about a legal proceeding, though she couldn't imagine what it would be.

A man in a blue suit handed each of them a sealed white envelope and had them sign a receipt. Lilith froze when she saw the ornately embossed letterhead. The U.S. Senate seal.

"What the…?" Ralen said.

"Indeed." Lilith unfolded the first page and checked Seth and Ralen for their responses. "Is yours about a hearing on Renu day after tomorrow?"

They nodded with grim expressions.

Seth looked up after reading the second page. "And there's a gag order compelling witnesses to not discuss the issue prior to the hearing."

Lilith stared at the papers. "We can't even talk about it here?"

"That's what it says." Ralen slapped the papers down on the foyer table. "Well, looks like we may as well continue with dinner."

Lilith's mind reeled as they returned to the table. How could they prepare if they couldn't even talk among themselves? Of course, that must be the intent.

"You're going to have testify in Washington?" Gemini asked shakily.

"It looks that way." Seth reached for a piece of bread.

"I know you can't talk about it, but that can't be good, can it?" Derek said.

"Yeah, I'll bet it's just another way to make sure people like Sadie can't get treated," Lacy snapped. "I wouldn't be surprised if Rev. Day is behind it."

The thought had already crossed Lilith's mind. Kate told her he had political connections, but she'd never expected it to be at this level.

The meal passed mostly in silence. The summons filled Lilith's thoughts, and Ralen and Seth seemed equally preoccupied. How had the server tracked them down at Gemini's house, unless they were being watched? What did that say about Day's influence? The tension in her neck returned with a vengeance, impossible to ignore after the few minutes of relief from being with her family. It had been the first break she'd had had in months—a taste of normalcy. Now this.

As they stood at the door to leave, Gemini hugged Lilith. "I know you have a lot to think about, so why don't you let me book your flights," she suggested.

"We'd appreciate that," Lilith said.

By the time they arrived home, an email with the tickets waited for them. Their flight would leave for D.C. mid-morning, with their appearance before the Special Committee on Aging slated for two-thirty the following afternoon.

Chapter 44

SALT LAKE CITY, UTAH—Jeremy Banks had just finished washing his hands when Rev. Day and the weasel arrived. At first, they'd been so focused on his mom, they hadn't noticed him in the corner of the warehouse's dimly lit utility closet. It would've been fine with him if they hadn't seen him at all. They just confused him.

After services Sunday, Jeremy had watched Rev. Day pay the weasel more cash than he'd ever seen. Why would Rev. Day have given him the money from the collection plates?

Everything had seemed so clear at first. Rev. Day told Jeremy his mother had brought God's vengeance upon herself and they were just His instruments. Now Jeremy wasn't so sure.

After the weasel made the 3 a.m. call to Lilith, Jeremy followed the Reverend's instructions and texted his mom on a burner phone the weasel had given him to use. The text had been simple. "Help me save your friends. Or you all die." Jeremy had met her in a park on the opposite side of town from the abandoned warehouse where he and the weasel were staying. For the past five days, she'd been here, too, tucked away in an oversized utility closet.

Jeremy felt vindicated. He had shown them he wasn't weak. Rev. Day had even praised his work. And unlike the weasel, Jeremy was a true believer.

"Get her ready to go." Rev. Day told him. "If her testimony

reveals the serum's true purpose, we won't have to use the explosives." Then he left with the weasel.

Jeremy removed the duct tape from his mom's ankles, then her wrists. He'd already brought in the carry-on bag from her car, which was parked inside the warehouse.

"Everything depends on you," Jeremy told her. "You heard Rev. Day—you can save your friends if you testify about Renu's true purpose."

"What's going on, Jeremy?" Kameitha rubbed her wrists and looked up at him. "Testify where?"

"At the hearings in Washington," Jeremy said. "You'll see."

A door slammed in the distance and the weasel's footsteps on the concrete floor grew louder as he neared.

"Don't trust them. They will blame you for everything!" His mother pleaded. "You need to tell the police."

Jeremy closed the closet door behind him so she could change. He didn't want to listen, but, for a moment, she sounded like the mother he knew and loved. After the weasel escorted his mom from the building, Jeremy saw the empty shelf. Where were the explosives? His stomach clenched. The more he thought about it, the less any of this made sense.

Desperate for guidance, he repeated aloud the scripture that had become his mantra:

"To everything there is a season, and a time to every purpose under the heaven: A time to be born, and a time to die..."

February 2030

SENATE SUBCOMMITTEE HEARING, DAY ONE, WASHINGTON, D.C.—Lilith stomped her feet and paced in a circle, trying to keep warm as she waited outside the Dirksen Senate Office Building with Seth and Ralen. The day had turned chilly and gray, matching her mood.

"Lil, you're not making the time go any faster," Seth chided when she checked her phone for the eighth time in as many minutes.

"I can't help it," she said. "They should've been here by now. I wanted all the Pioneers to at least go in together, but we can't wait much longer."

"You're right," Ralen said. "This building's huge. It's going to take us ten minutes or more to get to the hearing room. We don't want to cut it too close."

Lilith's phone vibrated. She read the text from Hector: "Stuck in traffic."

"Let's go," Seth said. He had already discovered the bronze doors on First Avenue were locked, so they went around the corner to a less ornate entry on Constitution Avenue. Once through security, Lilith checked a directory posted next to the elevators in a small lobby. They rode the elevators to the fifth floor and exited in a long hallway.

"This is like one of those nightmares with doors going on forever, and you don't know which to pick," Seth said.

"Except this nightmare is real," Ralen added.

Their footsteps, punctuated by the staccato clicks of Lilith's heels on the light gray marble floors, echoed in the silence. "There it is." She pointed to a door with 562 engraved on a brass plate.

A uniformed guard asked, "Your summons, ma'am? Sirs?" After reviewing their papers, he checked their names off a list on his tablet and motioned them toward wooden benches along both sides of the hallway. "You'll be called when it's your time to testify," he said. "Until then, have a seat."

Lilith checked her phone. Two fifteen.

"Ma'am." The guard frowned and motioned toward an orange sign on the wall with bold black lettering. It read: "No cell phones."

"Oh." Lilith switched off her phone and put it in her purse. "I hadn't noticed."

The elevator doors at the end of the hall opened and the other Pioneers emerged. "There," Hector said, pointing. He led them to where Lilith, Seth and Ralen sat. After they'd signed in and turned off their phones, Hector sat next to Lilith.

"Sorry we're late," he said. "We ran into Monique and the others downstairs at security. Some tourist in a Hawaiian shirt forgot he had a pocketknife, so the line was backed up."

Lilith chuckled softly. "That's Washington for you—tourists and politicians."

"And then there's us," Hector said grimly, looking down the hall at all the closed doors. "I'd rather be a dopey tourist."

Lilith silently agreed. Since receiving the summons, she'd spent her time trying to anticipate the questions they'd be asked and formulating answers. Everything depended on who was asking the questions, and why.

Had one of the pharmaceutical giants decided to pull strings to challenge the longevity serum? Or was this connected to Rev. Day and his claims that Renu was anti-family, and therefore anti-American? Even the Special Committee on Aging couldn't veer far from the party line when it came to family values.

She'd developed a list of key talking points, where she'd try to steer the discussion, if possible. Lilith had been tempted to check with the others—at least Seth and Ralen—to be sure their answers were consistent. But that in itself might be enough to create suspicion that they had violated the gag order. She didn't know which would be worse—being too alike or giving contradictory testimony.

A man in a black suit came to the door and gave the guard a list of names. "Yi Ling Tan," he called out, holding open one side of the massive double wooden doors.

Yi rose, giving the others a tentative smile as she entered the room, calling back, "Wish me luck!" Hector joined her, showing his identification papers to the guard, who closed the doors behind them.

Lilith was grateful Hector could act as their attorney during the hearings. At least she wouldn't be alone.

Thirty-minutes later, a paler version of Yi exited. With downcast eyes, she squeezed Karla's hand. "I'll see you back at the hotel," she mumbled.

"Yi, are you okay?" Karla said.

Yi shook her head and walked away.

The guard called the next name, "Karla Santos." Twenty minutes later, the scene repeated with Karla's abrupt departure.

"Lorenz Pedersen," the guard called out.

When Lorenz left for the hotel looking as shaken as the women had, it stoked Lilith's fear to new heights.

Next they called "Boris Shevchenko," then "Xavier Garcia."

As the hours passed, Lilith tried to focus on the book she'd brought, but couldn't. As the day progressed, she noticed a pattern. She silently replayed the list of everyone who had been called: Yi from Singapore, Karla from Brazil, Lorenz from Denmark, Boris from the Ukraine, and Xavier from Barcelona. So far, they'd only called those who weren't U.S. citizens. That meant Monique should be next. Even though she was naturalized, Monique maintained her French passport.

When Xavier came out, he left immediately for the hotel, as the others had. The guard called out, "Monique Dubois."

Why would they want to question the Pioneers from other countries first?

It was nearing six o'clock when the doors to the hearing room opened. After Monique left, the guard ushered the rest of them inside. He led them to an aisle behind a row of small desks with microphones, which faced the raised platform where the committee members sat. The center seat on the rostrum was vacant.

While they stood waiting for the committee chair to return, Lilith surveyed the walnut-paneled room. The remaining eighteen committee members were there, and more than a half-dozen people filled the boxed seating area labeled "Press." That surprised her. She thought the hearings were private since they hadn't been allowed in the room while the other Pioneers testified.

She also hadn't expected the spectators who filled about half the theater-style seats. At least fifty people watched them with mixed emotions playing on their faces—some looked sympathetic, while others seemed hostile.

A sense of dread filled Lilith when the flamboyant committee chairman, Sen. Reginald Archibald, entered the chambers. He wore his trademark "Mark Twain" white suit. The Georgia senator swept back his thick, silvery white hair with one hand as he took his seat, then glared down at the Pioneers.

"Before we adjourn today, I want to remind you not to talk among yourselves about the topic of this hearing, nor are you to watch, listen to, or read any media account of today's hearing," he drawled. "You will testify tomorrow to that effect, and if you perjure yourself, it will have legal repercussions. Do I make myself clear?"

They echoed Hector's "Yes, Chairman."

"Report back here tomorrow morning at nine o'clock," Sen. Archibald instructed, adjusting his red-checked bowtie.

Hector closed his tablet and slipped it into his briefcase before joining Lilith and the remaining Pioneers as they exited the hearing room.

"How did it go today?" Seth whispered to Hector on the elevator.

Hector shook his head and put a finger to his lips. When they reached the sidewalk, he flagged a cab before turning back to Seth. "I've called in additional counsel, if that tells you anything. Did you notice the only Pioneers called today weren't U.S. citizens?"

Lilith nodded. "Except for Monique, and she has dual citizenship."

A taxi pulled up, and Hector got in.

"Hang in there, buddy," Seth said.

Hector nodded. "I'm trying, but I got shut down on every motion I made." He turned to the driver. "The Four Seasons."

"See you tomorrow," Seth said.

Hector put two fingers to his forehead in a mock salute and pulled the door shut.

Ralen had flagged another cab, and they got in. On the way back to the Willard, he said, "Why do you think they focused on the non-citizens?"

"Maybe they're going to claim Renu is un-American?" Lilith guessed.

"But it's legally incorporated here—that can't be the issue," Ralen said.

"Perception can matter more than the truth," Lilith said. "That may be all they're going for. If you count Nan, who was a British citizen until the early 2000s, more than half of us aren't Americans."

"But longevity is a human issue, not a political one," Seth said.

Lilith and Ralen stared at him. "I hope you can say that after you testify tomorrow," Ralen said.

Remembering Sen. Archibald's parting words, Lilith tilted her head toward the driver. Thankfully, he seemed totally preoccupied with tuning the radio. "At any rate, it's nothing we can change."

Lilith stepped out of her heels before the door to their suite closed behind her. "I'm beat."

"Yeah, it's been a long day," Seth said.

"And all the drama," Ralen added.

"Let's order in," Lilith suggested, picking up the room service menu.

"Great idea," Ralen said.

Seth entered the order on the interactive console. A half-hour later, they sat down to a four-course meal in the suite's formal dining room. Midway into her second glass of chardonnay, Lilith began to unwind.

"I got a message from Gemini," she said. "They've been broadcasting the hearings on the Senate channel, and local news feeds are picking it up because of our involvement."

"What's her reaction?" Seth said.

"She knows we can't discuss it, so she didn't elaborate," Lilith said.

"That's probably wise," Ralen said. "I wouldn't doubt that they could have our phones monitored."

"Surely not." After her initial skepticism, doubt crept in. Lilith didn't know what they could do.

Ralen finished eating first. "Guess we better not watch the news."

"Guess not." Seth eyed the remote as he stood. "I'm going to turn in and read. Maybe I can stay out of trouble that way."

"Good idea." Ralen turned to Lilith. "Coming?"

She shook her head. "I'm still too wired." After they left, she paced the length of the living room, replaying in her mind the pale faces of the other Pioneers as they left the room. What had shaken them so much?

Only minutes passed before she heard stereo snoring coming from the bedroom. Lilith couldn't help but be a little jealous.

She was tempted to turn on the television or to check online for coverage of the hearings. But she wasn't good at lying, and she knew perjuring herself wouldn't help their case. She'd just have to wait and see for herself what the hearings were all about.

Lilith grabbed a pencil and opened the book of crossword puzzles she bought at the airport, trying to focus on something besides the hearings. After finishing a third puzzle, she laid it aside and checked the time. Two o'clock. She yawned and stared out the window at the lights along Pennsylvania Avenue.

46

February 2030

SENATE SUBCOMMITTEE HEARING, DAY TWO, WASHINGTON, D.C.—The next thing she knew, Seth jostled her awake. "Rise and shine!"

Lilith uncurled and stretched, wincing at the crick in her neck from sleeping in the chair. Now she wished she'd at least tried the bed.

"What time is it?" she asked.

"It's still early—only seven," Seth said. "But I knew you wouldn't want to rush."

"That's true." Still a bit groggy as she headed to the unoccupied second bathroom, she told herself she must find a way to thank the hotel angels. Someone must be looking out for them to have gotten this suite on such short notice. She'd always liked the idea of parking angels, so why not the hotel equivalent? She grinned at the thought, but quickly sobered when she recalled what lay ahead that day.

Forty-five minutes later, Lilith was at breakfast with Ralen and Seth in the hotel restaurant when Kate stopped by their table.

"I didn't know you were going to be here, too," Lilith said, the unease suddenly returning full force.

"My summons came yesterday after you'd left," she said. "As well as one for Dr. J."

Seth left a tip and stood. "Sounds like it's going to be a busy day."

"Want to head over with us?" Lilith asked. "We'll be leaving in about ten minutes."

"Sure," Kate said.

When they reached the lobby, Kate and Dr. J stood by the doorman, who had a cab waiting.

"Welcome to the party," Seth said, as they climbed in.

Dr. J grunted. "I can think of about a million other places I'd rather be."

"Can't we all!" Ralen said.

Lilith nodded when Nan was the first to be called. Yesterday's pattern continued. After each Pioneer testified, they'd left the room shaken. Ralen and Seth were no exception. When each returned from testifying, they'd confirmed plans to meet back at the hotel and quickly left.

That evening before Lilith left the Senate chambers, Sen. Archibald had again cautioned those who hadn't yet testified to not speak with anyone about Renu.

When she arrived at their hotel room, a half-dozen empty bottles from the mini bar littered the counter. Ralen and Seth obviously had a head-start on happy hour. "What's going on?" She gathered their testimony hadn't gone as well as they would've liked, but she wasn't prepared for their dismal expressions.

Seth shrugged. "I just don't know what to say without violating the gag order, so have a drink." He handed her a vodka tonic. "You'll understand tomorrow."

"Ralen?"

"What he said." Ralen tilted his head toward Seth and lifted his glass in a toast. "John Milton must be tossing in his grave."

Puzzled, Lilith waited until Ralen explained.

"His famous quote—'Let truth and falsehood grapple, for whoever knew Truth put to the worse in a free and open encounter.' Obviously, he never encountered anyone like our illustrious senator from Georgia."

"Indeed," Seth said, tilting his glass in Ralen's direction. The men soon became immersed in a football game on television, leaving Lilith to her thoughts.

47

February 2030

SENATE SUBCOMMITTEE HEARING, DAY THREE, WASHINGTON, D.C.—Lilith sat before the microphone, the last of the Pioneers to be called to testify. Senator Archibald cleared his throat and shuffled through papers on the table in front of him. "You call yourselves Pioneers?"

"The Methuselah Pioneers," she said. "Our group was the first to receive this treatment at the Renu Center. And while I can only speak for myself, I find the Senate's scrutiny of a treatment that brings health and well-being to your constituents to be quite puzzling."

She glanced at their attorneys, who didn't look happy with her. The only guidance Hector had given them was to answer only the question asked and to not offer anything more. She'd have to try harder.

"Various members of our committee were contacted by those very constituents," he said. "Indeed, a group called Natural Order demanded oversight of Renu's practices. When we heard their concerns, we agreed."

No surprise there, she thought, remembering Rev. Day's connections to the Natural Order.

"Ms. Davidson, you do realize lying to the court is perjury, a criminal offense for which you can be fined and imprisoned?"

She nodded. "Yes, of course."

"Yet, you reported your age as ninety-two. Would you like to correct the record at this time?"

"No, I wouldn't," she said. "That is my correct age."

Sen. Archibald raised his voice. "I repeat, lying to this committee is perjury." He glared down at her.

Hector gave her an almost imperceptible shrug.

"I cannot offer a different age because that *would* be perjury," she insisted. "Actually, my birthday was eight months ago, so I'm almost ninety-three."

The senator scoffed. "And I suppose you also have swamp land in Florida you want to sell me?" He allowed a round of laughter from the spectators before holding up his hand for quiet.

"No, Senator, I do not." Lilith bit back a sarcastic remark of her own. Following Hector's advice was proving much harder than she expected.

Sen. Archibald studied her face like she was an alien from another planet. "And you were one of the first people to undergo the treatment at Renu?"

"Yes. The first dozen of us were chosen because of our long-time support of the project. We all had terminal cancer. Doctors say I would've been dead by now without the treatment," she said.

"You claim you had cancer?" He sneered.

"I had one of the most aggressive forms—Stage Four pancreatic cancer," she said.

"Or maybe that just makes a good story Renu can advertise?" he said.

Anger flared, bringing a hot edge to Lilith's voice. "You don't have to take my word for it. I filled out the medical release forms, so you can access my records from Renu and the Mayo Clinic."

"I'm sure such things can be forged..."

"Not if you get them directly," she interrupted, "as I encourage you to do."

"Be assured, we will thoroughly investigate your age and the claims about your prior medical conditions," the senator said.

Hector stood.

Sen. Archibald sighed. "Yes, Counselor?"

"Again, I refer to the exhibits, offered as proof of Mrs. Davidson's age, along with the official records of the other Pioneers."

"Sit down."

"I also provided birth certificates not only for her, but for her children and grandchildren," Hector said, his voice strident. "Marriage licenses. Social Security and tax records. Driver's and professional licenses."

"You won't get another warning," Sen. Archibald barked. "One more word and you'll be held in contempt."

Hector glared at the senator, then slowly sat. Lilith's heart pounded. If he wouldn't accept official documents as evidence, what defense did they have?

The senator faced Lilith as two images appeared in front of the rostrum. "Do you confirm these are accurate holograms taken of you prior to and after the treatment?"

She examined the two images, momentarily surprised at how different she had looked. In the first hologram, she was a gray-haired elderly woman, obviously in failing health, with a pallid complexion and many wrinkles. How quickly she had put all that behind her. In the second, she looked much as she did today, with strawberry blonde hair and smooth skin glowing with health. She looked at least forty years younger.

"Yes, those are accurate images of me," she said.

"And you maintain the changes were solely due to the Renu treatment, not to plastic surgery, Botox, or other treatments?" he asked.

"I do," Lilith responded.

He paused a moment, then asked, "When do you tell applicants about the *true* purpose of the treatment?"

Puzzled by his question, Lilith said, "Applicants are told up-front that Renu's treatment is designed to alleviate the degenerative effects of aging, which include illnesses such as cancer."

"Come now!" Sen. Archibald scolded. "You are under oath. Previous testimony from the other so-called Pioneers makes the true goal of the treatment clear. Renu is a sex cult."

"What?" Lilith said. "That's ridiculous!"

"I object." A dark-skinned man sitting next to Hector stood.

"Counselor?" Sen. Archibald said, with a warning in his voice.

"Your allegation is inflammatory and totally unsubstantiated."

"Indeed?" the senator said. "This treatment breaks down the God-given, natural sexual instincts and supplants them with degenerate appetites. Yesterday's testimony clearly showed that."

"My clients' private lives do not affect the public interest, and therefore are not under this special committee's purview," he said.

"Quite the contrary," Sen. Archibald said. "As a matter of public trust, we are obliged to monitor people who pose a threat to national safety."

"How does saving lives threaten the nation?" he said.

Red-faced, the senator pointed at the attorney. "Sir, take your seat."

Hector's co-counsel took a deep breath and sat.

"Mrs. Davidson, do you deny that you and Kameitha Banks became lovers as a result of the treatment?"

She bit her lip. Hector turned his palms up. "We began our relationship after the treatment, but not because of it," she said.

"And your other so-called houseguest is your husband's lover?" A sequence of images showed behind him, including private moments shot within their home.

"How did you get those images? That's... illegal," she said.

The attorney stood again. "I object to this line of questioning. Those images are of a personal nature and not in the public interest."

"You are testing my patience, Counselor." Sen. Archibald motioned for him to sit. "The courts authorized the surveillance because this cult clearly poses a threat to our American way of life. To the very sanctity of our family values. Mrs. Davidson, isn't it true that the four of you now live together and swap partners?"

"How does that harm anyone, much less threaten the nation?" she asked.

"Answer the question, Mrs. Davidson," Sen. Archibald said.

Hector began to stand, but his co-counsel placed a hand on Hector's arm, halting him.

Lilith swallowed hard. "For several months, Ralen Alexander and Kameitha Banks have lived with my husband Seth and me."

"And why is that?" the senator asked.

"Those of us who took the first treatment decided to build a new home where we will all live and work together. It's much closer to the Renu Research Center," she said. "Several of the group, including Ralen and Kameitha, have already put their homes up for sale to help raise money needed to fund this project."

"Now Mrs. Davidson, isn't your sexual relationship with both of them the primary reason for their change of residence."

Frustration seeped into her voice. "I already said we're lovers."

The senator shook his head, then looked beyond Lilith to the spectators. "Families are the bedrock of our society. And families are undermined when a so-called palliative treatment fundamentally changes sexuality."

The attorneys rose to their feet, but before they could respond, a woman yelled, "Home wreckers!"

"Perverts!" a man jeered.

The senator pounded his gavel and demanded silence. He motioned to Hector and the new attorney to sit. When he didn't order the security guards to remove the protesters, Lilith figured their outburst had been staged for the benefit of the vidcams.

"That will be all, Mrs. Davidson," the senator told Lilith, then turned to the guard. "Please bring in the next witness."

As she walked out, Lilith realized why the others had look shell-shocked when they left the chambers. She could've said so much—in fact, she'd wanted to share her experience with Renu—but hadn't had the opportunity. Obviously, the hearings weren't about finding truth or providing the American public information about the new procedure.

Hector stood. "And the gag order… is it still in effect for those who've already testified?"

The senator looked down at a paper in front of him. "No, they are released. We have no further need for their testimony." He nodded to the guard, who escorted Lilith to the door and called out, "Kate Flowers."

Kate paused in the doorway and met her eyes. Lilith wondered at Kate's expression—a mixture of pity and resolve—until she looked across the hall and saw Kameitha sitting between Jeremy and Rev, Day.

Lilith halted mid-stride, trying to process what she was seeing. Kameitha looked lovely but vulnerable, a petite waif between the tall men dressed in black who flanked her. The familiar spark of attraction flashed in Kameitha's eyes for only a moment before her face became expressionless and cold.

What had they done to her? Anger and heartache flooded Lilith's senses in equal measure.

"Be strong," Kate whispered, squeezing Lilith's hand before she entered the hearing room.

Lilith heard the door close behind her as she walked across the hall and stood in front of Kameitha. "Why are you here with them?"

"Obviously, she's here to testify," Rev. Day said, standing. "And under the gag order, she's not allowed to talk about why she's here."

"I wasn't talking to you," Lilith snapped, then refocused on Kameitha. "I've been worried about you. Why didn't you return my calls?"

Kameitha looked away.

Jeremy smirked. "You see, she doesn't want to talk with you."

How could the woman she loved—the woman who loved her—be so cruel? Kameitha still loved her, didn't she?

"Kameitha, look at me!" Lilith pleaded.

Kameitha bit her lip and closed her eyes. "Please go," she said quietly.

Lilith's mouth fell open. *Please go. That was all she had to say?* Lilith shook her head and stepped back. She turned and walked in a daze down the hall. *Please go.* The words kept echoing in her mind.

She pushed the elevator button, then found herself on the street in front of the building. She kept walking, going with the flow on the crowded sidewalks, thinking only of Kameitha. Trying to make sense of what was happening. *Why had Kameitha left her? Why?*

Lilith ignored the phone vibrating in her pocket. The car honking at her when she walked in front it barely registered.

Please go.

Gravel crunched beneath her shoes. She walked around the mall, oblivious to the cold, drizzling rain.

The past months replayed in Lilith's thoughts—their first lingering kiss at the Research Center, the morning at Kameitha's home when they first made love. And their lovemaking only two days ago with Seth and Ralen. The tenderness. The sweetness.

And now it was all gone. Lilith kept walking. Maybe their love hadn't been real at all, but merely chemicals. Had the side effect simply run its course? If so, why didn't she feel differently? Or Ralen? Or Seth?

"Lilith."

At the sound of Seth's voice, she stopped walking and turned around.

He wrapped his arms around her. "Come back to the hotel with me."

Lilith leaned into his embrace. The warmth of his body made her realize how cold she was.

He guided her toward a waiting cab and slid in beside her. "Willard Hotel," he told the driver and pulled her close to him. "You're cold as ice." He took her hands and placed them between his, rubbing them together. "It took me a while to track you down. You walked more than a mile in those heels."

"I saw Kameitha."

"I know," Seth said. "Kate texted me. I tried to get there before you finished testifying."

"She told me to go." Lilith's voice broke. "She wouldn't even look at me."

Lilith buried her face against Seth's shoulder. She squeezed her eyes shut, trying to hold back the tears.

He held her close to him, making soft shushing noises. "I'm so sorry, Lil."

The cab stopped, and Seth paid the driver. When they reached the room, Ralen handed them towels. "C'mon, let's get you out of those wet clothes." Ralen gestured toward the sofa where he'd laid out dry clothes for both of them.

Lilith's teeth chattered as her brain fully registered the cold. She pulled off her soaked clothes, unceremoniously dropping them on the parquet floor in her hurry to dress. Dry clothes had never felt so good.

Ralen took their dripping clothes to the bathroom, while Seth guided her to the couch. Ralen had a carafe of coffee ready for them, sitting on a tray next to single-serve bottles of brandy. Seth poured one of the small bottles of brandy into a steaming cup of coffee. "Here, baby, you need to get warmed up on the inside, too."

Lilith took a sip, grimacing at the taste, but sighed as its fiery warmth soothed her throat. She closed her eyes and took a deep breath. Still, she couldn't quit thinking about Kameitha. She even thought she heard her talking.

Lilith opened her eyes and stared at the vid screen on the opposite wall. She hadn't imagined it. Kameitha's face filled the screen.

"Oh my god." Lilith pointed. They all stared at the screen.

"Volume up three clicks," Ralen instructed, and Kameitha's voice filled the room.

"Yes, we called it a 'side effect,' but it was more than that. As I look back at how things happened, I'm sure the medical team manipulated the serum to cause it."

Lilith gasped.

Shaking his head, Ralen said, "Why would she say that?"

"And you believe the Renu treatment is designed to change the sexual preference of those who are treated," Sen. Archibald said.

Kameitha gave a sidelong glance at Jeremy, then quietly said, "Yes."

Seth slammed his glass down on the table. "That's just crazy."

"What makes you think that?" the senator asked her.

"Our group worked with the medical team for about fifteen years, through all the project's phases. As remote viewers, we are generally kept blind to the real target so we won't just make guesses. I only recently learned that some of our targets had to do with sexual preference."

"How did you get that information?" the senator asked.

"A member of the medical staff at Renu provided a copy to my son, who shared the information with me," she said.

"And how long have you known this?" he asked.

"Since last week," she replied.

"Did this change your opinion about the work done by the Renu Research Center?" he asked.

Kameitha looked down at her lap. "Yes, it did."

"In what way?"

"They tricked me, both while I was helping develop the serum and later as a test subject. At no time was I told the serum was designed to change sexual preference." As she spoke, Kameitha stared at Jeremy and Rev. Day, who sat on the front row of spectators.

"If you had it all to do over again, would you?" the senator asked.

"No," she said, her tone robotic. "The treatment saved a life, but it wasn't *my* life. I lost the person I had been. I was no longer myself, as my son tried to tell me."

Lilith couldn't believe what she was hearing. "She doesn't mean that. She can't!"

"Somehow, Rev. Day has her in his pocket," Ralen said. "I just don't know how."

As the testimony continued, Lilith shivered. What had happened to make Kameitha say such things? Was she in danger?

Chapter 48

When Lilith next looked at the screen, a distraught elderly woman had replaced Kameitha.

"The treatment broke up our family," she told the senator. Images flashed on the screen of her with a sickly looking, gray-haired man. Surrounding them were about a dozen people of various ages.

"Those are your children and grandchildren?" he asked.

She nodded.

"It took all our savings, plus we had to get a loan. The treatment cost $600,000, but it was our only chance to save his life," the woman said. "The cancer was cured when he returned two weeks later, but he not only looked different, he was different."

After-treatment images showed her spouse looking as young as their middle-aged children.

"And who is this?" The senator pointed to an image of her spouse with a young man.

"That is his lover—the man he now lives with." She didn't try to hide her bitterness.

"So, the treatment changed his sexual preference?"

"It did," the woman said.

Lilith exchanged confused glances with Seth and Ralen. "Had you heard of anything like this?"

"We know how disruptive it's been for our own families, so it doesn't surprise me," Ralen said.

Hector stood and addressed the witness. "I'm sorry to hear of your problems. I know how upsetting family matters can be, but isn't it true your husband had previous affairs?"

She pursed her lips and looked toward Sen. Archibald for guidance.

"What happened prior to the treatment is not subject to public inquiry," Sen. Archibald stated.

"I only bring up such a delicate matter because it is relevant," Hector said. "As Dr. J testified earlier, the serum is not a love potion that makes you fall in love with someone you otherwise wouldn't find attractive. It merely strengthens tendencies you already have."

"He was certainly no homo," the woman scoffed. "He hated queers. That's why I know it was Renu what did it!"

Hector tilted his head to the side. "Psychological studies as far back as 2012 show those who are homophobic often have implicit desires."

She glared at him. "Believe me, the only 'implicit' desires he had were for females. I could give you the names of plenty of women who'd testify he was one-hundred percent a ladies' man."

"Then you're saying he did have affairs?"

"Never with men!" she added hotly.

"Whoa!" Lilith said. "Looks like Hector finally got a point across."

"To be fair, though, we could've been in the same situation if only one of us had taken the treatment," Seth suggested.

Lilith shook her head. "I don't think so. The treatment didn't change how I felt about you."

Seth laughed. "Well, it would've been a short-term problem. With my old decrepit body, I wouldn't have lasted a week trying to keep up with your revved-up libido."

She grinned at him.

"I told you before to limit your questions to the issue at hand," the senator told Hector before turning back to the woman. "Thank you for testifying, ma'am."

Senator Archibald called the next witness, a balding, middle-aged man.

"My name is Paul Black," he said. "I'm a senior economist

employed at the Roger's Institute, an internationally renowned think tank."

"What is your assessment of the impact this treatment could have?" Senator Archibald said.

"Those initially seeking treatment with Renu are elderly, but as clinics become more widely available, that will change," he said. "When you consider that half of all men and a third of women are likely to contract cancer in their lifetimes, that ailment alone could push significant numbers through Renu's doors on a continuing basis."

"Based on your analysis, is it safe to say the treatment's so-called side effect would have a negative impact on the economy?" the senator asked.

The economist paused, then pointed to a chart hologram. "Based on the number of clinics Renu has announced plans to open within the year and the current treatment rate, we project the number of nontraditional households to at least triple by the end of the year because of the bisexuality side effect."

"And how would that affect the economy?" the senator prodded.

"I'd point to two major economic benefits of nuclear families—those with a husband and wife—versus nontraditional households," he said. "First, being married has roughly the same effect on reducing poverty that adding five to six years to a parent's education has. And second, roughly three-quarters of welfare assistance currently goes to single-parent families."

"That's so transparent!" Lilith said. "Anyone can see he's targeting single mothers and same-sex couples."

A woman's voice drew Lilith's attention back to the screen.

"Have your studies taken into account the economic *benefits* this treatment could have, not only for individuals but for the country?" The nameplate identified her as Sen. Carmichael, ranking committee member.

Black flipped through pages on his tablet, then said, "Work-loss figures for cancer alone show costs exceeding $160 billion per year in the U.S. The loss of life and productivity worldwide accounts for about 1.5 percent of the GDP—that's the global gross domestic product."

"Can you explain what that means in terms we can understand?" she asked.

"Well, the American Institute of Cancer Research estimates that last year Americans lost 100 million years of healthy life because of cancer deaths and disabilities."

"And these costs—both personal and financial—would be mitigated if the treatment cures cancer, isn't that right?" she asked.

"I would have to do my own analysis, but generally I've found AICR data to be reliable," he said.

"Thank you, Mr. Black," she said.

Sen. Archibald cleared his throat. "Back to the point you were making about the financial impact of nontraditional families. Welfare costs will increase?"

"Certainly," he said.

Sen. Archibald gave Sen. Carmichael a sidelong glance. "How do expenditures for welfare compare to the financial costs from cancer you just described?"

"Without including such things as Medicaid, welfare costs for families are about $600 billion annually," Black said.

"So, almost four times as much?"

"That's correct. But the longevity aspect has an even greater potential impact," the economist said.

"How is that?" the senator asked.

"Even if you bypass the huge issue of population growth due to fewer people dying, if there is no change in work and retirement patterns, the ratio could quickly rise to roughly one older, economically inactive person for every worker."

"And this would have an immediate impact on the entitlement programs?" the senator asked.

"Everything from pensions and insurance to medical care and even education—it would have sweeping repercussions across the government and private sectors," Black said. "Already, people past age fifty control 70 percent of the nation's disposable income."

Ralen shut off the vid screen. "I can't take any more of this!"

"But we need to know what they're saying," Lilith protested, looking to Seth for support.

"Why?" Ralen said. "What can we do? All our work to bring this cure to the world and look what happens. These narrow-minded fools don't deserve to live."

"I can't argue with that, but they aren't the only ones affected," Seth said. "If we can't find a way to defend against this witch-hunt, no one will be able to get the treatment."

Lilith paced across the room. "I don't know. Maybe the treatment isn't everything we thought it was."

"It's not perfect, Lilith, but we'd be dead now," Seth said. "Would that really be better?"

She threw her hands up. "No, I guess not, but they make it sound so bad. I just want these people out of my life."

"I'm sure Kate and Peter are already working on how to do that," Seth said, checking his vibrating phone. "In fact, it looks like they've set a meeting for tomorrow afternoon. Let's pack. It's time for us to get home."

Lilith checked her text messages, heartened by Gemini's "Hang in there," and even by Lacy's "Senate living down to expectations. Par for the course." It was good to know they cared enough to watch the hearings.

As she closed her packed suitcase and rolled it toward the door, Lilith wondered where Kameitha was. She didn't know why Kameitha left them or why she said what she did at the hearing, but until Lilith had answers—*real* answers—she wasn't giving up on her.

Chapter 49

RENU RESEARCH CENTER, OGDEN RIVER SCENIC BYWAY—By the time the limo came to take them to the Research Center, Lilith already had her fill of drama. Protests at the just-opened Renu clinics around the country topped the news, along with clips from the Senate hearings.

In the Renu conference room, Kate sent each Pioneer links to the hearing transcript and video. Lilith didn't know if she could ever make herself watch it, so she was grateful to have the written copy. At least she could skim the highlights without having to sit through the whole thing.

"Let's get started." Hector motioned for everyone to take a seat. "We have a lot to cover. First, I want to assure you that all the clinics are open today, and none of next week's participants have canceled. Furthermore, since the hearings began, we've had ten times more inquiries about Renu than the previous week."

"Once again, the old adage proves true," Kate said. "There's no such thing as bad publicity."

"Of the thousands who are scheduled for treatment later this year, only nineteen have changed their minds," Hector continued.

"That's all good, but when are we going to be able to get our side of the story out?" Xavier asked.

"As it happens, we had already begun working with 'Science America,'" Kate said. "To take advantage of the heightened interest, they've decided to bump the cover story up to next week instead of waiting."

"Do you think you'll be able to show the benefits Renu offers?" Karla asked.

"Without a doubt," Kate said. "Plus, we need to bring you up to date on what will be the centerpiece of their story—the new protocol."

Lilith blinked in surprise. This must have happened while they were in D.C. The last she'd heard, the new protocol was just a teaser, not the article's focus.

Dr. J stood. "The new serum you helped develop can be taken by people with the usual ailments of middle and old age. It will not cure a life-threatening illness like the serum you took, but it can 'reset' the body to a healthier state. Some would call it a 'younger' state."

"And it doesn't have the side effect you experience with the original longevity serum," Kate said.

Now Lilith was beginning to see the reasoning behind the shift of focus.

"Recipients will experience enhanced libido, but only because of restored overall health," Kate said.

"This is based on our first four trials, so four dozen people," Dr. J said. "We've seen reversals of a variety of ailments—everything from high blood pressure and diabetes to the early stages of lupus and cancer. In other words, things that could become life-threatening are eliminated."

"It's a much quicker process, too," Kate said. "Now we're doing extensive diagnostics up front and monitoring afterward, so it's taking three days. After we've reached a level of statistical significance, we'll be able to do these treatments in one day, and for a fraction of the cost of the five-day longevity treatment."

"This is going to change everything," Peter said. "As you'll recall, we're only converting half of the Xtreme Care Clinics to handle those with life-threatening illnesses. We can convert the other 3,500 clinics to provide this preventative treatment."

Kate nodded. "Eventually, once everyone is getting these treatments, we'll be able to phase out the longevity serum. Then all the clinics can provide the preventative treatment."

As Lilith listened, she tried to picture how Rev. Day would view what they were saying. It certainly addressed one of the issues that kept coming up in the hearings—how spouses were left behind. The key would be getting early treatment, before either spouse developed a life-threatening disease. The new treatment would also sidestep the issue of enhanced sexuality, which had become the focus of the protesters and politicians. But would it be enough?

"You say this is going to be less expensive," Lilith said. "How will this compare to current medical procedures?"

"Do you mean are we going to go head-to-head with the current health care and pharmaceutical industries?" Kate asked. "The answer's yes, and we can expect much more opposition than we've already seen. The multi-billion-dollar industry we now have is based on people being sick. This will bring an end to that."

"That's the beauty of it," Dr. J said. "It's reversing the process—focusing on keeping people healthy, not on treating ailments."

"People will live longer without what we now think of as the unavoidable decline due to aging," Kate said.

"Seems like you'd want to get this news out now instead of waiting for the 'Science America' article,'" Nan said. "Things are out of control."

"It's a concern," Kate agreed, "but we need the credibility 'Science America' will bring. Otherwise, it's just us talking about how good the treatments are."

"Anyway, we're only talking about delaying a matter of days," Dr. J added.

"What if the Senate decides to shut us down?" Seth asked.

"I wouldn't be surprised if they find a way to make us suspend the treatments, but the Senate doesn't move quickly," Kate said. "The longer it takes, the closer we'll be to the tipping point, with enough people who have personally benefitted from the treatment."

"To lessen the impact on spouses and families of those getting the longevity treatments, they'll be the first offered the new preventative serum," Dr. J said. "I know you've all had issues with your families accepting your changed appearance. Now they'll be able to undergo similar rejuvenation. I think it should really help."

Lilith immediately thought of Gemini—would she take the treatment? It would remove the awkwardness of having parents who looked more like her children.

"We can handle three dozen people a week here, which will get us started until we rollout those new clinics Peter talked about,"

Kate said. "You each have a packet that tells what all is involved; I hope you'll share it with your family members."

"I like this plan a lot," Monique said. "But I don't think it really addresses the emotions the hearing stirred up. And even before that —the threat Lilith, Seth, Ralen and Kameitha got."

"You're right," Hector said. "I've been in touch with Detective Roberts in Park City. He's coordinating with Ogden and Eden police to supplement the private security we have monitoring our homes and the patrols at Eden clinic."

"He's concerned the hearings may encourage the caller to act," Kate said. "It's almost like the Senate painted a red bull's eye on us."

The Pioneers shifted in their seats, nodding heads, and leaning over to share whispered words with each other.

Ralen addressed the group. "Since security will be much easier when we're all living together, I talked with our contractor before the meeting. Everett assures me they'll be working around the clock on our new home, starting today. It's going to cost extra, of course, but they're close enough to completion that we should be able to move in by the end of the week."

The others visibly relaxed at the news.

As the meeting drew to a close, Kate pulled Lilith aside, sympathy showing on her face. "Seth told me Kameitha didn't want to talk with you. I'm so sorry. How are you holding up?"

Lilith shrugged. "I'm still trying to make sense of it. Do you think there's a chance the serum wore off and that's why she pulled away from our relationship?"

Kate tilted her head, questioningly. "You mean, to cause the physical attraction to end? No, that's not how it works. If that was the case, she wouldn't be the only one affected."

"Unless she's just the first to change—maybe her body chemistry is different," Lilith suggested. "I don't know. I'm just trying to find something—anything—to explain what's happened."

"Don't blame the serum." Dr. J said. Despite his defensive tone, he gave Lilith's hand a reassuring squeeze. "All our models show the treatment is stable for at least fifty years and probably much longer. That's one problem we don't need to worry about."

Chapter 50

PARK CITY, UTAH—When they returned home, Lilith dropped her handbag on the table in the foyer and wandered into the living room. The hollow feeling inside didn't go away, no matter how she tried to distract herself. Her thoughts shifted to darker images— Kameitha sitting on the bench outside the hearing room, telling her "please go."

Lilith picked up the remote for the video system. She tapped the link to the hearings Kate had given them and began scrolling through the footage. She hit play when it reached Sen. Archibald's closing remarks.

"I called for this hearing because of my firm belief that the most fundamental responsibility of our government is to ensure the safety of its people, and to protect and ensure our national security. Like five-star general Douglas MacArthur said more than a century ago, I believe the biggest threat to the security of our great nation are the insidious forces working from within that so drastically alter the character of our free institutions—those institutions we proudly call the American way of life."

Seth and Ralen joined her on the sofa.

"As I called each successive witness, it struck me how many of these so-called Pioneers are not American," Sen. Archibald continued. "I perceived a double-threat. This treatment strikes at the core of our family life by changing God-given sexual preferences. And more than half of those on the leading edge of this attack—and I call it an attack because that is what it is—come from outside our nation's borders.

"I have investigated remote viewing—the so-called scientific protocol they use. It is nothing more than a diversion. They don't want you to question how they got their information, so they trot out this shadowy technique that dates back to the Cold War era. They may as well have said it was alchemy.

"To be sure, the treatment they offer is seductive. Who isn't lured by the promise of longevity? Of youthful vigor? But don't be fooled. As experts in plastic surgery and holographic manipulation testified, the treatment is not what they would have you believe.

"Renu is making war on the natural order—the God-given attraction between men and women. That not only challenges the family values we hold sacred, but our security as a nation."

Lilith pressed the remote again, shutting off the screen. "I had no idea it was that bad. No wonder people are protesting the clinics."

Seth and Ralen looked as incredulous as she felt.

Ralen growled, "The only 'natural order' he's concerned about is the payola he gets from Big Pharma."

"That may be true," Seth said, "but it takes a lot of courage for people to embrace new ways of living. I don't know if most people have what it takes."

"We've all been there. Deciding to take the treatment wasn't easy, even if the alternative was death," Lilith said. "You have to let go of the familiar, which, at the time, seems secure."

"Well, it looks like Gemini's got a life-changing decision to make, too," Seth said.

Lilith examined the packet containing brochures about the new serum and nodded. "No time like the present. Let's see if she's home."

———

THE PHONE RANG, waking Lilith from a deep sleep. It was still dark. She checked the time. Three o'clock. Feeling a sense of deja vu, she checked the caller ID, then shook Seth. "Wake up!"

The phone rang again.

He grumbled, then propped up on his elbows.

"No caller ID," Lilith noted. She held her breath in anticipation as she handed him the phone.

Seth pressed the speaker button and said, "Yes?"

"You were warned," a steely male voice said. "The blood is on your hands."

Before Seth could respond, the caller disconnected.

Ralen switched on the bedside lamp. "He didn't sound happy."

"Don't joke," Lilith said sternly as she tried to rein-in her fear.

Seth punched in a number. "Detective Roberts?" Seth asked, when a groggy voice answered. "Sorry to bother you, but you said to call if we got another threat."

After Seth finished relaying the message, the detective said, "I'll have it traced, though it's likely another disposable phone. Have you noticed anything suspicious?"

"Nothing," Seth said. "We just got back from the hearings in Washington, so we've been out of touch with the clinics. But I'm sure they would've let us know if anything significant happened."

"Even something minor could be important," the detective said. He cleared his throat. "Speaking of the hearings, I've taken Ms. Banks off the missing persons' list."

Lilith buried her face in her pillow. That meant no one would be looking for Kameitha's car now. Not that it mattered. Even if Lilith learned where she was, Kameitha had made it clear she didn't want to be with her.

"I understand." Seth disconnected and turned to Lilith. "Hey, Lil, chin up."

Lilith clenched her jaws, holding in the hurt.

Ralen moved to Lilith's other side and put his arms around her. "I've known Kameitha a long time, and you've known her long enough to know that wasn't like her yesterday. Someone or something has her running scared or she wouldn't be doing this. In your heart, you know that's true."

Tears welled in Lilith's eyes. She couldn't talk for the lump in her throat. She shook her head, then took a deep breath and whispered, "I want to believe that."

"Trust me."

She leaned back against Ralen and let his warmth dispel the coldness she felt inside.

Seth stroked Lilith's hair. "We'll get to the bottom of this."

"He's right," Ralen said. "Kameitha's one of us. That hasn't changed."

Seth picked up his phone again. "I better let the others know about the call." He texted Kate and the other Pioneers.

"Right now, we need to focus on this caller," Ralen said. "Okay?"

Lilith pressed her lips together and nodded.

"Well, after we move to our new home, it will be a lot harder for anyone to breach our security," Seth said.

"Everything's operational?" Lilith wiped a tear from her cheek. She'd been so preoccupied the day before when they walked the punch list, she hadn't thought to ask.

Seth nodded. "Ralen and I did a thorough security run-through yesterday, too."

"The scanners all worked perfectly," Ralen said. "We got feedback from all the infrared sensors and thermographic monitors. Nothing's going to get past that system."

"I'm glad." Lilith rose, suddenly wanting time to herself. "Guess I may as well get up. There's no way I could get back to sleep now."

———

THEY HAD JUST FINISHED breakfast when the phone rang again. Lilith froze when she saw the caller's name.

"Kameitha?"

She pushed the holovid button and Kameitha's form wavered in the air. She stood in a darkened room, her mussed hair and wild eyes barely visible in the dim light.

"You have to leave the house. NOW!" Kameitha whispered. "Hurry!" Then the line went dead.

Ralen and Seth jumped to their feet, their eyes wide.

Lilith hit redial but reached voice mail. She threw her hands up, exasperated. "No!"

"C'mon, let's go," Ralen said.

"Yeah, she sounded scared," Seth said. "I think we should take it seriously."

Still rattled, Lilith followed them toward the garage. She felt silly about leaving their home like this—overly dramatic—but Kameitha's warning had raised a sense of dread she couldn't shake.

Along the way, they grabbed coats from the mud room. Seth

pushed the button to open the garage door and they walked briskly toward Lilith's Escalade. As soon as their car doors closed, Lilith put the car in reverse. The garage's overhead light flickered. A blinding light flared, blocking everything around them from view.

A roar louder than a jet engine rocked the car. Reacting instinctively, Lilith slammed her foot on the gas. Heavy boards and debris showered down around them. A board struck the middle of the windshield, shattering the glass with a loud pop. Wood scraped the hood as the car rocketed backward, out of the collapsing structure. The board dropped to the floor with other debris, filling the space where the car had sat moments before.

Another explosion sent a plume of orange and yellow flames into the still-dark sky. Lilith shifted into drive and sped down the circle driveway, away from the burning building.

"That was too close," Ralen said breathlessly.

"9-1-1," an operator voice answered.

"There's been an explosion." Seth gave their address. "We need assistance."

"Is anyone hurt?" the dispatcher asked.

Seth eyed Lilith and Ralen before replying, "No."

"Stay on the line." In the background, the dispatcher requested assistance, then she returned. "They're on the way. Until help gets there—it should be only a few minutes—tell me what's happening. How many are with you?"

"Two," Seth said.

As he continued to answer her questions, Ralen told Lilith, "We need to tell Detective Roberts." He punched in a text message.

Lilith switched off the car and leaned her forehead against the steering wheel, silently giving thanks for their escape. If it hadn't been for Kameitha…

She looked up as the first fire engine arrived. The blaze had already spread to the other side of the house. Flames danced as high as nearby treetops.

They opened the car doors, but Lilith fell back onto the seat when she tried to stand. Her legs shook.

Seth leaned against the side of the car next to her open door. "You're fine where you are."

A fireman came over. "Everyone out of the house?" They nodded. "Any injuries?" He stared at Lilith.

"I'm just a little shaken," she said.

He nodded. "What happened?"

Seth told him about the explosion, then repeated the story when Detective Roberts arrived a few minutes later.

Uniformed police put up barricades to divert the early-morning traffic, which was backing up as commuters slowed to stare. By the time the sun rose, the firemen were retracting their flexible white hoses and loading other equipment back onto the trucks.

All that remained of the house were charred and broken studs, bricks, and smoldering debris. The stench of burned plastic and wet ashes filled the air.

"I'm sure it comes as no surprise that we found accelerant. The arsonist intended the blaze to be fast-moving, which it was," the fireman said. "If you hadn't already been in the car, there's no way you could've outrun it."

"We have Kameitha to thank for that," Lilith said. "She warned us to get out of the house."

"I'm afraid she may be in danger," Ralen told Detective Roberts. "She sounded scared."

"Obviously, she's had contact with whoever did this, and they're not the kind of people you want to mess around with," the detective said. "This changes things. We'll put her back on the missing persons' list, and I'll check Ms. Banks' call records to see if we can find out where she called from."

"Thank you," Lilith said. "It makes me feel much better to know you're looking for her."

They walked around the perimeter with the detective and fire chief, staying outside the yellow tape encircling where the house had been. It had "do not cross" in large black letters, repeating continuously.

Seth kicked a small chunk of debris out of the way. "Nothing's left."

Lilith couldn't comprehend all they had lost. Maybe she was in shock? The keepsakes were the hardest to lose, but even those were trivial compared to their safety. At least everyone was okay. Now if they could find Kameitha.

Chapter 51

RENU RESEARCH CENTER, OGDEN RIVER SCENIC BYWAY—Lilith spotted Gemini in the lobby as they drove up the circular drive in front of the Renu Research Center several hours later. But she looked far different from the woman they'd dropped off three days before to take the new treatment.

Lilith had forgotten how much Lacy looked like her mother, but now they easily could pass for sisters. Gemini looked closer to thirty-five than sixty-eight. The laugh wrinkles around her mouth and eyes had smoothed, and her skin glowed. Lilith noticed how effortlessly Gemini walked; the limp that had plagued her was gone.

"You're moving so much better." Lilith gave Gemini a hug.

"And you look great!" Seth added.

"I have much more energy," Gemini said, laughing. "I had no idea how much I'd slowed down. And the sciatica is gone… what a relief!"

"Are you ready to go home?"

Gemini nodded, and they walked together toward the car. "I wasn't expecting all three of you. I feel honored."

Seth cleared his throat. "Well, we *are* all very happy for you, but why we're all here today is a rather long story."

Gemini cocked her head.

"Yeah," Lilith suddenly found it hard to talk. "Our home is… gone." She grimaced and brushed away a tear.

"What?" Gemini asked. They opened the car doors and slid in.

Lilith rested her head on the steering wheel for a moment and took a deep breath.

"It was bombed this morning," Ralen explained. "The house burned to the ground."

As Lilith began to drive away, Kate ran from the building, waving and yelling, "Stop! Stop!"

"What the hell?" Seth said.

Lilith braked. Kate ran to the car as Lilith lowered the driver-side window. "It wasn't just your house," Kate said, panting. "They bombed six of our clinics, too."

They followed Kate back into the Center's conference room.

"Was anyone hurt?" Ralen asked.

"At least ten are dead," Kate said breathlessly. "I don't know how many more are injured." She clicked the vid screen on. It filled with images of smoke billowing from a collapsed building.

"That's the clinic in Eden!" Lilith scooted to the edge of her seat.

"The director was killed," Hector said as he entered. "The whole front half of the building exploded."

"No!" Lilith exclaimed. "She was so young." In fact, she had reminded Lilith of an older version of Faye. Lilith's heart twisted at such a senseless waste of life, a pain that intensified when she let the scope of the attack sink in. Ten dead.

"The fire marshal said something went wrong with the device or it would've destroyed the rest of the building and killed all of the dozen people undergoing treatment."

Lilith reached for Gemini's hand, quivering at what might have been if the bomber's target had been different.

Horrified, they watched footage of protesters ringing a fallen building in Virginia Beach. Picketers' signs proclaimed: "Death to Renu," "Natural Order, not Renu," and "Say No to Renu." Police and firemen combed the rubble.

"The Natural Order claimed credit for the bombings," Hector said.

On the screen, a young woman carrying a "Fight for Families" placard at the Seattle facility told a reporter, "It's the American way to fight for what you believe. And that's what we're doing."

"By bombing this facility?" the reporter asked.

"It's a war," she said. "If you don't act, you get acted upon. The

American dream is not about communes and free sex. We have values."

"Even if people get killed?" the reporter countered.

"Look, they would've killed the America I love." She glared defensively into the camera. "The only way to stop those people is by showing you are not going to stand by and let them get away with it. We've let it go too far, and now it's time to take our country back."

Ralen pounded his fist on the conference table. "What's wrong with those people?"

"Sadly, it's nothing new," Seth said.

"If history's taught us one thing, it's that zealots don't give up," Gemini added. "Think of all the years protesters have attacked abortion clinics. And they're still at it."

Kate's phone vibrated. She checked the message, then left the room. A few minutes later, she returned with Detective Roberts. And Kameitha.

Lilith gasped. She stood and took a step forward, then froze, suddenly unsure how to react. She was both thrilled to see Kameitha and angry with her. Her call had saved them, but the words still echoed from the last time she saw Kameitha: *Please go.*

Seth walked over and hugged Kameitha. "You saved us!"

Ralen followed him, giving Kameitha another hug and a kiss on her forehead.

Kameitha walked over to Lilith. "I'm so sorry for everything I put you through."

Lilith pressed her lips together and stared at her.

"Jeremy texted me right after you got the 3 a.m. call and said we might be able to stop them from hurting anyone."

"And you believed him?" Lilith asked.

"I had to try," Kameitha said. "When they said you'd be safe if I testified at the hearings, what choice did I have?"

"What made you call us this morning?" Seth asked.

"I overheard the Reverend talking with a blond-haired man, who said in just a few minutes, the 'ones who started it all' wouldn't be a problem any longer."

Seth frowned. "Guess that meant us."

"Exactly what I thought."

Kameitha shivered. "I still can't believe Jeremy's involved in something like this." She looked from Seth to Ralen, then met

Lilith's eyes. "I never wanted to hurt you, Lilith. Or any of you." She gave the slightest of smiles. "I wanted to protect you. That's what I still want to do."

"Have you told the police everything?" Seth said.

Kameitha lowered her head and nodded.

Lilith saw tears in her eyes. She wanted to reach out and comfort Kameitha, knowing how hard she had taken her son's involvement when it was far less serious than this. Now it must be crushing. But, how could she? *Please go.*

"Jeremy's in custody, but Rev. Day is already out on bail," Kameitha said.

"The man has connections!" Hector said.

Kameitha took a seat next to Ralen across the table from her.

Lilith forced herself to focus on the vidscreen. More scenes of devastation, switching between cities. Her emotions churned, both from what she watched and from Kameitha's nearness. Her proximity stole Lilith's breath.

Gemini put a comforting hand on Lilith's shoulder.

Within the hour, the other Pioneers joined them.

"Thanks for coming so quickly," Hector told them. "We'll go together from here to our new home. There's no sense taking any chances until the police get this under control."

"We've had security teams do a complete sweep today to ensure everything is pristine before activating the alarm systems," Ralen said.

"Great," Monique said. "After everything that's happened today, I don't feel safe in Park City anymore."

"Or in Ogden," Hector agreed.

"Detective Roberts and the fire chief are doing a bomb sweep at your homes with dogs and other detectors to make sure they're clear before the movers come tomorrow," Seth said.

"And we kept the paper trail blurred, so no one can track the ownership of our new home," Hector said.

"We'll take mattresses from the storeroom so you'll have a place to sleep until your furniture arrives," Kate said.

After the coverage started repeating for the third time, they called for the limo.

Lilith reached into her purse and handed Gemini the car keys. "Looks like we won't be able to give you a lift home after all."

Gemini took the keys and pulled Lilith into a hug. "Just stay safe, Mom."

"We will," Lilith said. "I'm so thankful you weren't harmed. The bomb could've been here instead of the clinic in Eden."

Gemini squeezed her hand. "We'll all get through this." Seth and Ralen said their goodbyes, then Gemini walked over to Kameitha. "Thanks for warning them." She gave her a hug and left the conference room.

The Pioneers followed Gemini out to the driveway. Kameitha stood next to Lilith as they watched her drive away. She whispered in Lilith's ear, "Can I come home?"

Lilith paused and bit her lip. She wanted to say "yes," but she was afraid to let her guard down. She couldn't put aside everything that had happened, even if Kameitha had saved them.

Behind her, Ralen sighed. "Come on, Kami." He escorted her to the limo, which had just pulled up in front of them. "We'll figure it all out later."

Chapter 52

NEAR EDEN, UTAH—Lilith followed the other Pioneers into the large, octagonal room at the heart of their new home. They expressed appreciation with "oohs" and "ahhs," which echoed along with the sounds of the footsteps against the hard surfaces of the native stone tiles and insulated glass walls.

Behind them, Renu workers carried in mattresses. When they started toward the corridors leading to each of the three wings, Ralen stopped them and addressed the other Pioneers. "I don't know about the rest of you, but tonight, I'd like it if we all stayed in this room together."

"That's a great idea," Monique said. The others agreed.

After the workers left, they arranged the mattresses in a circle and unloaded groceries Kate brought. They made sandwiches and returned to sit on the mattresses.

Nan held up a bottle of water and toasted: "To brighter days ahead."

"To brighter days ahead," the others repeated.

When lunch was done, Hector led the way to the large theatre adjoining the great room. He turned on the vid screen, entered a search for Renu, and pulled up the news feed.

One clip showed a reporter stopping Sen. Archibald on the steps of the Capitol.

"Some claim your hearings were the catalyst for today's bombings of the Renu clinics. What do you have to say to that?"

Sen. Archibald adjusted his purple bowtie and glared at the reporter. "That's a perfect example of 'killing the messenger.' Perhaps the media should carry that burden for covering my hearings."

The reporter paled. Before he could ask another question, the Senator continued. "I regret people died, but any war has casualties. We need to think long and hard about what it means to be a patriot."

Lilith gripped the arms of her chair, her emotions swinging between fury and disbelief. How dare he use the word "patriot" to describe such actions! How could a government leader justify using such incendiary rhetoric?

"Yeah, it's definitely not over," Xavier said.

"No," Hector agreed. He sped through more clips, showing the cleanup beginning at the various clinics, then shut off the vid screen.

"C'mon," Seth said to the group. "We'll give you the grand tour." He and Ralen led them through all three levels, pointing out the security and energy-saving features.

"This is more like it," Xavier said when they came to the indoor pool. He stripped down to his briefs and jumped in. The others followed. An hour later, they grabbed towels from the pool lockers and returned to the central hub.

"I needed that," Lilith said. Swimming laps had drained her excess tension, leaving her pleasantly tired. After dinner and a few hours in the theatre, she finally felt drowsy. Seth and Ralen chose mattresses on either side of hers. Kameitha joined them a few minutes later, giving Lilith a questioning look before taking the mattress next to Ralen.

Lying there, Lilith gazed up the length of the three-story river-stone fireplace to the beamed cathedral ceiling. Then Seth pressed a button on a remote and panels between the beams slid aside to reveal the night sky. The Milky Way shone brightly above their isolated mountain retreat.

She lay there, listening to the others' breathing change as they slipped off to sleep. Except for her. And Kameitha. The hours passed slowly.

———

THE LIMO TOOK Lilith to get her car at Gemini's early the next morning. She made a quick trip to the nearby discount store for a few essentials. The other Pioneers had loaned them clothing. The rest of the shopping could wait.

By the time she returned to the house, the first moving van had arrived. Lilith focused her efforts on unloading boxes of dishes from Hector's house in the spacious new kitchen in the central hub.

Around noon, she checked in with Kate. "Anything new?"

"You have to ask?" Kate said. "Do you want the good or the bad news?"

"You mean there's good news?"

Kate chuckled.

Lilith sighed. "The bad news?"

"The subcommittee is working more efficiently than usual. They've ordered us to shut down the clinics."

"What!" The others stopped shuffling boxes so they could hear. Lilith pressed the hologram projector. "Go on—the others are listening, too."

"We'll shut the clinics down after this week's treatments conclude tomorrow," she continued. "And we're not going to be able to open the next three hundred clinics on schedule, either."

"That *is* bad news," Lilith said, wondering at the matter-of-fact way Kate had delivered the news. Why wasn't she devastated, after all the work they'd done?

Hector joined Kate in the projection. "We were having trouble ensuring adequate security anyway," he said.

"BUT the good news is really good," Kate said with an infectious grin. "The 'Science America' article is out, and we've been bombarded with inquiries from all over the world."

"What exactly does that mean?" Seth asked.

"It's going to be a slower process, but this new treatment will get us to the same place in terms of changing the medical model from sickness to wellness," Kate said. "We'll reopen the clinics next week, offering the new serum instead of the longevity one you took."

"We can already see it doesn't have the same stigma as the original serum," Hector added. "We'll be able to offer the longevity treatment for those with terminal illness after the Senate gets pressured by enough influential people."

"That probably won't take long," Ralen said.

"It's tragic the article didn't come out a day earlier," Nan said.

"I doubt it would've made any difference," Seth said.

"Whether Sen. Archibald admits it or not, the hearings stirred up a lot of fear," Monique said. "Some people only know how to cope with fear through violence."

"Well, it's up to us to lead them in a different direction," Kate said. "And we'll explore those overseas options we identified earlier. As I said, the calls we've been receiving confirm the interest is there."

"But that's not all," Hector said. "They've taken Rev. Day back into custody."

"How did that happen?" Seth asked.

"Detective Roberts convinced Jeremy to talk," Hector said. "With what Kameitha had already shared about her captivity and the conversation she overheard, they added charges of attempted murder and domestic terrorism, and denied bail. But the bomber still hasn't been found."

"And Jeremy?" Lilith asked.

Hector shook his head. "He may get a lighter sentence for cooperating, but he still faces serious charges."

Lilith looked for Kameitha, but she had left the room.

Chapter 53

As the sun began to set, Lilith bundled up against the chill and walked down the steep path to the pond. She held her hands above the steam rising from the hot spring, remembering her last visit here. Remembering Kameitha's touch.

Yesterday as they left the Research Center, she had longed to tell Kameitha everything was all right between them. If only she could make it so by saying it!

"It's been quite a year," a familiar voice said behind her.

Lilith's heart raced.

"This time last year, you and I were in our separate homes in Park City, wondering if we would live another month."

Lilith turned. Kameitha glowed, radiantly beautiful in the setting sun's orange light.

"I hadn't been able to take a walk like this in decades," Kameitha said.

"Me, either." Lilith had to remind herself to breathe.

"It really puts things into perspective," Kameitha said. "We not only have our health, but we have each other, too. If you'll have me."

Lilith pressed her lips together and nodded. She would follow her heart.

Kameitha wrapped her arms around Lilith and pulled her close. Kameitha's hair smelled of lilacs. Lilith placed a finger under her chin, gently guiding Kameitha's face upward. Their lips met in a lingering kiss, which tasted salty from their tears.

When she finally pulled away, Kameitha said, "I'm so sorry for what I said at the hearings. And for leaving home without any explanation."

"I know you acted out of love," Lilith said. "Still, it's kind of like a sunburn—I'll get over the sting, but for now, I'm still tender."

"I promise to be gentle." Kameitha grinned.

"There you two are," Seth called out. He and Ralen stepped off the trail at the bottom of the ridge and walked toward them.

"We were just thinking how far we've come since this time last year," Kameitha said.

They linked arms, completing a circle. "Well personally, I'd rather look to the future than the past," Ralen said.

Noting the Tree of Life insignia on their sweatshirts, Lilith smiled. "We are the future."

Acknowledgments

Sometimes an idea just won't let go of you.

Twenty-three years ago at the Clarion Science Fiction and Fantasy Writers' Workshop, I wrote a story called "The Fourth Treatment" about a longevity serum. In the critique session, I took a lot of grief from the other writers about how the story couldn't be classified as science fiction because science had proven we weren't descended from Neanderthals. Fast-forward to the Twenty-first Century and I can tell you what percentage of my DNA is Neanderthal. Life is strange like that!

In 2007, a revised version of "The Fourth Treatment" took first place in the writing contest at TuckerCon, the 9th North American Science Fiction Convention. My short story "Origin of the Species," which explores the outcome of the Fourth Treatment, took second place for horror in a Writer's Digest competition in 2011.

Four years later, I wrote about the longevity serum's First Treatment in a short story called "Methuselah's Legacy." Over the next couple of years, my amazing critique partners Brad R. Cook, Cole Gibsen and Jennifer Lynn helped me transform it into a novel.

The longer length allowed me to weave in another bit of science —remote viewing (RV), an intuitive-based protocol for precognitive predictions. Hopefully it won't take decades before RV's great potential is common knowledge.

I first learned about Associative Remote Viewing (ARV) in 2009 at a Monroe Institute class on intuitive investing taught by Marty Rosenblatt and Paul Elder. Since then, I've been a member of Marty's online group (Applied Precognition Project), and I'm honored to call him a friend. Over the years, I've also studied extensively with Lori Williams (Intuitive Specialists) and learned from many other luminaries in the field such as Angela Thompson Smith, Tom McNear, Lyn Buchanan, Joe McMoneagle, Paul Smith, Sean McNamara, Gail Husick, and Daz Smith. I'm grateful for all my wonderful friends in the RV community—too many to name.

After completion of the novel's first draft, I took *Methuselah's Legacy* to the next level with assistance from my insightful online critique buddies—Terri Bruce, Jeremy Hughes, Diana Davis Olsen, Christopher Ross, Leann Orris, and Angi Shearstone.

I got more excellent feedback in 2018 from Beta readers Jon Knowles, Jeanne Felfe, Michele Oyola, Peter Green, Bob Shuman, and Marguerite Devers, who's been a close friend since Clarion days.

This list is never complete without acknowledging my husband, family and friends—especially Jeanne Palmer and Mary Ferronato —for their support. To my publisher, Soul Song Press, thanks for appreciating and encouraging my wyrdness!

And finally, my heartfelt thanks to you for reading this story. Your time is precious, and I appreciate you spending some of it with me exploring this idea.

About the Author

T.W. Fendley is an award-winning author whose published works include *Zero Time*, a historical fantasy novel for adults, and young adult speculative fiction novels, *Moonblood* and *The Labyrinth of Time*. Teresa's short stories are available on Kindle and Audible.

She fell in love with ancient American cultures while researching story ideas at the 1997 Clarion Science Fiction and Fantasy Writers' Workshop. Since then, Teresa has trekked to archeological sites in the Yucatan, Peru, and American Southwest.

She began writing fiction in 2007 after working more than 25 years in journalism and corporate communication. When she's not writing, Teresa explores the boundaries of consciousness through remote viewing and shamanism. She currently lives near St. Louis with her artist husband and his pet fish. Learn more at https://twfendley.com and on her remote viewing website, www.arv4fun.com

T.W. Fendley hopes you liked *Methuselah's Legacy*. If you did, please consider leaving a review online. Even one or two sentences can help future readers decide if it's a book they'd also enjoy. The author appreciates your support!

facebook.com/teresa.schnellmann

twitter.com/twfendley

instagram.com/t.w.fendley

Also by T.W. Fendley

Zero Time Chronicles:

Zero Time

Jaguar Hope

The Mother Serpent's Daughter

Young Adult:

Moonblood

The Labyrinth of Time

Short Stories:

Solar Lullaby

The Mentor

And I Feel Fine

The Fourth Treatment

Audiobooks:

Moonblood

The Labyrinth of Time

Jaguar Hope

The Mother Serpent's Daughter

Solar Lullaby

CPSIA information can be obtained
at www.ICGtesting.com
Printed in the USA
LVHW031604100221
678949LV00002B/241